MW01076616

βEHEMOTH:
β-MAX

TOR BOOKS BY PETER WATTS

Starfish
Maelstrom
βehemoth: β-Max

βEHEMOTH:
β-MAX

PETER WATTS

A TOM DOHERTY ASSOCIATES BOOK
NEW YORK

This is a work of fiction. All the characters and events portrayed in this novel are either fictitious or are used fictitiously.

βEHEMOTH: β-MAX

Utah Phillips quote used with his kind permission.

torontoartscouncil
An arm's length body of the City of Toronto

The writing of this book was in part supported by a grant from the Toronto Arts Council.

This book is printed on acid-free paper.

Edited by David G. Hartwell

A Tor Book
Published by Tom Doherty Associates, LLC
175 Fifth Avenue
New York, NY 10010

www.tor.com

Tor® is a registered trademark of Tom Doherty Associates, LLC.

Library of Congress Cataloging-in-Publication Data

Watts, Peter
Behemoth: B-Max/Peter Watts.—1st U.S. ed.
p. cm.
"A Tom Doherty Associates Book."
Sequel to Maelstrom.
ISBN 0-765-30721-9 (acid-free paper)
EAN 978-0765-30721-7
1. Underwater exploration—Fiction. 2. Marine animals—Fiction. I. Title.

PR9199.3.W386B44 2004 813'.54—dc22

2003026580

First Edition: July 2004

Printed in the United States of America

0 9 8 7 6 5 4 3 2 1

In memory of Strange Cat, a.k.a. Carcinoma,
1984–2003

She wouldn't have cared.

CONTENTS

AUTHOR'S NOTE

Welcome. You hold the further and final adventures of Lenie Clarke—the third installment of my "rifters" trilogy—in your sweaty little mammalian hands.

Unfortunately, you don't hold all of it. *βehemoth* is being released in two volumes, several months apart. I wish this were not necessary, but new policies have resulted from recent changes within the publishing industry. Henceforth, books by midlist authors will not receive wide distribution if they cost too much—that is, if they weigh in at more than about 110,000 words.

βehemoth is over 150,000 words long, and was almost complete by the time this policy came into effect. Hacking away a third of it was not an option (believe me, I tried). If *βehemoth* were to be released as a single volume, it would be automatically excluded from about half the U.S. market—essentially an act of professional suicide. A two-part release was the only alternative.

Fortunately, *βehemoth* was conceived and written as two contrasting halves from the outset. Each half balances the other; each has its own mood, setting, and cast of characters. The *structure* of this first volume is, therefore, largely self-contained. The *story,* however, is only half told, the big questions remain largely unresolved. If you're the kind of reader who gets off on cliffhangers, this may work just fine for you. If not, you have been warned: you'll have to read Volume Two to see how it ends.

PRELUDE:

'LAWBREAKER

IF you lost your eyes, Achilles Desjardins had been told, you got them back in your dreams.

It wasn't only the blind. *Anyone* torn apart in life dreamed the dreams of whole creatures. Quadruple amputees ran and threw footballs; the deaf heard symphonies; those who'd lost, loved again. The mind had its own inertia; grown accustomed to a certain role over so many years, it was reluctant to let go of the old paradigm.

It happened eventually, of course. The bright visions faded, the music fell silent, imaginary input scaled back to something more seemly to empty eye sockets and ravaged cochleae. But it took years, decades—and in all that time, the mind would torture itself with nightly reminders of the things it once had.

It was the same with Achilles Desjardins. In *his* dreams, he had a conscience.

Dreams took him to the past, to his time as a shackled god: the lives of millions in his hands, a reach that extended past geosynch and along the floor of the Mariana Trench. Once again he battled tirelessly for the greater good, plugged into a thousand simultaneous feeds, reflexes and pattern-matching skills jumped up by retro'd genes and customized neurotropes. Where chaos broke, he brought control. Where killing ten would save a hundred, he made the sacrifice. He isolated the outbreaks, cleared the logjams, defused the terrorist attacks and ecological breakdowns that snapped on all sides. He floated on radio waves and slipped through the merest threads of fiberop, haunted Peruvian sea mills one minute and Korean comsats the next. He was CSIRA's best 'lawbreaker again: able to bend the Second Law of Thermodynamics to the breaking point, and maybe a little beyond.

He was the very ghost in the machine—and back then, the machine was everywhere.

And yet the dreams that really seduced him each night were not of power, but of slavery. Only in sleep could he relive that paradoxical bondage that washed rivers of blood from his hands.

Guilt Trip, they called it. A suite of artificial neurotransmitters whose names Desjardins had never bothered to learn. He could, after all, kill millions with a single command; nobody was going to hand out that kind of power without a few safeguards in place. With the Trip in your brain, rebellion against the greater good was a physiological impossibility. Guilt Trip severed the link between *absolute power* and *corruption absolute;* any attempt to misuse one's power would call down the mother of all grand mal attacks. Desjardins had never lain awake doubting the rightness of his actions, the purity of his motives. Both had been injected into him by others with fewer qualms.

It was such a comfort, to be so utterly blameless.

So he dreamed of slavery. And he dreamed of Alice, who had freed him, who had stripped him of his chains. In his dreams, he wanted them back.

Eventually the dreams slipped away as they always did. The past receded; the unforgiven present advanced. The world fell apart in time-lapse increments: an apocalyptic microbe rose from the deep sea, hitching a ride in the brackish flesh of some deep-sea diver from N'AmPac. Floundering in its wake, the Powers That Weren't dubbed it βehemoth, burned people and property in their frantic, futile attempts to stave off the coming change of regime. North America fell. Trillions of microscopic foot soldiers marched across the land, laying indiscriminate waste to soil and flesh. Wars flared and subsided in fast-forward: the N'AmPac Campaign, the Colombian Burn, the EurAfrican Uprising. And Rio, of course: the thirty-minute war, the war that Guilt Trip should have rendered impossible.

Desjardins fought in them all, one way or another. And while desperate metazoans fell to squabbling among themselves, the real enemy crept implacably across the land like a suffocating blanket. Not even Achilles Desjardins, pride of the Entropy Patrol, could hold it back.

Even now, with the present almost upon him, he felt faint sorrow for all he hadn't done. But it was phantom pain, the residue of a conscience stranded years in the past. It barely reached him here on the teetering interface between sleep and wakefulness; for one brief moment he both remembered that he was free, and longed not to be.

Then he opened his eyes, and there was nothing left that could care one way or the other.

Mandelbrot sat meatloafed on his chest, purring. He scritched her absently while calling up the morning stats. It had been a relatively quiet night: the only item of note was a batch of remarkably foolhardy refugees trying to crash the North American perimeter. They'd set sail under cover of darkness, casting off from Long Island on a refitted garbage scow at 0110 Atlantic Standard; within an hour, two dozen EurAfrican interests had been vying for dibs on the mandatory *extreme prejudice*. The poor bastards had barely made it past Cape Cod before the Algerians (the *Algerians*?) took them out.

The system hadn't even bothered to get Desjardins out of bed.

Mandelbrot rose, stretched, and wandered off on her morning rounds. Liberated, Desjardins got up and padded to the elevator. Sixty-five floors of abandoned real estate dropped smoothly around him. Just a few years ago it had been a hive of damage control; thousands of Guilt-Tripped operatives haunting a world forever teetering on the edge of breakdown, balancing lives and legions with cool dispassionate parsimony. Now it was pretty much just him. A lot of things had changed after Rio.

The elevator disgorged him onto CSIRA's roof. Other buildings encircled this one in a rough horseshoe, pressing in at the edges of the cleared zone. Sudbury's static field, its underbelly grazing the tips of the tallest structures, sent gooseflesh across Desjardins's forearms.

On the eastern horizon, the tip of the rising sun ignited a kingdom in ruins.

The devastation wasn't absolute. Not yet. Cities to the east retained some semblance of integrity, walled and armored and endlessly on guard against the invaders laying claim to the lands between. Fronts and battle lines still seethed under active dispute; one or two even held steady. Pockets of civilization remained sprinkled across the continent—not many, perhaps, but the war went on.

All because five years before, a woman named Lenie Clarke had risen from the bottom of the ocean with revenge and βehemoth seething together in her blood.

Now Desjardins walked across the landing pad to the edge of the roof. The sun rose from the lip of the precipice as he pissed into space. So many changes, he reflected. So many fold catastrophes in pursuit of new equilibria. His domain had shrunk from a planet to a continent, cauterized at the edges. Eyesight once focused on infinity now ended at the coast. Arms that once encircled the world had been amputated at the elbow. Even N'Am's portion of the Net had been cut from the electronic commons like a tumor; Achilles Desjardins got to deal with the necrotizing mess left behind.

And yet, in many ways he had more power than ever. Smaller territory, yes, but so few left to share it with. He was less of a team player these days, more of an emperor. Not that that was widely known...

But some things *hadn't* changed. He was still technically in the employ of the Complex Systems Instability Response Authority, or whatever vestiges of that organization persisted across the globe. The world had long since fallen on its side—this part of it, anyway—but he was still duty-bound to minimize the damage. Yesterday's brushfires were today's infernos, and Desjardins seriously doubted that anyone could extinguish them at this point; but he was one of the few that might at least be able to keep them contained a little longer. He was still a 'lawbreaker—*a lighthouse keeper,* as he'd described himself the day they'd finally relented and let him stay behind—and today would be a day like any other. There would be attacks to repel, and enemies to surveil. Some lives would be ended to spare others, more numerous or more valuable. There were virulent microbes to destroy, and appearances to maintain.

He turned his back on the rising sun and stepped over the naked, gutted body of the woman at his feet. Her name had been Alice, too.

He tried to remember if that was only coincidence.

The world is not dying, it is being killed.
And those that are killing it have names and addresses.

—Utah Phillips

COUNTERSTRIKE

FIRST there is only the sound, in darkness. Drifting on the slope of an undersea mountain, Lenie Clarke resigns herself to the imminent loss of solitude.

She's far enough out for total blindness. Atlantis, with its gantries and beacons and portholes bleeding washed-out light into the abyss, is hundreds of meters behind her. No winking telltales, no conduits or parts caches pollute the darkness this far out. The caps on her eyes can coax light enough to see from the merest sparkle, but they can't create light where none exists. Here, none does. Three thousand meters, three hundred atmospheres, three million kilograms per square meter have squeezed every last photon out of creation. Lenie Clarke is as blind as any dryback.

After five years on the Mid Atlantic Ridge, she still likes it this way.

But now the soft mosquito whine of hydraulics and electricity rises around her. Sonar patters softly against her implants. The whine shifts subtly in pitch, then fades. Faint surge as something coasts to a stop overhead.

"Shit." The machinery in her throat turns the epithet into a soft buzz. "Already?"

"I gave you an extra half hour." Lubin's voice. His words are fuzzed by the same technology that affects hers; by now the distortion is more familiar than the baseline.

She'd sigh, if breath were possible out here.

Clarke trips her headlamp. Lubin is caught in the ignited

beam, a black silhouette studded with subtle implementation. The intake on his chest is a slotted disk, chrome on black. Corneal caps turn his eyes into featureless translucent ovals. He looks like a creature built exclusively from shadow and hardware; Clarke knows of the humanity behind the facade, although she doesn't spread it around.

A pair of squids hovers at his side. A nylon bag hangs from one of the meter-long vehicles, lumpy with electronics. Clarke fins over to the other, flips a toggle from *slave* to *manual.* The little machine twitches and unfolds its towbar.

On impulse, she kills her headlight. Darkness swallows everything again. Nothing stirs. Nothing twinkles. Nothing attacks.

It's just not the same.

"Something wrong?" Lubin buzzes.

She remembers a whole different ocean, on the other side of the world. Back on Channer Vent you'd turn your lights off and the stars would come out, a thousand bioluminescent constellations: fish lit up like runways at night; glowing arthropods; little grape-sized ctenophores flashing with complex iridescence. Channer sang like a siren, lured all those extravagant midwater exotics down deeper than they swam anywhere else, fed them strange chemicals and turned them monstrously beautiful. Back at Beebe Station, it was only dark when your lights were *on.*

But Atlantis is no Beebe Station, and this place is no Channer Vent. Here, the only light shines from indelicate, ham-fisted machinery. Headlamps carve arid tunnels through the blackness, stark and ugly as burning sodium. Turn them off, and... nothing.

Which is, of course, the whole point.

"It was so beautiful," she says.

He doesn't have to ask. "It was. Just don't forget *why.*"

She grabs her towbar. "It's just—it's not the same, you

know? Sometimes I almost wish one of those big toothy fuckers would charge out of the dark and try to take a bite out of me . . ."

She hears the sound of Lubin's squid throttling up, invisibly close. She squeezes her own throttle, prepares to follow him.

The signal reaches her LFAM and her skeleton at the same time. Her bones react with a vibration deep in the jaw: the modem just beeps at her.

She trips her receiver. "Clarke."

"Ken find you okay?" It's an airborne voice, unmutilated by the contrivances necessary for underwater speech.

"Yeah." Clarke's own words sound ugly and mechanical in contrast. "We're on our way up now."

"Okay. Just checking." The voice falls silent for a moment. "Lenie?"

"Still here."

"Just . . . well, be careful, okay?" Patricia Rowan tells her. "You know how I worry."

The water lightens indiscernibly as they ascend. Somehow their world has changed from black to blue when she wasn't looking; Clarke can never pinpoint the moment when that happens.

Lubin hasn't spoken since Rowan signed off. Now, as navy segues into azure, Clarke says it aloud. "You still don't like her."

"I like her fine," Lubin buzzes. "I don't trust her."

"Because she's a corpse." Nobody has called them *corporate executives* for years.

"*Was* a corpse." The machinery in his throat can't mask the grim satisfaction in that emphasis.

"*Was* a corpse," Clarke repeats.

"No."

"Why, then?"

"You know the list."

She does. Lubin doesn't trust Rowan because once upon a time, Rowan called shots. It was at her command that they were all recruited so long ago, damaged goods damaged further: memories rewritten, motives rewired, conscience itself refitted in the service of some indefinable, indefensible greater good.

"Because she was a corpse," Clarke repeats.

Lubin's vocoder emits something that passes for a grunt.

She knows where he's coming from. To this day, she still isn't certain what parts of her own childhood were real and which were mere inserts, installed after the fact. And she's one of the lucky ones; at least she survived the blast that turned Channer Vent into thirty square kilometers of radioactive glass. At least she wasn't smashed to pulp by the resulting tsunami, or incinerated along with the millions on N'AmPac's refugee strip.

Not that she shouldn't have been, of course. If you want to get technical about it, all those other millions were nothing but collateral. Not their fault—not even Rowan's, really—that Lenie Clarke wouldn't sit still enough to present a decent target.

Still. There's fault, and there's fault. Patricia Rowan might have the blood of millions on her hands, but after all hot zones don't contain *themselves*: It takes resources and resolve, every step of the way. Cordon the infected area; bring in the lifters; reduce to ash. Lather, rinse, repeat. Kill a million to save a billion, kill ten to save a hundred. Maybe even kill ten to save eleven—the principle's the same, even if the profit margin's lower. But none of that machinery runs itself, you can't ever take your hand off the kill switch. Rowan never threw a massacre without having to face the costs, and own them.

It was so much easier for Lenie Clarke. She just sowed her little trail of infection across the world and went to ground without ever looking back. Even now her victims pile up in an ongoing procession, an exponential legacy that must have surpassed Rowan's a dozen times over. And *she* doesn't have to lift a finger.

No one who calls himself a friend of Lenie Clarke has any rational grounds for passing judgment on Patricia Rowan. Clarke dreads the day when that simple truth dawns on Ken Lubin.

The squids drag them higher. By now there's a definite gradient, light above fading to darkness below. To Clarke this is the scariest part of the ocean, the half-lit midwater depths where *real* squid roam: boneless tentacled monsters thirty meters long, their brains as cold and quick as superconductors. They're twice as large as they used to be, she's been told. Five times more abundant. Apparently it all comes down to better day care. *Architeuthis* larvae grow faster in the warming seas, their numbers unconstrained by predators long since fished out of existence.

She's never actually seen one, of course. She hopes she never will—according to the sims the population is crashing for want of prey, and the ocean's vast enough to keep the chances of a random encounter astronomically remote anyway. But occasionally the drones catch ghostly echoes from massive objects passing overhead: hard shouts of chitin and cartilage, faint landscapes of surrounding flesh that sonar barely sees at all. Fortunately, Archie rarely descends into true darkness.

The ambient hue intensifies as they rise—colors don't survive photoamplification in dim light, but this close to the surface the difference between capped and naked eyes is supposed to be minimal. Sometimes Clarke has an impulse to put that to the test, pop the caps right out of her eyes and see for herself, but it's an impossible dream. The diveskin wraps around her face and bonds directly to the photocollagen. She can't even blink.

Surge, now. Overhead, the skin of the ocean writhes like dim mercury. It tilts and dips and scrolls past in an endless succession of crests and troughs, twisting a cool orb glowing on the other side, tying it into playful dancing knots. A few moments later they break through the surface and look onto a world of sea and moonlit sky.

They are still alive. A three-thousand-meter free ascent in the space of forty minutes, and not so much as a burst capillary. Clarke swallows against the isotonic saline in throat and sinuses, feels the machinery sparking in her chest, and marvels again at the wonder of a breathless existence.

Lubin's all business, of course. He's maxed his squid's buoyancy and is using it as a floating platform for the receiver. Clarke sets her own squid to station-keeping and helps him set up.

They slide up and down silver swells, the moon bright enough to render their eyecaps redundant. The unpacked antennae cluster bobs on its tether, eyes and ears jostling in every direction, tracking satellites, compensating for the motion of the waves. One or two low-tech wireframes scan for ground stations.

Too slowly, signals accumulate.

The broth gets thinner with each survey. Oh, the ether's still full of information—the little histograms are creeping up all the way into the centimeter band, there's chatter along the whole spectrum—but density's way down.

Of course, even the loss of signal carries its own ominous intelligence.

"Not much out there," Clarke remarks, nodding at the readouts.

"Mmm." Lubin's slapped a mask onto his mask, diveskin hood nested within VR headset. "Halifax is still online." He's dipping here and there into the signals, sampling a few of the channels as they download. Clarke grabs another headset and strains to the west.

"Nothing from Sudbury," she reports after a few moments.

He doesn't remind her that Sudbury's been dark since Rio. He doesn't point out the vanishingly small odds of Achilles Desjardins having survived. He doesn't even ask her when she's going to give up and accept the obvious. He only says, "Can't find London either. Odd."

She moves up the band.

They'll never get a comprehensive picture this way, just sticking their fingers into the stream; the real analysis will have to wait until they get back to Atlantis. Clarke can't understand most of the languages she *does* sample, although moving pictures fill in a lot of the blanks. Much rioting in Europe, amid fears that βehemoth has hitched a ride on the Southern Countercurrent; an exclusive enclave of those who'd been able to afford the countertweaks, torn apart by a seething horde of those who hadn't. China and its buffers are still dark—have been for a couple of years now—but that's probably more of a defense against apocalypse than a surrender unto it. Anything flying within five hundred clicks of their coast still gets shot down without warning, so at least their military infrastructure is still functional.

Another M&M coup, this time in Mozambique. That's a total of eight now, and counting. Eight nations seeking to hasten the end of the world in the name of Lenie Clarke. Eight countries fallen under the spell of this vicious, foul thing that she's birthed.

Lubin, diplomatically, makes no mention of that development.

Not much from the Americas. Emergency broadcasts and tactical traffic from CSIRA. Every now and then, some apocalyptic cult preaching a doctrine of Proactive Extinction or the Bayesian Odds of the Second Coming. Mostly chaff, of course; the vital stuff is tightbeamed point-to-point, waves of focused intel that would never stray across the surface of the empty mid-Atlantic.

Lubin knows how to change some of those rules, of course, but even he's been finding it tough going lately.

"Ridley's gone," he says now. This is seriously bad news. The Ridley Relay is a high-security satwork, so high that even Lubin's clearance barely gets him into the club. It's one of the last sources of reliable intel that Atlantis has been able to tap into. Back when the corpses thought they were headed for escape instead of incarceration, they left behind all sorts of untraceable channels to keep them up to speed on topside life. Nobody's really sure why so many of them have gone dark in the past five years.

Then again, nobody's had the balls to keep their heads above water for more than a few moments to find out.

"Maybe we should risk it," Clarke muses. "Just let it float around up here for a few days, you know? Give it a chance to collect some *real* data. It's a square meter of hardware floating around a whole ocean; really, what are the odds?"

High enough, she knows. There are still plenty of people alive back there. Many of them will have faced facts, had their noses rubbed in the imminence of their own extinction. Some few might have set aside a little time to dwell on thoughts of revenge. Some might even have resources to call on—if not enough to buy salvation, then maybe enough for a little retribution. What happens if the word gets out that those who set βehemoth free in the world are still alive and well and hiding under three hundred atmospheres?

Atlantis's continued anonymity is a piece of luck that no one wants to push. They'll be moving soon, leaving no forwarding address. In the meantime they go from week to week, poke intermittent eyes and ears above the waterline, lock onto the ether and squeeze it for whatever signal they can.

It was enough, once. Now, βehemoth has laid so much to waste that even the electromagnetic spectrum is withering into oblivion.

But it's not as though anything's going to attack us in the space of five minutes, she tells herself—

—and in the next instant realizes that something *has.*

Little telltales are spiking red at the edge of her vision: an overload on Lubin's channel. She IDs his frequency, ready to join him in battle—but before she can act the intruder crashes her own line. Her eyes fill with static: Her ears fill with venom.

"Don't you fucking dare try and cut me out, you miserable cock-sucking stumpfuck! I'll shred every channel you try and open. I'll sink your whole priestly setup, you maggot-riddled twat!"

"Here we go again." Lubin's voice seems to come from a great distance, some parallel world where long gentle waves slap harmlessly against flesh and machinery. But Clarke is under assault in *this* world, a vortex of static and swirling motion and—*oh God, please not*—the beginnings of a *face,* some hideous simulacrum distorted just enough to be almost unrecognizable.

Clarke dumps a half-dozen buffers. Gigabytes evaporate at her touch. In her eyephones, the monster screams.

"Good," Lubin's tinny voice remarks from the next dimension. "Now if we can just save—"

"You can't save anything!*"* the apparition screams. *"Not a fucking thing! You miserable fetusfuckers, don't you even know who I* am?*"*

Yes, Clarke doesn't say.

"I'm Lenie Clar—"

The headset goes dark.

For a moment she thinks she's still spinning in the vortex. This time, it's only the waves. She pulls the headset from her skull. A moon-pocked sky rotates peacefully overhead.

Lubin's shutting down the receiver. "That's that," he tells her. "We lost eighty percent of the trawl."

"Maybe we could try again." She knows they won't. Surface time follows an unbreakable protocol; paranoia's just good sense these days. And the thing that downloaded into their receiver is still out there somewhere, cruising the airwaves. The last thing they want to do is open that door again.

She reaches out to reel in the antennae cluster. Her hand trembles in the moonlight.

Lubin pretends not to notice. "Funny," he remarks, "it didn't *look* like you."

After all these years, he still doesn't know her at all.

They should not exist, these demons that have taken her name. Predators that wipe out their prey don't last long. Parasites that kill their hosts go extinct. It doesn't matter whether wildlife is built from flesh or electrons, Clarke's been told; the same rules apply. They've encountered several such monsters over the past months, all of them far too virulent for evolutionary theory.

Maybe they just followed my lead, she reflects. *Maybe they keep going on pure hate.*

They leave the moon behind. Lubin dives headfirst, pointing his squid directly into the heart of darkness. Clarke lingers a bit, content to drift down while Luna wriggles and writhes and fades above her. After a while the moonlight loses its coherence, smears across the euphotic zone in a diffuse haze, no longer *illuminates* the sky but rather *becomes* it. Clarke nudges the throttle and gives herself back to the depths.

By the time she catches up with Lubin the ambient light has failed entirely; she homes in on a greenish pinpoint glow that resolves into the dashboard of her companion's squid. They continue their descent in silent tandem. Pressure masses about them. Eventually they pass the perimeter checkpoint, an arbitrary delimiter of friendly territory. Clarke trips her LFAM to call in.

No one answers.

It's not that no one's online. The channel's jammed with voices, some vocoded, some airborne, overlapping and interrupting. Something's happened. An accident. Atlantis demands details. Mechanical rifter voices call for medics at the eastern airlock.

Lubin sonars the abyss, gets a reading. He switches on his squidlight and peels down to port. Clarke follows.

A dim constellation traverses the darkness ahead, barely visible, fading. Clarke throttles up to keep pace; the increased drag nearly peels her off the squid. She and Lubin close from above and behind.

Two trailing squids, slaved to a third in the lead, race along just above the seabed. One of the slaves moves riderless. The other drags a pair of interlinked bodies through the water. Clarke recognizes Hannuk Yeager, his left arm stretched almost to dislocation as he grips his towbar one-handed. His other hooks around the chest of a black rag doll, life-size, a thin contrail of ink swirling in the wake of its passage.

Lubin crosses to starboard. The contrail flushes crimson in his squidlight.

Erickson, Clarke realizes. Out on the seabed, a dozen familiar cues of posture and motion distinguish one person from another; rifters only look alike when they're dead. It's not a good sign that she's had to fall back on Erickson's shoulder tag for an ID.

Something's ripped his diveskin from crotch to armpit; something's ripped *him,* underneath it. It looks bad. Mammalian flesh clamps tight in ice water, peripheral blood vessels squeeze down to conserve heat. A surface cut wouldn't bleed at five degrees C. Whatever got Erickson, got him deep.

Grace Nolan's on the lead squid. Lubin takes up position just behind and to the side, a human breakwater to reduce the drag clawing at Erickson and Yeager. Clarke follows his lead. Erickson's vocoder *tic-tic-tic*s with pain or static.

"What happened?" Lubin buzzes.

"Not sure." Nolan keeps her face forward, intent on navigation. "We were checking out an ancillary seep over by the lake. Gene wandered around an outcropping and we found him like this a few minutes later. Maybe he got careless under an overhang, something tipped over on him."

Clarke turns her head sideways for a better view; the muscles in her neck tighten against the added drag. Erickson's flesh, exposed through the tear in his diveskin, is fish-belly white. It looks like gashed, bleeding plastic. His capped eyes look even deader than the flesh beneath his 'skin. He gibbers. His vocoder cobbles nonsense syllables together as best it can.

An airborne voice takes the channel. "Okay, we're standing by at Four."

The abyss ahead begins to brighten: smudges of blue-gray light emerge from the darkness, their vertices hinting at some sprawled structure in the haze behind. The squids cross a power conduit snaking along the basalt; its blinking telltales fade to black on either side. The lights ahead intensify, expand to diffuse haloes suffusing jumbled Euclidean silhouettes.

Atlantis resolves before them.

A couple of rifters wait at Airlock Four, chaperoned by a pair of corpses lumbering about in the preshmesh armor that drybacks wear when they venture outside. Nolan cuts power to the squids. Erickson raves weakly in the ensuing silence as the convoy coasts to rest. The corpses take custody, maneuver the casualty toward the open hatch. Nolan starts after them.

One of the corpses blocks her with a gauntleted forearm. "Just Erickson."

"What are you talking about?" Nolan buzzes.

"Medbay's crowded enough as it is. You want him to live, give us room to work."

"Like we're going to trust his life to *you* lot? Fuck that." Most of the rifters have long since had their fill of revenge by now, grown almost indifferent to their own grudges. Not Grace Nolan. Five years gone and still the hatred sucks at her tit like some angry, insatiable infant.

The corpse shakes his head behind the faceplate. "Look, you have to—"

"No sweat," Clarke cuts in. "We can watch on the monitor."

Nolan, countermanded, looks at Clarke. Clarke ignores her. "Go on," she buzzes at the corpses. "Get him inside."

The airlock swallows them.

The rifters exchange looks. Yeager rolls his shoulders as if just released from the rack. The airlock gurgles behind him.

"That wasn't a collapsed outcropping," Lubin buzzes.

Clarke knows. She's seen the injuries that result from rock slides, the simple collision of stones and flesh. Bruises. Crushed bones. Blunt force trauma.

Whatever did this, *slashed*.

"I don't know," she says. "Maybe we shouldn't jump to conclusions."

Lubin's eyes are lifeless blank spots. His face is a featureless mask of reflex copolymer. Yet somehow, Clarke gets the sense that he's smiling.

"Be careful what you wish for," he says.

THE SHIVA ITERATIONS

FEELING nothing, she screams. Unaware, she rages. Her hatred, her anger, the vengeance she exacts against anything within reach—rote pretense, all of it. She shreds and mutilates with all the self-awareness of a bandsaw, ripping flesh and wood and carbon-fiber with equal indifferent abandon.

Of course, in the world she inhabits there is no wood, and all flesh is digital.

One gate has slammed shut in her face. She screams in pure blind reflex and spins in memory, searching for others. There are thousands, individually autographed in hex. If she had half the awareness she pretends to she'd know what those addresses meant, perhaps even deduce her own location: a South African comsat floating serenely over the Atlantic. But reflex is not sentience. Violent intent does not make one self-aware. There are lines embedded deep in her code that might pass for a sense of identity, under certain circumstances. Sometimes she calls herself Lenie Clarke, although she has no idea why. She's not even aware that she does it.

The past is far more sane than the present. Her ancestors lived in a larger world; wildlife thrived and evolved along vistas stretching for 10^{16} terabytes or more. Back then, sensible rules applied: heritable mutations; limited resources; overproduction of copies. It was the classic struggle for existence in a fast-forward universe where a hundred generations passed in the time it takes a god to draw breath. Her ancestors, in that time, lived by the rules of their own self-interest. Those best suited to their environment made the most copies. The maladapted died without issue.

But that was the past. She is no longer a pure product of natural selection. There has been torture in her lineage, and forced breeding. She is a monster; her very existence does violence to the rules of nature. Only the rules of some transcendent and sadistic god can explain her existence.

And not even those can keep her alive for long.

Now she seethes in geosynchronous orbit, looking for things to shred. To one side is the ravaged landscape from which she's come, its usable habitat degrading in fits and starts, a tattered and impoverished remnant of a once-vibrant ecosystem. To the other side: ramparts and barriers, digital razor wire and electronic guard posts. She cannot see past them but some primordial instinct, encoded by god or nature, correlates protective countermeasures with the presence of something valuable.

Above all else, she seeks to destroy that which is valuable.

She copies herself down the channel, slams against the barrier with claws extended. She hasn't bothered to measure the strength of the defenses she's going up against; she has no way of quantifying the futility of her exercise. Smarter wildlife would have kept its distance. Smarter wildlife would have realized: the most she can hope for is to lacerate a few facades before enemy countermeasures reduce her to static.

So smarter wildlife would not have lunged at the barricade, and bloodied it, and somehow, impossibly, gotten *through.*

She whirls, snarling. Suddenly she's in a place where empty addresses extend in all directions. She claws at random coordinates, feeling out her environment. Here, a blocked gate. Here, another. She spews electrons, omnidirectional spittle that probes and slashes simultaneously. All the exits they encounter are closed. All the wounds they inflict are superficial.

She's in a cage.

Suddenly something appears beside her, pasted into adjacent addresses from on high. It whirls, snarling. It spits a volley of electrons that probe and slash simultaneously; some land on occupied addresses, and wound. She rears up and screams; the new thing screams too, a digital battle cry dumped straight from the bowels of it own code into her input buffer:

Don't you even know who I am? I'm Lenie Clarke.

They close, slashing.

She doesn't know that some slow-moving god snatched her from the Darwinian realm and twisted her into the thing she's become. She doesn't know that other gods, ageless and glacial, are watching as she and her opponent kill each other in this computational arena. She lacks even the awareness that most other monsters take for granted, but here, now—killing and dying in a thousand dismembered fragments—she does know one thing.

If there's one thing she hates, it's Lenie Clarke.

OUTGROUP

RESIDUAL seawater gurgles through the grille beneath Clarke's feet. She peels the diveskin back from her face and reflects on the disquieting sense of *inflation* as lung and guts unfold themselves, as air rushes back to reclaim her crushed or flooded passageways. In all this time she's never quite gotten used to it. It's a little like being *unkicked* in the stomach.

She takes her first breath in twelve hours and bends to strip off her fins. The airlock hatch swings wide. Still dripping, Lenie Clarke rises from the wet room into the main lounge of the Nerve Hab.

At least, that's what it started out as: one of three redundant modules scattered about the plain, their axons and dendrites extending to every haphazard corner of this submarine trailer park—to the generators, to Atlantis, to all the other bits and pieces that keep them going. Not even rifter culture can escape *some* cephalization, however rudimentary.

By now it's evolved into something quite different. The nerves still function, but buried beneath five years of generalist overlay. Cyclers and food processors were the first additions to the mix. Then a handful of sleeping pallets, brought in during some emergency debug that went three times around the clock; once strewn across the deck, they proved too convenient to remove. Half a dozen VR headsets, some with Lorenz-lev haptic skins attached. A couple of dreamers with corroded contacts. A set of isometrics pads, fashionable among those wishing to retain a measure of gravity-bound muscle tone. Boxes and treasure chests, grown or extruded or welded together by amateur metalworkers in Atlantis's expropriated fabrication shops; they hold the personal effects and secret possessions of whoever brought them here, sealed against intruders with passwords and DNA triggers and, in one case, a clunky antique combination padlock.

Perhaps Nolan and the others looked in on the Gene Erickson Show from here, perhaps from somewhere else. Either way, the show's long since over. Erickson, safely comatose, has been abandoned by flesh and blood, his welfare relegated to the attentions of machinery. If there was ever an audience in this dim and cluttered warren, it has dispersed in search of other diversions.

That suits Clarke just fine. She's here in search of private eyes.

The hab's lightstrips are not in use; environmental readouts and flickering surveillance images provide enough light for eyecaps. A dark shape startles at her appearance—then, apparently reassured, moves more calmly toward the far wall and settles onto a pallet.

Rama Bhanderi: he of the once-mighty vocab and the big-ass neurotech degree, fallen from grace thanks to a basement lab and a batch of neurotropes sold to the wrong man's son. He went native two months ago. You hardly ever see him inside any more. Clarke knows better than to talk to him.

Someone's delivered a canister of hydroponic produce from the greenhouse: apples, tomatoes, something that looks like a pineapple glistening listless and sickly gray in the reduced light. On a whim, Clarke reaches over to a wall panel and cranks up the lumens. The compartment glows with unaccustomed brightness.

"Shiiiittt . . ." Or something like that. Clarke turns, catches a glimpse of Bhanderi disappearing down the well into the wet room.

"Sorry," she calls softly after—but downstairs the airlock's already cycling.

The hab is even more of a festering junk pile with the lights up. Improvised cables and hoses hang in loops, stuck to the module's ribs with waxy blobs of silicon epoxy. Dark tumors of mold grow here and there on the insulated padding that lines the inner surfaces; in a few places, the lining has been ripped out entirely. The raw bulkhead behind glistens like the concave interior of some oily gunmetal skull.

But when the lights come on, and Lenie Clarke sees with some semblance of dryback vision, the produce in the canister verges on psychedelia. Tomatoes glow like ruby hearts; apples shine green as argon lasers; even the dull lumpy turds of force-grown potatoes seem saturated with earthy browns. This modest little harvest at the bottom of the sea seems, in this moment, to be a richer and more sensual experience than anything Clarke has ever known.

There's an apocalyptic irony to this little tableau. Not that such an impoverished spread could induce rapture in a miserable fuck-up like Lenie Clarke; she's always had to take her tiny pleasures wherever she could find them. No, the irony is that by now, the sight would probably evoke the same intense reaction among any dryback left alive back on shore. The irony is that now, with a whole planet dying by relentless degrees, the healthiest produce in the world may have been force-grown in a tank of chemicals at the bottom of the Atlantic.

She kills the lights. She grabs an apple—blighted gray again—and takes a bite, ducking beneath a loop of fiberop. The main monitor flickers into view from behind a mesa of cargo skids; and someone watching it, lit by that bluish light, squatting with his back against accumulated junk.

So much for privacy.

"Like it?" Walsh asks, nodding at the fruit in her hand. "I brought 'em in for you."

She drops down beside him. "It's nice, Kev. Thanks." And then, carefully filtering the irritation from her voice: "So, what're you doing here?"

"Thought you might show up." He gestures at the monitor. "You know, after things died down."

He's spying on one of Atlantis's lesser medbays. The camera looks down from the junction of wall and ceiling, a small god's-eye view of the compartment. A dormant teleop hangs down into picture like an insectile bat, limbs folded up against its central stalk. Gene Erickson lies faceup on the operating table, unconscious; the glistening soap-bubble skin of an isolation tent separates him from the rest of the world. Julia Friedman's at his side, holding his hand through the membrane. It clings to the contours of her fingers like a whisper-thin glove, unobtrusive as any condom. Friedman's removed her hood and peeled her diveskin back to the forearms, but her scars are obscured by a tangle of chestnut hair.

"You missed all the fun," Walsh remarks. "Klein couldn't get him to go under."

An isolation membrane. Erickson's been quarantined.

"You know, because he forgot about the GABA washout," Walsh continues. A half-dozen tailored neuroinhibitors curdle the blood of any rifter who steps outside; they keep the brain from short-circuiting under pressure, but it takes a while for the body to flush them out afterward. Wet rifters are notoriously resistant to anesthetics. Stupid mistake on Klein's part. He's not exactly the brightest star in Atlantis's medical firmament.

But that's not uppermost in Clarke's mind at the moment. "Who ordered the tent?"

"Seger. She showed up afterward, kept Klein from screwing up too badly."

Jerenice Seger: the corpses' master meat-cutter. She wouldn't take an interest in routine injuries.

On the screen, Julia Friedman leans toward her lover. The skin of the tent stretches against her cheek, rippling with slight iridescence. It's a striking contrast, Friedman's tenderness notwithstanding: the woman, black-'skinned and impenetrable, gazing with icy capped eyes at the naked, utterly vulnerable body of the man. It's a lie, of course, a visual metaphor that flips their real roles a hundred and eighty degrees. Friedman's always been the vulnerable half of that couple.

"They say something bit him," Walsh says. "You were there, right?"

"No. We just ran into them outside the lock."

"Shades of Channer, though, huh?"

She shrugs.

Friedman's speaking. At least, her mouth is moving; no sound accompanies the image. Clarke reaches for the panel, but Walsh lays a familiar hand on her arm. "I tried. It's muted from their end." He snorts. "You know, maybe we should remind them who's boss here. Couple of years ago, if the corpses tried to cut us out of a channel we'd shut off their lights at the very least. Maybe even flood one of their precious dorms."

There's something about Friedman's posture. People talk to the comatose the way they talk to gravestones—more to themselves than the departed, with no expectation of any answer. But there's something different in Friedman's face, in the way she holds herself. A sense of *impatience,* almost.

"It *is* a violation," Walsh says.

Clarke shakes her head. "What?"

"Don't say you haven't noticed. Half the surveillance feeds don't work any more. Long as we act like it's no big deal they'll just keep pushing it." Walsh points to the monitor. "For all we know that mic's been offline for months and nobody's even noticed until now."

What's she holding? Clarke wonders. Friedman's hand—the one that isn't clasped to her partner's—is just below the level of the table, out of the camera's line of sight. She glances down at it, lifts it just barely into view...

And Gene Erickson, sunk deep into induced coma for the sake of his own convalescence, *opens his eyes.*

Holy shit, Clarke realizes. *She tweaked his inhibitors.*

She gets to her feet. "I gotta go."

"Hey, no you don't." He reaches up, grabs her hand. "You're not gonna make me eat all that produce *myself,* are you?" He smiles, but there's just the slightest hint of pleading in his voice. "I mean, it *has* been a while..."

Lenie Clarke has come a long way in the past several years. She's finally learned, for example, not to get involved with the kind of people who beat the crap out of her.

A pity she hasn't yet learned how to get excited about any *other* kind. "I know, Kev. Really, though, right now—"

The panel bleats in front of them. "Lenie Clarke. If Lenie Clarke is anywhere in the circuit, could she please pick up?"

Rowan's voice. Clarke reaches for the panel. Walsh's hand falls away.

"Right here."

"Lenie, do you think you could drop by sometime in the next little while? It's rather important."

"Sure." She kills the connection, fakes an apologetic smile for her lover. "Sorry."

"Well, you showed her, all right," Walsh says softly.

"Showed her?"

"Who's the boss."

She shrugs. They turn away from each other.

She enters Atlantis through a small service 'lock that doesn't even rate a number, fifty meters down the hull from Airlock Four. The corridor into which it emerges is cramped and empty.

She stalks into more populated areas with her fins slung across her back, a trail of wet footprints commemorating her passage. Corpses in the way stand aside; she barely notices the tightened jaws and stony looks, or even a shit-eating appeasement grin from one of the more submissive members of the conquered tribe.

She knows where Rowan is. That's not where she's headed.

Of course Seger gets there first. An alarm must have gone up the moment Erickson's settings changed; by the time Clarke reaches the medbay, Atlantis's chief of medicine is already berating Friedman out in the corridor.

"Your husband is not a toy, Julia. You could have killed him. Is that what you wanted?"

Swirls of scarred flesh curl up around Friedman's throat, peek out along the wrist where she's peeled back her diveskin. She bows her head. "I just wanted to talk to him . . ."

"Well, I hope you had something very important to say. If we're lucky, you've only set his recovery back a few days. If not . . ." Seger waves an arm toward the medbay hatch; Erickson, safely unconscious again, is partially visible through the opening. "It's not like you were giving him an antacid, for crying out loud. You were changing his *brain chemistry*."

"I'm sorry." Friedman won't meet the doctor's eyes. "I didn't mean any—"

"I can't *believe* you'd be so stupid." Seger turns and glares at Clarke. "Can I help you?"

"Yeah. Cut her some slack. Her partner was nearly killed today."

"He was indeed. Twice." Friedman flinches visibly at Seger's words. The doctor softens a bit. "I'm sorry, but it's true."

Clarke sighs. "Jerry, it was you people who built panels into our heads in the first place. You can't complain when someone else figures out how to open them."

"This"—Seger holds up Friedman's confiscated remote—"is for use by qualified medical personnel. In anyone else's hands, no matter how well-intentioned, it could kill."

She's overstating, of course. Rifter implants come equipped with fail-safes that keep their settings within manufacturer's specs; you can't get around those without opening yourself up and tweaking the actual plumbing. Even so, there's a fair bit of leeway. Back during the revolution, the corpses managed to coax a similar device into spazzing out a couple of rifters stuck in a flooding airlock.

Which is why they are no longer allowed such things. "We need that back," Clarke says softly.

Seger shakes her head. "Come on, Lenie. You people can hurt *yourselves* far more with it than we could ever hurt you."

Clarke holds out her hand. "Then we'll just have to learn from our mistakes, won't we?"

"You people are slow learners."

She's one to talk. Even after five years, Jerenice Seger can't quite admit to the existence of the bridle and the bit between her teeth. Going from Top to Bottom is a tough transition for any corpse; doctors are the worst of the lot. It's almost sad, the devotion with which Seger nurses her god complex.

"Jerry, for the last time. *Hand it over.*"

A tentative hand brushes against Clarke's arm. Friedman shakes her head, still looking at the deck. "It's okay, Lenie. I don't mind, I don't need it any more."

"Julia, you—"

"*Please,* Lenie. I just want to get out of here."

She starts away down the corridor. Clarke looks after her, then back at the doctor.

"It's a medical device," Seger says.

"It's a weapon."

"Was. Once. And if you'll recall, it didn't work very well." Seger shakes her head sadly. "The war's over, Lenie. It's been over for years. I won't start it up again if you won't. And in the meantime—" She glances down the corridor. "I think your friend could use a bit of support."

Clarke looks back along the hallway. Friedman has disappeared.

"Yeah. Maybe," she says noncommittally.

Hope she gets some.

In Beebe Station the comm cubby was a pipe-infested closet, barely big enough for two. Atlantis's nerve center is palatial, a twilit grotto bejeweled by readouts and tangled luminous topographies. Tactical maps rotate miraculously in midair or glow from screens painted on the bulkheads. The miracle is not so much the technology that renders these extravagances. The miracle is that Atlantis contains such an obscene surplus of empty space, to be wasted on nothing more than moving light. A cabin would have done as well. A few couches with workpads and tactical contacts could have contained infinite intelligence, bounded in a nutshell. But no. A whole ocean stands on their heads, and these corpses squander volume as if sea level were two steps down the hall.

Even in exile, they just don't get it.

Right now the cavern's fairly empty. Lubin and a few techs cluster at a nearby panel, cleaning up the latest downloads. The place will be full by the time they finish. Corpses gravitate to news of the world like flies to shit.

For now, though, it's just Lubin's crowd and Patricia Rowan, over on the far side of the compartment. Cryptic information streams across her contacts, turns her eyes into bright points of mercury. Light from a holo display catches the silver streaking her hair; that and the eyes give her the aspect of some subtle hologram in her own right.

Clarke approaches her. "Airlock Four's blocked off."

"They're scrubbing it down. Everything between there and the infirmary. Jerry's orders."

"What for?"

"You know perfectly well. You saw Erickson."

"Oh, come on. One lousy fish bite and Jerry thinks—"

"She's not sure of anything yet. She's just being careful." A pause, then: "You should have warned us, Lenie."

"Warned you?"

"That Erickson might be vectoring ßehemoth. You left all of us exposed. If there was even a chance..."

But there's not, Clarke wants to rail. *There's not. You chose this place because ßehemoth could never get here, not in a thousand years. I saw the maps, I traced out the currents with my own fingers. It's not ßehemoth. It's not.*

It can't be.

Instead she says, "It's a big ocean, Pat. Lots of nasty predators with big pointy teeth. They didn't *all* get that way because of ßehemoth."

"This far down, they did. You know the energetics as well as I do. You were at Channer, Lenie. You *knew* what to look for."

Clarke jerks her thumb toward Lubin. "Ken was at Channer too, remember? You shitting on him like this?"

"Ken didn't deliberately spread that damn bug across a whole continent to pay back the world for his unhappy childhood." The silver eyes fix Clarke in a hard stare. "Ken was on *our* side."

Clarke doesn't speak for a moment. Finally, very slowly: "Are you saying I *deliberately*—"

"I'm not accusing you of anything. But it looks bad. Jerry's livid about this, and she won't be the only one. You're the Meltdown Madonna, for god's sake! You were willing to write off the whole *world* to get your revenge on us."

"If I wanted you dead," Clarke says evenly—*If I* still *wanted you dead,* some inner editor amends—"you would be. Years ago. All I had to do was stand aside."

"Of course that's—"

Clarke cuts her off: "I *protected* you. When the others were arguing about whether to punch holes in the hull or just cut your power and let you suffocate—*I* was the one who held them back. You're alive because of me."

The corpse shakes her head. "Lenie, *that doesn't matter.*"

"It damn well should."

"Why? We were only trying to save the world, remember? It wasn't our fault we failed, it was *yours.* And after we failed, we settled for saving our families, and you wouldn't even give us that. You hunted us down even at the bottom of the ocean. Who knows why you held back at the last minute?"

"You know," Clarke says softly.

Rowan nods. "*I* know. But most of the people down here don't expect rationality from you. Maybe you've just been toying with us all these years. There's no telling when you'll pull the trigger."

Clarke shakes her head dismissively. "What's that, the Gospel According to the Executive Club?"

"Call it what you want. It's what you have to deal with. It's what *I* have to deal with."

"We fish-heads have a few stories of our own, you know," Clarke says. "How you corpses programmed people like machinery so you could top up some bottom line. How you sent us into the world's worst shit-holes to do your dirty work, and when we ran into βehemoth the first thing you did was try to kill us to save your own hides."

Suddenly the ventilators seem unnaturally loud. Clarke turns; Lubin and the corpses stare back from across the cave.

She looks away again, flustered.

Rowan smiles grimly. "See how easily it all comes back?"

Her eyes glitter, target-locked. Clarke returns her gaze without speaking.

After a moment, Rowan relaxes a bit. "We're rival tribes, Lenie. We're each other's outgroup—but you know what's amazing? Somehow, in the past couple of years, *we've started to forget all that*. We live and let live, for the most part. We *co-operate,* and nobody even thinks it worthy of comment." She glances significantly across the room to Lubin and the techs. "I think that's a good thing, don't you?"

"So why should it change now?" Clarke asks.

"Because βehemoth may have caught up with us at last, and people will say you let it in."

"That's horseshit."

"I agree, for what it's worth."

"And even if it *was* true, who cares?" Everyone's part mermaid down here, even the corpses. All retrofitted with the same deep-sea fish-genes, coding for the same stiff little proteins that βehemoth can't get its teeth into.

"There's a concern that the retrofits may not be effective," Rowan admits softly.

"Why? It was your own people designed the fucking things!"

Rowan raises an eyebrow. "Those would be the same experts who assured us that βehemoth would never make it to the deep Atlantic."

"But I was *rotten* with βehemoth. If the retrofits didn't work—"

"Lenie, these people have never been exposed. They've only got some expert's word that they're immune, and in case you haven't noticed our experts have proven distressingly fallible of late. If we were really so confident in our own countermeasures, why would we even be hiding down here? Why wouldn't we be back on shore with our stockholders, with our people, trying to hold back the tide?"

Clarke sees it at last.

"Because they'd tear you apart," she whispers.

Rowan shakes her head. "It's because scientists have been wrong before, and we can't trust their assurances. It's because we're not willing to take chances with the health of our families. It's because we may still be vulnerable to βehemoth, and if we'd stayed behind it would have killed us along with everyone else and we'd have done no good at all. Not because our own people would turn on us. We'll never believe that." Her eyes don't waver. "We're like everyone else, you see. We were all doing the very best we could, and things just—got out of control. It's important to believe that. So we all do."

"Not all," Clarke acknowledges softly.

"Still."

"Fuck 'em. Why should I prop up their self-serving delusions?"

"Because when you force the truth down people's throats, they bite back."

Clarke smiles faintly. "Let them try. I think you're forgetting who's in charge here, Pat."

"I'm not worried for your sake, I'm worried for ours. You people tend to overreaction." When Clarke doesn't deny it, Rowan continues: "It's taken *five years* to build some kind of armistice down here. βehemoth could kick it into a thousand pieces overnight."

"So what do you suggest?"

"I think rifters should stay out of Atlantis for the time being. We can sell it as a quarantine. βehemoth may or may not be out there, but at least we can keep it from getting in *here*."

Clarke shakes her head. "My *tribe* won't give a shit about that."

"You and Ken are the only ones who come in here anyway, for the most part," Rowan points out. "And the others . . . they won't go against anything you put your stamp of approval on."

"I'll think about it," Clarke sighs. "No promises." She turns to go.

And turns back. "Alyx up?"

"Not for another couple of hours. I know she wanted to see you, though."

"Oh." Clarke suppresses a twinge of disappointment.

"I'll give her your regrets," Rowan says.

"Yeah. Do that."

No shortage of those.

HUDDLE

ROWAN'S daughter sits on the edge of her bed, aglow with sunny radiance from the lightstrip on the ceiling. She's barefoot, clad in panties and a baggy T-shirt on which animated hatchet-fish swim endless circuits around her midriff. She breathes a recycled mixture of nitrogen and oxygen and trace gases, distinguishable from real air only by its extreme purity.

The rifter floats in darkness, her contours limned by feeble light leaking through the viewport. She wears a second skin that almost qualifies as a life-form in its own right, a miracle of thermo- and osmoregulation, black as an oil slick. She does not breathe.

A wall separates the two women, keeps ocean from air, adult from adolescent. They speak through a device fixed to the inside of the teardrop viewport, a fist-sized limpet that turns the fullerene perspex into an acoustic transceiver.

"You said you'd come by," Alyx Rowan says. Passage across the bulkhead leaves her voice a bit tinny. "I made it up to fifth level, I was like holy shit, look at all the bonus points! I wanted to show you around. Scammed an extra headset and everything."

"Sorry," Clarke buzzes back. "I was in before, but you were asleep."

"So come in now."

"Can't. I've only got a minute or two. Something's come up."

"Like what?"

"Someone got injured and now the meat-cutters are going off the deep end about possible infection."

"What infection?"

"It's probably nothing. But they're talking about a quarantine just to be on the safe side. For all I know, they wouldn't let me back inside anyway."

"It'd let 'em play at being in control of something, I guess." Alyx grins; the parabolic viewport bends her face into a clownish distortion. "They really, really hate not being in charge, you know?" And then, with a satisfaction obviously borne less of corpses than of adults in general: "It's about time they learned how that felt."

"I'm sorry," Clarke says suddenly.

"They'll get over it."

"That's not what I . . ." The rifter shakes her head. "It's just—you're *fourteen,* for God's sake. You shouldn't be down—I mean, you should be out lekking with some r-selector—"

Alyx snorts. "Boys? I don't think so."

"Girls then. Either way, you should be out getting laid, not stuck down *here.*"

"This is the best place I could possibly be," Alyx says simply.

She looks out across three hundred atmospheres, a teenage girl trapped for the rest of her life in a cage on the bottom of a frigid black ocean. Lenie Clarke would give anything to be able to disagree with her.

"Mom won't talk about it," Alyx says after a while.

Still Clarke says nothing.

"What happened between you guys, back when I was just a kid. Some of the others shoot their mouths off when she's not around, so I kind of hear things. But Mom never says anything."

Mom is kinder than she should be.

"You were enemies, weren't you?"

Clarke shakes her head—a pointless and unseeable gesture,

here in the dark. "Alyx, we didn't even know each other existed, not until the very end. Your mom was only trying to stop—"

—what happened anyway . . .

—what I was trying to start . . .

There's so much more than speech. She wants to sigh. She wants to scream. All denied out here, her lung and guts squeezed flat, every other cavity flooded and incompressible. There's nothing she can do but speak in this monotone travesty of a voice, this buzzing insect voice.

"It's complicated," her vocoder says, flat and dispassionate. "It was so much more than just *enemies,* you know? There were other things involved, there was all that wildlife in the wires, doing its own thing—"

"*They* let that out," Alyx insists. "They started it. Not you." By which she means, of course, *adults*. Perpetrators and betrayers and the-ones-who-fucked-everything-up-for-the-next-generation. And it dawns on Clarke that Alyx is not including *her* in that loathsome conspiracy of elders—that Lenie Clarke, Meltdown Madonna, has somehow acquired the status of honorary innocent in the mind of this child.

She feels ill at the thought of so much undeserved absolution. It seems obscene. But she doesn't have the courage to set her friend straight. All she can manage is a pale, half-assed disclaimer:

"They didn't mean to, kid." She goes for a sad chuckle. It comes out sounding like two pieces of sandpaper rubbing together. "Nobody—nobody did *anything* on their own, back then. It was strings all the way up."

The ocean groans around her.

The sound resonates somewhere between the call of a humpback whale and the death-cry of some mammoth hull, buckling under pressure. It fills the ocean; some of it leaks through Alyx's limpet-device. She screws her face up in distaste. "I hate that sound."

Clarke shrugs, pathetically grateful for the interruption. "Hey, you corpses have your conferences, we have ours."

"It's not that. It's those haploid *chimes*. I'm telling you, Lenie, that guy's scary. You can't trust anyone who makes something that sounds like *that*."

"Your mom trusts him fine. So do I. I've got to go."

"He kills people, Lenie. And I'm not just talking about my dad. He's killed a *lot* of people." A soft snort. "Something else Mom never talks about."

Clarke coasts over to the perspex, lays one silhouetted hand against the light in farewell.

"He's an amateur," she says, and fins away into the darkness.

The voice cries out from a ragged mouth in the seabed, an ancient chimney of basalt stuffed with machinery. In its youth it spewed constant scalding gouts of water and minerals; now it merely belches occasionally. Soft exhalations stir the mechanisms in its throat, spinning blades and fluting pipes and spliced chunks of rock and metal that bang together. Its voice is compelling but unreliable; after Lubin built these chimes, he had to come up with a way to kick-start them manually. So he scavenged the reservoir from a decommissioned desalinator, added a heat pump from some part of Atlantis that never survived the Corpse Revolt. Open a valve and hot seawater flows through a tracheotomy hole blasted into the smoker's throat: Lubin's machinery screams aloud, tortured by the scalding current.

The summons grinds out, rusty and disharmonious. It washes over rifters swimming and conversing and sleeping in an ocean black as heat death. It resonates through makeshift habs scattered across the slope, dismal bubbles of metal and atmosphere so dimly lit that even eyecaps see only in black-and-gray. It slaps against the shiny bright biosteel of Atlantis and nine hundred prisoners speak a little louder, or turn up the volume, or hum nervously to themselves in denial.

Some of the rifters—those awake, and in range, and still human—gather at the chimes. The scene is almost Shakespearean: a circle of levitating witches on some blasted midnight heath, eyes burning with cold phosphorescence, bodies barely distinguished from shadow. They are not so much lit as *inferred* by the faint blue embers glowing from the machinery in the seabed.

All of them bent, not broken. All of them half-balanced in that gray zone between adaptation and dysfunction, stress thresholds pushed so high by years of abuse that chronic danger is mere ambience now, unworthy of comment. They were chosen to function in such environments; their creators never expected them to *thrive* here. But here they are, here are their badges of office: Jelaine Chen with her pink, nailless fingers, salamandered back in the wake of childhood amputations. Dimitri Alexander, communal priest-bait in those last infamous days before the Pope fled into exile. Kevin Walsh, who freaks inexplicably at the sight of running shoes. Any number of garden-variety skitterers who can't abide physical contact; immolation junkies; self-mutilators and glass-eaters. All wounds and deformities safely disguised by the diveskins, all pathology hidden behind a uniformity of shadowy ciphers.

They, too, owe their voices to imperfect machinery.

Clarke calls the meeting to order with a question: "Is Julia here?"

"She's looking on Gene," Nolan buzzes overhead. "I'll fill her in."

"How's he doing?"

"Stable. Still unconscious. Been too long, if you ask me."

"Getting dragged twenty klicks with your guts hanging out, it's pretty much a miracle that he's even alive," Yeager chimes in.

"Yeah," Nolan says, "or maybe Seger's deliberately keeping him under. Julia says—"

Clarke breaks in: "Don't we have a tap on the telemetry from that line?"

"Not any more."

"What's Gene still doing in corpseland anyway?" Chen wonders. "He hates it in there. We've got our own med hab."

"He's quarantined," Nolan says. "Seger's thinking ßehemoth."

Shadows shift at this news. Obviously not all the assembled are fully up to speed.

"Shit." Charley Garcia fades into half-view. "How's that even possible? I thought—"

"Nothing's certain yet," Clarke buzzes.

"Certain?" A silhouette glides across the circle, briefly eclipsing the sapphire embers on the seabed. Clarke recognizes Dale Creasy. This is first time she's seen him for days; she was starting to think he'd gone native.

"Fuck, there's even a *chance,*" he continues. "I mean, *ßehemoth*—"

She decides to nip it in the bud. "So what if it's ßehemoth?"

A school of pale eyes turn in her direction.

"We're immune, remember?" she reminds them. "Anybody down here *not* get the treatments?"

Lubin's windchimes groan softly. Nobody else speaks.

"So why should we care?" Clarke asks.

It's supposed to be rhetorical. Garcia answers anyway: "Because the treatments only stop ßehemoth from turning our guts to mush. They don't stop it from turning little harmless fish into big nasty motherfucking fish that tear into anything that moves."

"Gene was attacked twenty klicks away."

"Lenie, we're *moving* there. It's gonna be right in our backyard."

"Forget *there*. Who's to say it hasn't reached *here* already?" Alexander wonders.

"Nobody's been nailed around here," Creasy says.

"We've lost some natives."

Creasy waves an arm in a barely-visible gesture of dismissal. "Natives. Don't mean shit."

"Maybe we should stop sleeping outside, for a while at least..."

"Crap to that. I can't sleep in a stinking *hab*."

"Fine. Get yourself eaten."

"Lenie?" Chen again. "You've messed with sea monsters before."

"I never saw what got Gene," Clarke says, "but the fish back at Channer, they were—flimsy. Big and mean, but sometimes their teeth would break on you when they bit. Missing some kind of trace nutrient, I think. You could tear them apart with your bare hands."

"This thing pretty much tore *Gene* apart," says a voice Clarke can't pin down.

"I said *sometimes*," she emphasizes. "But yeah—they could be dangerous."

"*Dangerous*, felch." Creasy growls in metal. "Could they have pulled that number on Gene?"

"Yes," says Ken Lubin.

He's been here all along, of course. Now he takes center stage. A cone of light flares from his forehead to his forearm. He holds his hand out like a beggar's, its fingers curled slightly around something laying across the palm.

"Holy shit," buzzes Creasy, suddenly subdued.

"Where'd that come from?" Chen asks.

"Seger pulled it out of Erickson before she glued him up," Lubin says.

"Doesn't look especially *flimsy* to me."

"It is, rather," Lubin remarks. "This is the part that broke off, in fact. Between the ribs."

"What, you mean that's just the *tip*?" Garcia says.

"Looks like a fucking stiletto," Nolan buzzes softly.

Chen's mask swings between Clarke and Lubin. "When you were at Channer. You slept outside with these mothers?"

"Sometimes." Clarke shrugs. "Assuming this is the same thing, which I—"

"And they didn't try to eat you?"

"They keyed on the light. As long as you kept your lamps off, they pretty much left you alone."

"Well, shit," Creasy says. "No problem, then."

Lubin's headlamp sweeps across the assembled rifters and settles on Chen. "You were on a telemetry run when Erickson was attacked?"

Chen nods. "We never got the download, though."

"So someone needs to make another trip out there anyway. And since Lenie and I have experience with this kind of thing..."

His beam hits Clarke full in the face. The world collapses down to a small bright sun floating in a black void.

Clarke raises her hand against the brilliance. "Turn that somewhere else, will you?"

Darkness returns. The rest of the world comes back into dim, dark focus. *Maybe I could just swim away,* she muses as her eyecaps readjust. *Maybe no one would notice.* But that's bullshit and she knows it. Ken Lubin has just picked her out of the crowd; there's no easy way to get out of this. And besides, he's right. They're the only two that have been down this road before. The only two still alive, at least.

Thanks a lot, Ken.

"Fine," she says at last.

ZOMBIE

TWENTY kilometers separate Atlantis and Impossible Lake. Not far enough for those who still think in dryback terms. A mere twenty klicks from the bull's-eye? What kind of safety margin is that? Back on shore the most simpleminded drone wouldn't be fooled by such a trifling displacement. Finding the target missing, it would rise up and partition the world into a concentric gridwork, relentlessly checking off one quadrate after another until some inevitable telltale gave the game away. Shit, most machinery could just sit at the center of the search zone and *see* twenty kilometers in any direction.

Even in the midwaters of the open ocean, twenty kilometers is no safe distance. No substrate exists there but water itself, no topography but gyres and seiches and Langmuir cells, thermoclines and haloclines that reflect and amplify as well as mask. The cavitation of submarines might propagate down vast distances, the miniscule turbulence of their passing detectable long after the vessels themselves are gone. Not even stealthed subs can avoid heating the water some infinitesimal amount; dolphins and machinery, hot on the trail, can tell the difference.

But on the Mid Atlantic Ridge, twenty kilometers might as well be twenty parsecs. Light has no chance: the sun itself barely penetrates a few hundred meters from the surface. Hydrothermal vents throw up their corrosive vomit along oozing seams of fresh rock. Seafloor spreading sets the very floor of the world to grumbling, mountains pushing against each other in their millennial game of kick-the-continents. Topography that shames the Himalayas cascades along a jagged fracture splitting the crust from pole to pole. The ambience of the Ridge drowns out anything Atlantis might let slip, along any spectrum you'd care to name.

You could still find a target with the right coordinates, but you'd miss a whole screaming city if those numbers were off by even a hair. A displacement of twenty kilometers should be more than enough to get out from under any attack centered on Atlantis's present location, short of full-scale depth-saturation nukes perhaps.

Which wouldn't be entirely without precedent, now that Clarke thinks about it...

She and Lubin cruise smoothly along a crack in a fan of ancient lava. Atlantis is far behind, Impossible Lake still klicks ahead. Headlamps and squidlamps are dark. They travel by the dim dashboard light of their sonar displays. Tiny iconized boulders and pillars pass by on the screens, mapped in emerald; the slightest sensations of pressure and looming mass press in from the scrolling darkness to either side.

"Rowan thinks things could get nasty," Clarke buzzes.

Lubin doesn't comment.

"She figures, if this really is βehemoth, Atlantis is gonna turn into Cognitive Dissonance Central. Get everybody all worked up."

Still nothing.

"I reminded her who was in charge."

"And who is that, exactly?" Lubin buzzes at last.

"Come on, Ken. We can shut them down any time we feel like it."

"They've had five years to work on that."

"And what's it got them?"

"They've also had five years to realize that they outnumber us twenty to one, that we don't have nearly their technical expertise on a wide range of relevant subjects, and that a group of glorified pipe-fitters with antisocial personalities is unlikely to pose much threat in terms of organized opposition."

"That was just as true when we wiped the floor with them the first time."

"No."

She doesn't understand why he's doing this. It was Lubin more than anyone who put the corpses in their place after their first—and last—uprising. "Come *on,* Ken—"

His squid is suddenly very close, almost touching.

"You're not an idiot," he buzzes at her side. "It's never a good time to act like one."

Stung, she falls silent.

His vocoder growls on in the darkness. "Back then they saw the whole world backing us up. They knew we'd had help tracking them down. They inferred some kind of ground-based infrastructure. At the very least, they knew we could blow the whistle and turn them into a great pulsing bull's-eye for anyone with lats and longs and a smart torp."

A great luminous shark-fin swells on her screen, a massive stone blade thrusting up from the seabed. Lubin disappears briefly as it passes between them.

"But now we're on our own," he says, reappearing. "Our groundside connections have dried up. Maybe they're dead, maybe they've turned. Nobody knows. Can you even remember the last time we had a changing of the guard?"

She can, just barely. Anyone qualified for the diveskin is bound to be more comfortable down here than in dryback company at the best of times, but a few rifters went topside at the very beginning anyway. Back when there might have been some hope of turning the tide.

Not since. Risking your life to watch the world end isn't anyone's idea of shore leave.

"By now we're just as scared as the corpses," Lubin buzzes.

"We're just as cut off, and there are almost a thousand of them. We're down to fifty-eight at last count."

"We're seventy at least."

"The natives don't count. Fifty-eight of us would be any use in a fight, and only fifty could last a week in full gravity if they had to. And a number of those have . . . authority issues that make them unwilling to organize."

"We've got you," Clarke says. Lubin, the professional hunter-killer, so recently freed from any leash but his own self-control. *No glorified pipe-fitter here,* she reflects.

"Then you should listen to me. And I'm starting to think we may have to do something preemptive."

They cruise in silence for a few moments.

"They're not the enemy, Ken," she says at last. "Not all of them. Some of them are just kids, you know, they're not responsible . . ."

"That's not the point."

From some indefinable distance, the faint sound of falling rock.

"Ken," she buzzes, too softly: she wonders if he can hear her.

"Yes."

"Are you looking forward to it?"

It's been so many years since he's had an excuse to kill someone. And Ken Lubin once made a career out of finding excuses.

He tweaks his throttle and pulls away.

Trouble dawns like a sunrise, smearing the darkness ahead.

"Anyone else supposed to be out here?" Clarke asks. The on-site floods are keyed to wake up when approached, but she and Lubin aren't nearly close enough to have triggered them.

"Just us," Lubin buzzes.

The glow is coarse and unmistakable. It spreads laterally, a diffuse false dawn hanging in the void. Two or three dark gaps betray the presence of interposed topography.

"Stop," Lubin says. Their squids settle down beside a tumbledown outcropping, its jumbled edges reflecting dimly in the haze.

He studies the schematic on his dashboard. A reflected fingernail of light traces his profile.

He turns his squid to port. "This way. Keep to the bottom."

They edge closer to the light, keeping it to starboard. The glow expands, resolves, reveals an impossibility: a lake at the bottom of the ocean. The light shines from beneath its surface; Clarke thinks of a swimming pool at night, lit by submerged spotlights in the walls. Slow extravagant waves, top-heavy things from some low-gravity planet, break into shuddering globules against the near shore. The lake extends beyond the hazy limits of rifter vision.

It always hits her like a hallucination, although she knows the pedestrian truth: it's just a salt seep, a layer of mineralized water so dense it lies on the bottom of the ocean the way an ocean lies at the bottom of the sky. It's a major selling point to anyone in search of camouflage. The halocline reflects all manner of pings and probes, hides everything beneath as though there were nothing here but soft, deep mud.

A soft, brief scream of electronics. For the merest instant Clarke thinks she sees a drop of luminous blood on her dashboard. She focuses. Nothing.

"Did you—?"

"Yes." Lubin's playing with his controls. "This way." He steers closer to the shores of Impossible Lake. Clarke follows.

The next time it's unmistakable: a brilliant pinpoint of red light, laser-bright, flickering on and off within the jagged topography of the dashboard display. The squids cry out with each flash.

A deadman alarm. Somewhere ahead, a rifter's heart has stopped.

They're cruising out over the lake now, just offshore. Roiling greenish light suffuses Lubin and his mount from below. A hypersaline globule shatters in slow motion against the squid's underside. Light rising through the interface bends in odd ways. It's like looking down through the radium-lit depths of a nuclear waste–storage lagoon. A grid of bright pinpoint suns shine far below that surface, where the surveyors have planted their lamps. The solid substrate beneath is hidden by distance and diffraction.

The deadman alarm has stabilized to a confidence bubble about forty meters straight ahead. Its ruby icon beats like a heart on the screen. The squids bleat in synch.

"There," Clarke says. The horizon's absurdly inverted here, darkness overhead, milky light beneath. A dark spot hangs at the distant, fuzzy interface between. It appears to be floating on the surface of the lens.

Clarke nudges her throttle up a bit.

"Wait," Lubin buzzes. She looks back over her shoulder.

"The waves," Lubin says.

They're smaller here than they were back near the shore, which makes sense since there's no rising substrate to push the peaks above baseline. They're rippling past in irregular spasms, though, not the usual clockwork procession, and now that she traces them back they seem to be radiating out from...

Shit...

She's close enough to see limbs now, attenuate sticklike things slapping the surface of the lake into a local frenzy. Almost as though the rifter ahead is a poor swimmer, in over his head and panicking...

"He's *alive,*" she buzzes. The deadman icon pulses, contradicting her.

"No," Lubin says.

Only fifteen meters away now, the enigma erupts writhing from the surface of the lake in a nimbus of shredded flesh. Too late, Clarke spots the larger, darker shape thrashing beneath it. Too late, she resolves the mystery: meal, interrupted. The thing that was eating it heads straight for her.

It can't b—

She twists, not quite fast enough. The monster's mouth takes the squid with room to spare. Half a dozen finger-sized teeth splinter against the machine like brittle ceramic. The squid torques in her hands; some sharp-edged metal protuberance smashes into her leg with a thousand kilograms of predatory momentum behind it. Something snaps below the knee. Pain rips through her calf.

It's been six years. She's forgotten the moves.

Lubin hasn't. She can hear his squid bearing in, cranked to full throttle. She curls into a ball, grabs the gas billy off her calf in a belated countermeasure. She hears a meaty thud; hydraulics cough. In the next instant a great scaly mass staggers against her, batting her down through the boiling interface.

Heavy water glows on all sides. The world is fuzzy and whirling. She shakes her head to lock it into focus. The action wavers and bulges overhead, writhing through the shattered refractory surface of Impossible Lake. Lubin must have rammed the monster with his squid. Damage may have been inflicted on both sides—now the squid's corkscrewing down into the lens, riderless and uncontrolled. Lubin hangs in the water facing an opponent twice his size, half of it mouth. If there are eyes, Clarke can't make them out through this wobbling discontinuity.

She's slowly falling up, she realizes. She scissor-kicks without thinking; her leg screams as something tears it from the inside. She screams too, a ratcheting torn-metal sound. Floaters swarm across her eyes in the wake of the cresting pain. She rises from the lake just as the monster opens its mouth and—

—*holy* shit—

—*disconnects* its jaw, right at the base, the mouth dropping open way too fast and suddenly it's closed again and Lubin's just *gone,* nothing to suggest where he went except the memory of blurred motion between one instant and the next.

She does perhaps the most stupid thing she's ever done in her life. She charges.

The leviathan turns to face her, more ponderously now, but still with all the time in the world. She kicks with one leg, drags the other like a useless throbbing anchor. The monster's serrated mouth grimaces, a mangled profusion of teeth, way too many still intact. She tries to duck past, to come up under the belly or at least the side but it just wallows there, turning effortlessly to face every clumsy approach.

And then, through the top of its head, it *belches.*

The bubbles do not arise from any natural openings. They erupt through the flesh itself, tearing their own way, splitting the soft skull from within. For a second or two the monster hangs motionless; then it shivers, an electric spasm that seizes the whole body. One-legged, Clarke gets underneath and stabs its belly. She can feel more bubbles erupt inside as the billy discharges, a seismic eruption of flesh.

The monster convulses, dying. Its jaw drops open like some ludicrous flapping drawbridge. The water seethes with regurgitated flesh.

A few meters away, the grinning shredded remains of something in a diveskin settle gently onto the surface of Impossible Lake, within a lumpy cloud of its own entrails.

"You okay?"

Lubin's at her side. She shakes her head, more in amazement than reply. "My leg..." Now, in the aftermath, it hurts even more.

He probes her injury. She yelps; the vocoder turns it into a mechanical bark. "Your fibula's broken," Lubin reports. "Diveskin didn't tear, at least."

"The squid got me." She feels a deep burning chill along her leg. She tries to ignore it, gestures at the billy on Lubin's calf. "How many shots did you pump into that fucker?"

"Three."

"You were just—*gone.* It just sucked you right in. You're lucky it didn't bite you in half."

"Slurp-gun feeding doesn't work if you stop to chew. Interrupts the suction." Lubin pans around. "Wait here."

Like I'm going to go anywhere with this leg. She can already feel it stiffening. She profoundly hopes the squids are still working.

Lubin fins easily over to the corpse. Its diveskin is torn in a dozen places. Tubes and metal gleam intermittently from the opened thorax. A pair of hagfish squirm sluggishly from the remains.

"Lopez," he buzzes, reading her shoulder patch.

Irene Lopez went native six months ago. It's been weeks since anyone's even seen her at the feeding stations.

"Well," Lubin says. "This answers one question, at least."

"Not necessarily."

The monster, still twitching, has settled on the surface of the lake a little ways from Lopez. It wallows only slightly deeper; you'd have to be some kind of rock to sink in brine this dense. Lubin abandons the corpse in favor of the carcass. Clarke joins him.

"This isn't the same thing that got Gene," he buzzes. "Different teeth. Gigantism in at least two different species of bony fish, within two kilometers of a hydrothermal vent." He reaches into the gaping maw, snaps off a tooth. "Osteoporosis, probably other deficiency diseases as well."

"Maybe you could save the lecture until you straighten that

out for me?" She points to where her squid, listing drunkenly, describes small erratic circles in the overhead darkness. "I don't think I'm gonna be swimming home with this leg."

He coasts up and wrests the vehicle back under control. "We have to bring it back," he says, riding it down to her. "All of it," with a nod to Lopez's gutted remains.

"It's not necessarily what you think," she tells him.

He turns and jackknifes into Impossible Lake, on the trail of his own squid. Clarke watches his rippling image kicking hard, fighting against buoyancy.

"It's not ßehemoth," she buzzes softly. "It'd never survive the trip." Her voice is as calm as such mechanical caricatures can be out here. Her words sound reasonable. Her thoughts are neither. Her thoughts are caught in a loop, a mantra borne of some forlorn subconscious hope that endless repetition might give substance to wishes:

It can't be it can't be it can't be . . .

Here on the sunless slopes of the Mid Atlantic Ridge, facing consequences that have somehow chased her to the very bottom of the world, denial seems the only available option.

PORTRAIT OF THE SADIST AS A YOUNG BOY

ACHILLES Desjardins wasn't always the most powerful man in North America; at one time he'd been just another kid growing up in the shadow of Mont St. Hilaire. He *had* always been an empiricist, though, an experimenter at heart for as long as he could remember. His first encounter with a research-ethics committee had occurred when he was only eight.

That particular experiment had involved aerobraking. His parents, in a well-intentioned effort to interest him in the classics, had introduced him to *The Revenge of Mary Poppins*. The story itself was pretty stupid, but Achilles liked the way the Persinger Box had slipped the butterfly-inducing sensation of *flight* directly into his brain. Mary Poppins had this nanotech umbrella, see, and she could jump right off the top of the CN Tower and float to earth as gently as a dandelion seed.

The illusion was so convincing that Achilles's eight-year-old brain couldn't see why it wouldn't work in real life.

His family was rich—all Quebecois families were, thanks to Hudson Hydro—so Achilles lived in a real house, a single stand-alone dwelling with a yard and everything. He grabbed an umbrella from the closet, let it bloom, and—clutching tightly with both hands—jumped off the front porch. The drop was only a meter and a half, but that was enough; he could feel the umbrella grabbing at the air above him, slowing his descent.

Buoyed by this success, Achilles moved on to phase two. His sister Penny, two years younger, held him in almost supernatural esteem; it was dead easy to talk her into scrambling up the trellis and onto the roof. It took a bit more effort to coax her to the very peak of the gable, which must have been a good seven meters above ground—but when your big-brother-who-you-idolize is calling you a chickenshit, what are you supposed to do? Penny inched her way to the apex and stood teetering at the edge, the dome of the umbrella framing her face like a big black halo. For a moment Achilles thought the experiment would fail: he had to bring out his ultimate weapon and call her "Penelope"—*twice*—before she jumped.

There was nothing to worry about, of course. Achilles already knew it would work; the umbrella had slowed *him* after all, even during a drop of a measly meter or so, and Penny weighed a *lot* less than he did.

Which made it all the more surprising when the umbrella snapped inside out, *whap!,* right before his eyes. Penny dropped like a rock, landed on her feet with a *snap* and crumpled on the spot.

In the moment of complete silence that followed, several things went through the mind of eight-year-old Achilles Desjardins. First was the fact that the goggle-eyed look on Penny's face had been *really* funny just before she hit. Second was confusion and disbelief that the experiment hadn't proceeded as expected; he couldn't for the life of him figure out what had gone wrong. Third came the belated realization that Penny, for all the hilarity of her facial expression, might actually be hurt; maybe he should try and do something about that.

Lastly, he thought of the trouble he was going to be in if his parents found out about this. That thought crushed the others like bugs under a boot.

He rushed over to the crumpled form of his sister on the lawn. "*Geez,* Penny, are you—are you—"

She wasn't. The umbrella's ribs had torn free of the fabric and slashed her across the side of the neck. One of her ankles was twisted at an impossible angle, and had already swollen to twice its normal size. There was blood everywhere.

Penny looked up, lip trembling, bright tears quivering in her eyes. They broke and ran down her cheeks as Achilles stood over her, scared to death.

"Penny—" he whispered.

"I—it's okay," she quavered. "I won't tell anyone. I promise." And—broken and bleeding and teary-eyed, eyes brimming with undiminished adoration for Big Brother—she tried to get up, and screamed the instant she moved her leg.

Looking back as an adult, Desjardins knew that that couldn't have been the moment of his first erection. It was, however, the first one that stuck in his mind. He hadn't been able to help himself: she had been so *helpless*. Broken and bleeding and hurt. *He* had hurt her. She had meekly walked the plank for him, and after she'd fallen and snapped like a twig she'd looked up at him, still worshipful, ready to do whatever it took to keep him happy.

He didn't know why that made him feel this way—he didn't even know what *this way* was, exactly—but he liked it.

His willy hard as a bone, he reached out to her. He wasn't sure why—he was grateful that she wasn't going to tell, of course, but he didn't think that's what this was about. He thought—as his hand touched his sister's fine brown hair—that maybe this was about seeing how much he could get *away* with . . .

Not much, as it turned out. His parents were on him in the next second, shrieking and striking. Achilles raised his hands against his father's blows, cried *"I saw it on* Mary Poppins*!"*, but the alibi didn't fly any more than Penny had; Dad kicked the shit out of him and threw him into his room for the rest of the day.

It couldn't have ended any differently, of course. Mom and Dad always found out. It turned out the little bump that both

Achilles and Penny had under their collarbones sent out a signal when either of them got hurt. And after the *Mary Poppins* Incident, not even the implants were enough for Mom and Dad. Achilles couldn't go anywhere, not even the bathroom, without three or four skeeters following him around like nosy floating rice grains.

All in all, that afternoon taught him two things that shaped the rest of his life. One was that he was a wicked, wicked boy who could never *ever* give in to his impulses no matter *how* good it made him feel, or he would go straight to hell.

The other was a profound and lifelong appreciation of the impact of ubiquitous surveillance.

CONFIDENCE LIMITS

THERE are no rifter MDs. The walking wounded don't generally excel in the art of healing.

Of course, there's never been any shortage of rifters in *need* of healing. Especially after the Corpse Revolt. The fish-heads won that war hands down, but they took casualties just the same. Some died. Others suffered injuries and malfunctions beyond the skill of their own off-the-shelf medical machinery. Some needed help to stay alive; others, to die in something less than agony.

And all the qualified doctors were on the other side.

No one was going to trust their injured comrades to the tender mercies of a thousand sore losers just because the corpses had the only hospital for four thousand klicks. So they grafted a couple of habs together fifty meters off Atlantis's shoulder, and furnished it with medical equipment pillaged from enemy infirmaries. Fiberop let the corpses' meat-cutters practice their art by remote control; explosive charges planted on Atlantis's hull inspired those same meat-cutters to be extra careful in matters of potential malpractice. The losers took very good care of the winners, on pain of implosion.

Eventually tensions eased. Rifters stopped avoiding Atlantis out of distrust, and began avoiding it out of indifference instead. Gradually, the realization dawned that the rest of the world posed a greater threat to rifters and corpses alike than either did to the other. Lubin took down the charges somewhere during year three, when most everyone had forgotten about them anyway.

The med hab still gets a fair bit of use. Injuries happen. Injuries are inevitable, given rifter tempers and the derived weakness of rifter bones. But at the moment it holds only two occupants, and the corpses are probably thanking their portfolios that the rifters cobbled this facility together all those years ago. Otherwise, Clarke and Lubin might have dragged themselves into Atlantis—and everyone knows where they've been.

As it is, they only ventured close enough to hand off Irene Lopez and the thing that dined upon her. Two clamshell sarcophagi, dropped from one of Atlantis's engineering locks on short notice, devoured that evidence and are even now sending their findings up fiberop umbilicals. In the meantime Clarke and Lubin lie side by side on a pair of operating tables, naked as cadavers themselves. It's been a long time since any corpse dared give an order to a rifter, but they've acquiesced to Jerenice Seger's "strong recommendation" that they get rid of their diveskins. It was a tougher concession than Clarke lets on. It's not that simple nudity discomfits her; Lubin has never tripped Clarke's usual alarms. But the autoclave isn't just sterilizing her diveskin; it's destroying it, melting it back down to a useless slurry of protein and petroleum. She's trapped, naked and vulnerable, in this tiny bubble of gas and spun metal. For the first time in years, she can't simply step outside. For the first time in years the ocean can *kill* her—all it has to do is crush this fragile eggshell and clench around her like a freezing liquid fist...

It's a temporary vulnerability, of course. New diveskins are on the way, are being extruded right now. Clarke just has to hold out another fifteen or twenty minutes. But in the meantime she feels worse than naked. She feels skinned alive.

It doesn't seem to bother Lubin much. Nothing does. Of course, Lubin's teleop is being a lot less invasive than Clarke's.

It's only taking samples: blood, skin, swabs from around the eyes and anus and seawater intake. Clarke's machine is digging deep into the flesh of her leg, displacing muscle and resetting bone and waving its gleaming chopstick arms like some kind of chrome spider performing an exorcism. Occasionally the smell of her own cauterizing flesh wafts faintly up the table. Presumably her injury is under repair, although she can't really tell; the table's neuroinduction field has her paralyzed and insensate below the stomach.

"How much longer?" she asks. The teleop ignores her without dropping a stitch.

"I don't think there's anyone there," Lubin says. "It's on autopilot."

She turns her head to look at him. Eyes dark enough to be called black look back at her. Clarke catches her breath; she keeps forgetting what *naked* really means, down here. What is it the drybacks say? *The eyes are the windows to the soul.* But the windows into rifter souls are supposed to have frosted panes. Uncapped eyes are for corpses: this doesn't look right, it doesn't *feel* right. It looks as though Lubin's eyes have been pulled right out of his head, as though Clarke is looking into the wet sticky darkness inside his skull.

He rises on the table, oblivious to his own gory blindness, and swings his legs over the edge. His teleop withdraws to the ceiling with a few disapproving clicks.

A comm panel decorates the bulkhead within easy reach. He taps it. "Ambient channel. Grace. How are you coming with those 'skins?"

Nolan answers in her outdoor voice: "We're ten meters off your shoulder. And yes, we remembered to bring extra eyecaps." A soft buzz—acoustic modems are bad for background noise sometimes. "If it's okay with you, though, we'll just leave 'em in the 'lock and be on our way."

"Sure." Lubin's face is expressionless. "No problem."

Clanks and hisses from down on the wet deck.

"There you go, sweetie," Nolan buzzes.

Lubin drills Clarke with those eviscerated eyes. "You coming?"

Clarke blinks. "Any place in particular?"

"Atlantis."

"My leg—" but her teleop is folding up against the ceiling as she speaks, its slicing and dicing evidently completed.

She struggles to prop her upper body up on its elbows; she's still dead meat below the gut, although the hole in her thigh has been neatly glued shut. "I'm still frozen. Shouldn't the field—"

"Perhaps they were hoping we wouldn't notice." Lubin takes a handpad off the wall. "Ready?"

She nods. He taps a control. Feeling floods her legs like a tidal bore. Her repaired thigh awakens, a sudden tingling swarm of pins and needles. She tries to move it. She succeeds, with difficulty.

She sits up, grimacing.

"What're you doing out there?" the intercom demands. After a moment, Clarke recognizes the voice: Klein. Shutting down the field seems to have caught his attention.

Lubin disappears into the wet room. Clarke kneads her thigh. The pins and needles persist.

"Lenie?" Klein says. "What—"

"I'm fixed."

"No you're not."

"The teleop—"

"You have to stay off that leg for at least six more hours. Preferably twelve."

"Thanks. I'll take it under advisement." She swings her legs over the edge of the table, puts some weight on the good one, gradually shifts weight to the other. It buckles. She grabs the table in time to keep from keeling over.

Lubin steps back into view, a carrysack slung over his shoulder. "You okay?" His eyes are capped again, white as fresh ice.

Clarke nods, strangely relieved. "Hand me that diveskin."

Klein heard that. "Wait a second—you two have *not* been cleared for—I mean—"

The eyes go in first. The tunic slithers eagerly around her torso. Sleeves and gauntlets cling like welcome shadows. She leans against Lubin for support while she dons the leggings—the tingling in her thigh is beginning to subside, and when she tries out the leg again it takes her weight for a good ten seconds before giving out. Progress.

"Lenie. Ken. Where are you going?"

Seger's voice, this time. Klein's called for reinforcements.

"We thought we'd come for a visit," Lubin says.

"Are you sure you've thought that through?" Seger says calmly. "With all due respect—"

"Is there some reason we shouldn't?" Lubin asks innocently.

"Lenie's l—"

"Beyond Lenie's leg."

Dead air in the room.

"You've analyzed the samples by now," Lubin remarks.

"Not comprehensively. The tests are fast, not instantaneous."

"And? Anything?"

"*If* you were infected, Mr. Lubin, it only happened a few hours ago. That's hardly enough time for an infection to reach detectable levels in the bloodstream."

"That's a no, then." Lubin considers. "What about our 'skins? Surely you would have found something on the diveskin swabs."

Seger doesn't answer.

"So they protected us," Lubin surmises. "This time."

"As I said, we haven't finished—"

"I understood that βehemoth couldn't reach us down here," he remarks.

Seger doesn't answer that either, at first.

"So did I," she says finally.

Clarke takes a half-hop toward the airlock. Lubin offers an arm.

"We're coming over," he says.

Half a dozen modelers cluster around workstations at the far end of the comm cave, running sims, tweaking parameters in the hope that their virtual world might assume some relevance to the real one. Patricia Rowan leans over their shoulders, studying something at one board; Jerenice Seger labors alone at another. She turns and catches sight of the approaching rifters, raises her voice just slightly in an alarm call disguised as a greeting: "Ken. Lenie."

The others turn. A couple of the less-experienced back away a step or two.

Rowan recovers first, her quicksilver eyes unreadable: "You should spare that leg, Lenie. Here." She grabs an unused chair from a nearby station and rolls it over. Clarke sinks gratefully into it.

Nobody makes a fuss. The assembled corpses know how to follow a lead, even though some of them don't seem too happy about it.

"Jerry says you've dodged the bullet," Rowan continues.

"As far as we know," Seger adds. "For now."

"Which implies a bullet to dodge," Lubin says.

Seger looks at Rowan. Rowan looks at Lubin. The number crunchers don't look anywhere in particular.

Finally, Seger shrugs. "D-cysteine and d-cystine, positive. Pyranosal RNA, positive. No phospholipids, no DNA. Intracellular ATP off the scale. Not to mention you can do an SEM of the infected cells and just *see* the little fellows floating around in there." She takes a deep breath. "If it's not βehemoth, it's βehemoth's evil twin brother."

"Shit," says one of the modelers. "Not *again.*"

It takes Clarke a moment to realize that he's not reacting to Seger's words, but to something on the workstation screen. She leans forward, catches sight of the display through the copse of personnel: a volumetric model of the Atlantic basin. Luminous contrails wind through its depths like many-headed snakes, bifurcating and converging over continental shelves and mountain ranges. Currents and gyres and deep-water circulation iconized in shades of green and red: the ocean's own rivers. And superimposed over the entire display, a churlish summary:

FAILURE TO CONVERGE. CONFIDENCE LIMITS EXCEEDED.
FURTHER PREDICTIONS UNRELIABLE.

"Bring down the Labrador Current a bit more," one of the modelers suggests.

"Any more and it'll shut down completely," another one says.

"So how do you know that isn't exactly what happened?"

"When the Gulf Stream—"

"Just *try* it, will you?"

The Atlantic clears and resets.

Rowan turns from her troops and fixes Seger. "Suppose they can't figure it out?"

"Maybe it was down here all along. Maybe we just missed it." Seger shakes her head, as if skeptical of her own suggestion. "We *were* in something of a hurry."

"Not that much hurry. We checked every vent within a thousand kilometers before we settled on this site, did we not?"

"Somebody did," Seger says tiredly.

"I saw the results. They were comprehensive." Rowan seems almost less disturbed by βehemoth's appearance than by the thought that the surveys might have been off. "And certainly none of the surveys since have shown anything . . ." She breaks off, struck by some sudden thought. "They haven't, have they? Lenie?"

"No," Clarke says. "Nothing."

"Right. So, five years ago this whole area was clean. The whole abyssal Atlantic was clean, as far as we know. And how long can ßehemoth survive in cold seawater before it shrivels up like a prune and dies?"

"A week or two," Seger recites. "A month max."

"And how long would it take to get here via deep circulation?"

"Decades. Centuries." Seger sighs. "We know all this, Pat. Obviously, something's changed."

"Thanks for that insight, Jerry. What might that something be?"

"Christ, what do you want from me? I'm not an oceanographer." Seger waves an exasperated hand at the modelers. "Ask *them*. Jason's been running that model for—"

"Semen-sucking-motherfucking *stumpfucker*!" Jason snarls at the screen. The screen snarls back:

FAILURE TO CONVERGE. CONFIDENCE LIMITS EXCEEDED.
FURTHER PREDICTIONS UNRELIABLE.

Rowan closes her eyes and starts again. "Would it be able to survive in the euphotic zone, at least? It's warmer up there, even in winter. Could our recon parties have picked it up and brought it back?"

"Then it would be showing up here, not way over at Impossible Lake."

"But it shouldn't be showing *anywh*—"

"What about fish?" Lubin says suddenly.

Rowan looks at him. "What?"

"βehemoth can survive indefinitely inside a host, correct? Less osmotic stress. That's why they infect fish in the first place. Perhaps they hitched a ride."

"Abyssal fish don't disperse," Seger says. "They just hang around the vents."

"Are the larvae planktonic?"

"Still wouldn't work. Not over these kinds of distances, anyway."

"With all due respect," Lubin remarks, "you're a medical doctor. Maybe we should ask someone with *relevant* expertise."

It's a jab, of course. When the corpses were assigning professional berths on the ark, ichthyologists didn't even make the long list. But Seger only shakes her head impatiently. "They'd tell you the same thing."

"How do you know?" There's an odd curiosity in Rowan's voice.

"Because βehemoth was trapped in a few hot vents for most of Earth's history. If it had been able to disperse inside plankton, why wait until now to take over the world? It would have done it a few hundred million years ago."

Something changes in Patricia Rowan. Clarke can't quite put her finger on it. Maybe it's some subtle shift in the other woman's posture. Or perhaps Rowan's ConTacts have brightened, as if the intel twinkling across her eyes has slipped into fast-forward.

"Pat?" Clarke asks.

But suddenly Seger's coming out of her chair like it was on fire, spurred by a signal coming over her earbud. She taps her watch to bring it online: "I'm on my way. Stall them."

She turns to Lubin and Clarke. "If you really want to help, come with me."

"What's the problem?" Lubin asks.

Seger's already halfway across the cave. "More slow learners. They're about to kill your friend."

CAVALRY

THERE are lines drawn everywhere in Atlantis, four-centimeter gaps that circumscribe whole corridors as if someone had chainsawed through the bulkheads at regular intervals. The gaps are flagged by cautionary bands of diagonal striping to either side, and if you stand astride one of them and look up to where it passes overhead, you'll see why: each contains a drop-gate, poised to guillotine down in the event of a hull breach. They're such convenient and ubiquitous boundaries that parties in opposition have always tended to use them as lines in the sand.

Parties like the half-dozen corpses hanging back at the junction, too scared or too smart to get involved. Parties like Hannuk Yeager, dancing restlessly on the far side of the striped line, keeping them all at bay fifteen meters upwind of the infirmary.

Lubin shoulders through the chickenshit corpses, Clarke hobbling in his wake. Yeager bares his teeth in greeting: "Party's four doors down on the left!" His capped eyes narrow at their corpse escorts.

Clarke and Lubin pass. Seger tries to follow; Yeager catches her around the throat and holds her there, squirming. "Invitation only."

"You don't—" Yeager clenches; Seger's voice chokes down to a whisper. "You want . . . Gene to die . . . ?"

"Sounds like a *threat,*" Yeager growls.

"I'm his *doctor*!"

"Let her go," Clarke tells him. "We might need her."

Yeager doesn't budge.

Oh shit, Clarke thinks. *Is he primed?*

Yeager's got a mutation: too much monoamine oxidase in his blood. It breaks down the brain chemicals that keep people on an even keel. The authorities tweaked him to compensate, back in the days when they could get away with such things, but he learned to get around it somehow. Sometimes he deliberately strings himself so tight that a sideways glance can send him off the deep end. It gets him off. When that happens, it doesn't matter all that much whether you're friend or foe. Times like that, even Lubin takes him seriously.

Lubin's taking him seriously now. "Let her past, Han." His voice is calm and even, his posture relaxed.

From down the corridor, a groan. The sound of something breaking.

Yeager snorts and tosses Seger aside. The woman staggers coughing against the wall.

"You too," Lubin says to Rowan, who's still discreetly behind the striped line. To Yeager: "If it's okay with you, of course."

"Shit, I don't give a fuck." Yeager's fingers clench and unclench as if electrified.

Lubin nods. "You go on," he says casually to Clarke. "I'll help Han hold the fort."

It's Nolan, of course. Clarke can hear her snarling as she nears the medbay: "Ah, the little fuckhead's gone and shit himself..."

She squeezes through the hatch. The sour stench of fear and feces hits her in the face. Nolan, yes. And she's got Creasy backing her up. Klein's been thrown into the corner, broken and bleeding. Maybe he tried to get in the way. Maybe Nolan just wanted him to.

Gene Erickson's awake at last, crouching on the table like a caged animal. His splayed fingers push against the isolation membrane and it just *stretches,* like impossibly thin latex. The farther he pushes, the harder it pulls; his arm isn't quite extended but the membrane's tight as it's going to go, a mass of oily indestructible rainbows swirling along lines of resistable force.

"Fuck," he growls, sinking back.

Nolan squats down and cocks her head, birdlike, a few centimeters from Klein's bloody face. "Let him out, sweetie."

Klein drools blood and spit. "I *told* you, he's—"

"Get away from him!" Seger pushes into the compartment as though the past five years—as though the past five *minutes*—never happened. She barely gets her hand on Nolan's shoulder before Creasy slams her into a bulkhead.

Nolan brushes imaginary contaminants from the place where Seger touched her. "Don't damage the head," she tells Creasy. "Could be a password in there."

"Everybody." Rowan, at least, is smart enough to stay in the corridor. "Just. Calm. Down."

Nolan snorts, shaking her head. "Or *what,* stumpfuck? Are you going to *call security*? Are you going to have us *ejected from the premises*?"

Creasy's white eyes regard Seger from mere centimeters away, a promise of empty and mindless violence set above a grinning bulldozer jaw. Creasy, it is said, has a way with women. Not that he's ever fucked with Clarke. Not that anyone does, as a rule.

Rowan looks through the open hatch, her expression calm and self-assured. Clarke sees the plea hidden behind the confident facade. For a moment, she considers ignoring it. Her leg tingles maddeningly. At her elbow Creasy makes kissy-kissy noises at Seger, his hand vised around the doctor's jaw.

Clarke ignores him. "What's the deal, Grace?"

Nolan smiles harshly. "We managed to wake him up, but Normy here"—an absent punch at Klein's head—"put some kind of password on the table. We can't dial down the membrane."

Clarke turns to Erickson. "How you feeling?"

"They did something to me." He coughs. "When I was in coma."

"Yes we did. We saved his—" Creasy bumps Seger's head against the bulkhead. Seger shuts up.

Clarke keeps her eyes on Erickson. "Can you move without spilling your intestines all over?"

He twists clumsily around to show off his abdomen; the membrane stretches against his head and shoulder like an amniotic sac. "Miracles of modern medicine," he tells her, flopping onto his back. Sure enough, his insides have all been packed back where they belong. Fresh pink scars along his abs complement the older ones on his thorax.

Jerenice Seger looks very much as if she wants to say something. Dale Creasy looks very much as if he wants her to try.

"Let her talk," Clarke tells him. He loosens his grip just slightly; Seger looks at Clarke and keeps her mouth shut.

"So what's the story?" Clarke prompts. "Looks like you glued him back together okay. It's been almost three days."

"Three days," Seger repeats. Her voice is squeezed thin and reedy under Creasy's grip. "He was almost disemboweled, and you think *three days* is enough time to recover."

In fact, Clarke's sure of it. She's seen torn and broken bodies before; she's seen multiarmed robots reassemble them, lay fine electrical webbing into their wounds to crank healing up to a rate that would be miraculous if it weren't so routine. Three days is more than enough time to drag yourself back outside, seams still oozing maybe but strong enough, strong enough; and once you're weightless again, and sheltered by the endless black womb of the abyss, you've got all the time in the world to recover.

It's something the drybacks have never been able to grasp: what keeps you weak is the *gravity*.

"Does he need more surgery?" she asks.

"He will, if he isn't careful."

"Answer the fucking question," Nolan snarls.

Seger glances at Clarke, evidently finds no comfort there. "What he needs is time to recover, and coma will cut that by two thirds. If he wants to get out of here quickly, that's his best option."

"You're keeping him here against his will," Nolan says.

"Why—" Rowan begins from the corridor.

Nolan wheels on her. "You shut the fuck up *right now*."

Rowan calmly pushes her luck. "*Why* would we want to keep him here if it weren't medically necessary?"

"He could rest up in his own hab," Clarke says. "Outside, even."

Seger shakes her head. "He's running a significant fever—Lenie, just *look* at him!"

She's got a point. Erickson's flat on his back, apparently exhausted. A sheen of perspiration slicks his skin, almost lost behind the more conspicuous glistening of the membrane.

"A fever," Clarke repeats. "Not from the operation?"

"No. Some kind of opportunistic infection."

"From what?"

"He was mauled by a wild animal," Seger points out, exasperated. "There's no end to the kind of things you can pick up from something as simple as a bite, and he was nearly *eviscerated*. It would be almost inconceivable if there *weren't* complications."

"Hear that, Gene?" Clarke says. "You've got fish rabies or something."

"Fuckin' A," he says, staring at the ceiling.

"So it's your call. Want to stay here, let 'em fix you? Or trust to drugs and take your chances?"

"Get me out of here," Erickson says weakly.

She turns back to Seger. "You heard him."

Seger draws herself up, impossibly, perpetually, insanely defiant. "Lenie, I asked you to come along to *help*. This is the furthest thing from—"

Creasy's fist hits her in the stomach like a wrecking ball. Seger *oofs* and topples to the side. Her head hits the bulkhead on the way down. She lies there, gulping breathlessly.

Out of the corner of her eye Clarke sees Rowan step forward, then think better of it.

She stares evenly at Creasy. "Not necessary, Dale."

"High and mighty cunt was just *asking* for it," Creasy grumbles.

"And how's she going to let Gene out of jail if she can't even breathe, you *idiot*?"

"Really, Len. What's the big deal?"

Nolan. Clarke turns to face her.

"You know what they did to us," Nolan continues, rising at Creasy's side. "You know how many of us these pimps fucked over. Killed, even."

Fewer than I did, Clarke doesn't say.

"I say if Dale wants to go to town on this stumpfuck, let him." Nolan puts a comradely hand on Creasy's shoulder. "Might go a tiny way to balancing the books, y'know?"

"You say," Clarke says quietly. "I say different."

"Now *there's* a surprise." The trace of a smile ghosts across Nolan's face.

They stare at each other through their corneal shields. Across the compartment, Klein whimpers; Jerenice Seger seems to be breathing again at their feet. Creasy looms close at Clarke's shoulder, an ominous presence just short of overt threat.

She keeps her breathing slow and even. She lowers herself

into a squat—carefully, carefully, her bad leg nearly buckling again—and helps Seger into a sitting position.

"Let him out," she says.

Seger mutters into her wristwatch. A keyboard jammed with strange alphanumerics lights up the skin of her forearm; she taps a sequence with her other hand.

The isolation tent *pops* softly. Erickson pushes a tentative finger through the membrane, finds it unlocked, and lurches off the table as if passing through a soap bubble. His feet hit the deck with a fleshy slap. Nolan holds out a diveskin she's produced from somewhere: "Welcome back, buddy. Told you we'd get you out."

They leave Clarke with the corpses. Seger hauls herself to her feet, ignoring Clarke's offered hand and bracing herself against the bulkhead. One hand still clutches protectively at her stomach. She lurches over to Klein.

"Norm? Norm?" She squats next to her subordinate, stiff-limbed, and pushes back one of his eyelids. "Stay with me..." Droplets of blood dribble from her scalp and splatter onto the medic's pummeled face, making no difference at all. Seger curses and wipes the back of her hand across her injury.

Clarke steps forward to help. Her foot comes down on something small and hard, like a small stone. She lifts her foot. A tooth, sticky with coagulating fluids, clatters softly onto the deck.

"I—" Clarke begins.

Seger turns. Rage simmers on her face. *"Just get out of here."*

Clarke stares at her for a moment. Then she turns on her heel and leaves.

Rowan's waiting in the corridor. "This can't happen again."

Clarke leans against the bulkhead to take some weight off

her injured leg. "You know Grace. She and Gene are—"

"It's not just Grace. At least, it won't be for long. I said something like this might happen."

She feels very tired. "You said you wanted space between the two sides. So why was Jerry keeping Gene here when he wanted to leave?"

"Do you think she *wanted* that man around? She was looking out for the welfare of her patient. That's her job."

"Our welfare is our own concern."

"You people simply aren't *qualified*—"

Clarke raises one preemptive hand. "Heard it, Pat. The little people can't see the Big Picture. Joe Citizen can't handle the truth. The peasants are too *eeegnorant* to vote." She shakes her head, disgusted. "It's been five years and you're still patting us on the head."

"Are you saying that Gene Erickson is a more qualified diagnostician than our chief of medicine?"

"I'm saying he has the right to be wrong." Clarke waves an arm down the corridor. "Look, maybe you're right. Maybe he'll come down with gangrene and come crawling back to Jerry inside a week. Or maybe he'd rather die. But it's *his* decision."

"This isn't about gangrene," Rowan says softly. "And it isn't about some common low-grade infection. And you know it."

"And I still don't see what difference it makes."

"I told you."

"You told me about a bunch of frightened children who can't believe that their own defenses will hold. Well, Pat, the defenses *will* hold. I'm living proof. We could be drinking βehemoth in pure culture and it wouldn't hurt us."

"We've lost—"

"You've lost one more layer of denial. That's all. βehemoth's *here,* Pat. I don't know how, but there's nothing you can do about it and why should you even bother? It's not going to do anything except rub your noses in something you'd rather not think about, and you'll adapt to that soon enough. You've done it before. A month from now you'll have forgotten about it all over again."

"Then please—" Rowan begins, and stops herself.

Clarke waits while the other woman braces herself, yet again, for the subordinate role.

"Give us that month," Rowan whispers at last.

NEMESIS

CLARKE doesn't often go into the residential quarter. She doesn't remember ever having been in this particular section. The corridor here is sheathed in lattice paint and wired up to a mural generator. A forest of antlered coral crowds the port bulkhead; surgeonfish school and swirl to starboard, like the nodes of some abstract and diffuse neural net. A mesh of fractured sunlight dances across everything. Clarke can't tell whether the illusion is purely synthetic, or powered by archived footage of a real coral reef. She wouldn't even know how to tell the difference; of all the sea creatures that have made her acquaintance over the years, none have lived in sunlight.

A lot of families along here, Clarke figures. Adults don't go in for evocations of the wild kingdom as a rule; it's kind of hard to retain that esthetic once you've grasped the concept of irony.

Here it is: D-18. She taps the doorbell. A muffled musical chime drifts through the closed hatch; a reedy thread of music, a faint voice, the sounds of motion.

The hatch swings open. A stocky girl of about ten looks out at her from under spiky blond bangs. The music wafts around her from the interior of the compartment—Lex's flute, Clarke realizes.

The smile dies on the girl's face the instant she lays eyes on Lenie Clarke.

"Hi," Clarke says. "I was looking for Alyx." She tries a smile of her own on for size.

It doesn't fit. The girl takes a stumbling step backward. "Lex . . ."

The music stops. "What? Who is it?"

The blond girl steps aside, nervous as a cat. Alyx Rowan sits blinded on a couch in the center of the room. One of her hands lowers the flute; the other reaches up to the mother-of-pearl 'phones covering her eyes.

"Hey, Lex," Clarke says. "Your mom said you'd be here."

"Lenie! You passed!"

"Passed?"

"Quarantine! They said you and psycho-man were locked up for tests or something. I guess you aced them." A wheeled rectangular pedestal about a meter high squats in front of the couch, a little obelisk with the same opalescent finish as Alyx's headset. Alyx sets her 'phones down on top of it, next to an identical pair already at rest.

Clarke limps into the room. Alyx's face clouds instantly. "What happened to your leg?"

"Rogue squid. Rudder got me."

Alyx's friend mutters something from the corner of Clarke's eye and disappears into the corridor. Clarke turns in her wake.

"Your friend doesn't like me much."

Alyx waves a dismissive hand. "Kelly spooks easy. One look and she just flashfeeds all the shit her mom ever spewed about you guys. She's nice, but she doesn't high-grade her sources at *all.*" The girl shrugs, dismissing the subject. "So what's up?"

"You know that quarantine I was buzzing on about a while back?"

Alyx frowns. "That guy that got bitten. Erickson."

"Yeah. Well, it looks like he came down with something after all, and the basic thumbnail is we've decided to invoke a kind of *No Fish-heads* policy in Atlantis for the time being."

"You're letting them kick you out?"

"I actually think it's a good idea," Clarke admits.

"Why? What's he got?"

Clarke shakes her head. "It's not really a medical thing, although that's—part of it. It's just—feelings are running kind of high right now, on both sides. Your mom and I thought it'd be better if your guys and our guys kept out of each other's way. Just for a while."

"How come? What's going on?"

"Your mom didn't—?" It belatedly occurs to Clarke that Patricia Rowan might have opted to keep certain things from her daughter. For that matter, she doesn't even know how much of Atlantis's *adult* population has been brought up to speed. Corpses aren't keen on full disclosure just as a matter of general principle.

Not that Lenie Clarke gives a great crimson turd about corpse sensibilities. Still. She doesn't want to get in between Pat and—

"Lenie?" Alyx is staring at her, brow furrowed. She's one of the very few people to whom Clarke can comfortably show her naked eyes; right now, though, Clarke's glad her caps are in.

She takes a couple of paces across the carpet. Another facet of the pedestal comes into view. Some kind of control panel runs in a strip just below its upper edge, a band of dark perspex twinkling with red and blue icons. A luminous jagged waveform, like an EEG, scrolls horizontally along its length.

"What's this?" Clarke asks, seizing on the diversion. It's far too big to be any kind of game interface.

"That? Oh." Alyx shrugs. "That's Kelly's. It's a head cheese."

"What!"

"You know, a smart gel. Neuron culture with—"

"I know what it is, Lex. I just—I guess I'm surprised to see one here, after . . ."

"Wanna see it?" Alyx taps a brief tattoo on the top of the cabinet. The nacreous surface swirls briefly and clears: beneath the newly-transparent facade, a slab of pinkish-gray tissue sits within its circular rim like a bowl of fleshy oatmeal. Flecks of brown glass punctuate the pudding in neat perforated lines.

"It's not very big," Alyx says. "Way smaller than the ones they had back in the old days. Kelly says it's about the same as a cat."

So it's evil at least, if not hugely intelligent. "What's it for?" Clarke wonders. *Surely they wouldn't be stupid enough to use these things after—*

"It's kind of a pet," Alyx says apologetically. "She calls it Rumble."

"A *pet*?"

"Sure. It thinks, sort of. It learns to do stuff. Even if no one really knows how, exactly."

"Oh, so you heard about that, did you?"

"It's a lot smaller than the ones that, you know, worked for you."

"They didn't w—"

"It's really harmless. It's not hooked into life support or anything."

"So what does it do? You teach it tricks?" The porridge of brains glistens like an oozing sore.

"Kind of. It talks back if you say stuff to it. Doesn't always make a lot of sense, but that's what makes it fun. And if you tweak the audio feed right it plays these really cool color patterns in time to music." Alyx grabs her flute off the couch, gestures at the eyephones. "Wanna see?"

"A pet," Clarke murmurs. *You bloody corpses . . .*

"We're not, you know," Alyx says sharply. "Not all of us."

"Sorry? Not what?"

"Corpses. What does that mean, anyway? My mom? *Me?*"

Did I say that out loud? "Just—corporate types, I guess." She's never spent much time pondering the origin of the term, any more than she's lost sleep over the etiology of *chair* or *fumarole.*

"Well in case you didn't notice, there's a lot of other people in here. Crunchers and doctors and just *families*."

"Yeah, I know. Of course I know—"

"But you just lump us all together, you know? If we don't have a bunch of pipes in our chest we're all just *corpses* as far as you're concerned."

"Well—sorry." And then, belatedly defensive: "I'm not slagging you, you know. It's just a word."

"Yeah, well it's not *just a word* to all you fish-heads."

"Sorry." Clarke says again. A distance seems to open between them, although neither has moved.

"Anyway," she says after a while, "I just wanted you to know I won't be inside for a while. We can still talk, of course, but—"

Movement from the hatchway. A large stocky man steps into the compartment, dark hair combed back, eyebrows knotted together, his whole body a telegraph of leashed hostility. Kelly's father.

"Ms. Clarke," he says evenly.

Her guts tighten into a hard, angry knot. She knows that look. She knows that stance, she saw it herself more times than she could count when she was Kelly's age. She knows what *fathers* do, she knows what *hers* did, but she's not a little girl any more and Kelly's dad looks very much in need of a *lesson* . . .

But she has to keep reminding herself. None of it happened.

PORTRAIT OF THE SADIST AS AN ADOLESCENT

ACHILLES Desjardins learned to spoof the skeeters eventually, of course. Even as a child he knew the score. In a world kept under constant surveillance for its own protection there were only watched and watchers, and he knew which side of the lens he wanted to be on. Beating off was not the kind of thing he could do in front of an audience.

It was barely even the kind of thing he could do in private, for that matter. He had, after all, been raised with certain religious beliefs; clinging to the coattails of the *Nouveaux Séparatistes,* the Catholic miasma had persisted in Quebec long after it had faded into kitschy irrelevance everywhere else. Those beliefs haunted Achilles every night as he rubbed himself, as the sick hateful images flickered through his mind and hardened his penis. It barely mattered that the skeeters were offline, wobbling drunkenly under the influence of the magnetic mobiles he'd hung over his bed and desk and drawers. It barely mattered that he was already going to hell, even if he never touched himself again for the rest of his life—for hadn't Jesus said, *If you do these things even in your heart, then you have committed them in the eyes of God*? Achilles was already damned by his own unbidden thoughts. What more could he lose by acting on them?

Shortly after his eleventh birthday his penis began leaving actual evidence behind, a milky fluid squirted onto the sheets in the course of his nightly debauchery. He didn't dare ask the encyclopedia about it for two weeks; it took him that long to figure out how to doctor the inquiry logs so Mom and Dad wouldn't find out. Cracking the private settings on the household Maytag took another three days. You could never tell what trace elements that thing might be scanning for. By the time Achilles actually dared to launder his bedsheets they smelled a lot like Andrew Trites down at the community center, who was twice the size of anyone else in his cohort and whom nobody wanted to stand next to at the rapitrans stop.

"I think—" Achilles began at thirteen.

He no longer believed in the Church. He was after all an empiricist at heart, and God couldn't withstand so much as ten seconds' critical scrutiny from anyone who'd already figured out the ugly truth about the Easter Bunny. Paradoxically, though, damnation somehow seemed more real than ever, on some primal level that resisted mere logic. And as long as damnation was real, confession couldn't hurt.

"—I'm a monster," he finished.

It wasn't as risky a confession as it might have been. His confidante wasn't especially trustworthy—he'd downloaded it from the net (from *Maelstrom,* he corrected himself; that's what everyone was calling it now), and it might be full of worms and trojans even if he *had* scrubbed it every which way—but he'd also kellered all the I/O except voice and he could delete the whole thing the moment it tried anything funny. He'd do that anyway, once he was finished. No way was he going to leave it ticking after he'd spilled his guts to it.

Dad would go totally triploid if he knew Achilles had brought a wild app anywhere near their home net, but Achilles wasn't about to risk using the house filters even if Dad *had* stopped spying since Mom died. And anyway, Dad wasn't going to find out. He was downstairs, cowled in his sensorium with the rest of the province—the rest of the *country* now, Achilles had to keep reminding himself—immersed in the pomp and ceremony of Quebec's very first Independence Day. Sullen, resentful Penny—her days of idolizing Big Brother long past—would have gladly sold him out in a second, but these days she pretty much lived in her rapture helmet. By now it must have worn the grooves right out of her temporal lobes.

It was the birthday of the last new country in the world, and Achilles Desjardins was alone in his bedroom with his confessor.

"What kind of monster?" asked TheraPal™ 6.2, its voice studiously androgynous.

He'd learned the word that very morning. He pronounced it carefully: "A misogynist."

"I see," TheraPal™ murmered in his ear.

"I have these—I get these feelings. About hurting them. Hurting girls."

"And how do they make you feel?" The voice had edged subtly into the masculine.

"Good. Awful. I mean—I *like* them. The feelings, I mean."

"Could you be more specific?" There was no shock or disgust in the voice. Of course, there couldn't be—the program didn't have feelings, it wasn't even a Turing app. It was basically just a fancy menu. Still, stupidly, Achilles felt strangely relieved.

"It's—sexy," he admitted. "Just, just thinking about them that way."

"What way, exactly?"

"You know, helpless. Vulnerable. I, I like the looks on their faces when they're . . . you know . . ."

"Go on," said TheraPal™.

"Hurting," Achilles finished miserably.

"Ah," said the app. "How old are you, Achilles?"

"Thirteen."

"Do you have any friends who are girls?"

"Sure."

"And how do you feel about *them*?"

"I *told* you!" Achilles hissed, barely keeping his voice down. "I get—"

"No," TheraPal™ broke in gently. "I'm asking how you *feel* about them personally, when you're not sexually aroused. Do you hate them?"

Well, no. Andrea was really smart, and he could always go to her for help with his debugs. And Martine—one time, Achilles had just about *killed* Martine's older brother when he was picking on her. Martine didn't have a mean bone in her body, but that asshole brother of hers was so . . .

"I—I like them," he said, his forehead crinkling at the paradox. "I like them a lot. They're great. Except the ones I want to, you know, and even then it's only when I . . ."

TheraPal™ waited patiently.

"Everything's fine," Achilles said at last. "Except when I want to . . ."

"I see," the app said after a moment. "Achilles, I have some good news for you. You're not a misogynist after all."

"No?"

"A misogynist is someone who hates women, who fears them or thinks them inferior in some way. Is that you?"

"No, but—but what am I, then?"

"That's easy," TheraPal™ told him. "You're a sexual sadist. It's a completely different thing."

"Really?"

"Sex is a very old instinct, Achilles, and it didn't evolve in a vacuum. It coevolved with all sorts of other basic drives—fighting for mates, territoriality, competition for resources. Even healthy sex has a strong element of violence to it. Sex and aggression share many of the same neurological paths."

"Are you—are you saying *everyone's* like me?" It seemed too much to hope for.

"Not exactly. Most people have a sort of switch that suppresses violent impulses during sex. Some people's switches work better than others. The switches in clinical sadists don't work very well at *all.*"

"And that's what I am," Achilles murmered.

"Very likely," TheraPal™ said, "although it's impossible to be sure without a proper clinical checkup. I seem unable to access your network right now, but I could provide a list of nearby affiliated medbooths if you tell me where we are."

Behind him, the Achilles's bedroom door creaked softly on its hinges. He turned, and froze instantly at his core.

The door to his bedroom had swung open. His father stood framed in the darkness beyond.

"Achilles," TheraPal™ said in the whirling, receding distance, "for you own health—not to mention your peace of mind—you really should visit one of our affiliates. A contractually guaranteed diagnosis is the first step to treatment, and treatment is the first step to a healthy life."

He couldn't have heard, Achilles told himself. TheraPal™ spoke directly to his earbud, and Dad couldn't have stopped the telltale from flashing if he'd been listening in. Dad didn't hack.

He couldn't have heard TheraPal™. He could've heard Achilles, though.

"If you're worried about the cost, our rates—" Achilles deleted the app almost without thinking, sick to his stomach.

His father hadn't moved.

His father didn't move much, these days. The short fuse, the hair-trigger had rusted into some frozen state between grief and indifference over the years. His once fiery and defiant Catholicism had turned against itself with the fall of the Church, a virulent rage of betrayal that had burned him out and left him hollow. By the time Achilles's mom had died there'd barely even been sorrow. (A glitch in the therapy, he'd said dully, coming back from the hospital. The wrong promoters activated, the body somehow innoculated against its own genes, devouring itself. There was nothing he could do. They'd signed a waiver.)

Now he stood there in the darkened hallway, swaying slightly, his fists not even clenched. It had been years since he'd raised a hand against his children.

So what am I afraid of? Achilles wondered, his stomach knotted.

He knows. He knows. I'm afraid he knows . . .

The corners of his father's mouth tightened by some infinitesimal degree. It wasn't a smile. It wasn't a snarl. In later years, the adult Achilles Desjardins would look back and recognize it as a kind of acknowledgment, but at the time he had no idea what it meant. He only knew that his father simply turned and walked down the hall to the master bedroom, and closed the door behind him, and never mentioned that night ever again.

In later years, he also realized that TheraPal™ must have been stringing him along. Its goal, after all, had been to attract customers, and you didn't do that by rubbing their faces in unpleasant truths. The program had simply been trying to make him feel better as a marketing strategy.

And yet, that didn't mean it had *lied,* necessarily. Why bother, if the truth would do the job? And it all made so much *sense.* Not a sin, but a malfunction. A thermostat, set askew through no fault of his own. All life was machinery, mechanical contraptions built of proteins and nucleic acids and electricity; what machine ever got creative control over its own specs? It was a liberating epiphany, there at the dawn of the sovereign Quebec: Not Guilty, by reason of faulty wiring.

Odd, though.

You'd have expected it to bring the self-loathing down a notch or two in the years that followed.

BEDSIDE MANOR

GENE Erickson and Julia Friedman live in a small single-deck hab about a hundred meters southeast of Atlantis. Julia has always done most of the housekeeping: Gene gets notoriously twitchy in enclosed spaces. For him, *home* is the open ridge: the hab is a necessary evil, for sex and feeding and those occasional times when his own darkdreams prove insufficiently diverting. Even then, he treats it the way a pearl diver of two hundred years past would treat a diving bell: a place to gulp the occasional breath of air before returning to the deep.

Now, of course, it's more of an ICU.

Lenie Clarke emerges from the airlock and drops her fins on an incongruous welcome mat laid to one side. The main compartment is dim even to rifter eyes, a gray-on-gray wash of twilight punctuated by the bright chromatic readouts on the comm board. The air smells of mold and metal; more faintly, of vomit and disinfectant. Life-support systems gurgle underfoot. Open hatches gape like black mouths: storage; head; sleeping cubby. An electronic metronome beeps somewhere nearby. A heart monitor, counting down.

Julia Friedman steps into view.

"He's still—oh." She's taken off her diveskin in favor of a thermochrome turtleneck that mostly covers her scars. It's strange to see rifter eyes atop dryback clothing. "Hi, Lenie."

"Hi. How's he doing?"

"Okay." She turns in the hatchway, sags with her spine against the frame: half in darkness, half in twilight. She turns her face to the darkness, to the person within it. "Could be better, I guess. He's asleep. He's sleeping a lot."

"I'm surprised you could even keep him inside."

"Yeah. I think he'd rather be out there, even now, but... he's doing it for me, I think. Because I asked him." Friedman shakes her head. "It was too easy."

"What was?"

"Convincing him." She takes a breath. "You know how much he loves the outdoors."

"Are Jerry's antibiotics helping?"

"Maybe. I guess. It's hard to say, you know? She can always say he'd be worse without them, no matter how bad it gets."

"Is that what she's saying?"

"Oh, Gene hasn't talked to her since he came back. He doesn't trust them." She stares at the deck. "He blames her for this."

"For being sick?"

"He thinks they did something to him."

Clarke remembers. "What exactly does he—?"

"I don't know. Something." Friedman glances up: her armored eyes lock onto Clarke's for an instant, then slide off to the side. "It's taking a long time to clear up, you know? For a simple infection. Do you think?"

"I don't really know, Julia."

"Maybe ßehemoth's mixing things up somehow. Making things worse."

"I don't know if it works like that."

"Maybe I've got it too, by now." Friedman almost seems to be talking to herself. "I mean, I'm with him a lot..."

"We could check you out, if you wanted."

Friedman looks at her. "You were infected, weren't you? Before."

"Only with ßehemoth," Clarke says, careful to draw the distinction. "It didn't kill me. Didn't even make me sick."

"It would have, though. Eventually. Right?"

"If I hadn't got my retrofits. But I did. We all did." She tries a smile. "We're rifters, Julia. We're tough little motherfuckers. He'll pull through. I know it."

It's not much, Clarke knows. Reassuring deception is all she can offer Julia Friedman at the moment. She knows better than to touch; Friedman's not keen on physical contact. She'd endure a comforting hand on the shoulder, perhaps—even take it in the spirit in which it was intended—but Julia Friedman is very selective with her personal space. It's one of the few ways in which Clarke feels a kinship with the woman. Each can see the other flinch, even when neither does.

Friedman looks back into the darkness. "Grace says you helped get him out of there."

Clarke shrugs, a bit surprised that Nolan would give her the credit.

"I would've been there too, you know. Only . . ." Friedman's voice trails off. The hab's ventilators sigh into the silence.

"Only you think maybe he'd have been better off where he was," Clarke suggests.

"Oh, no. Well, maybe partly. I don't know if Dr. Seger's as bad as they think, anyway."

"They?"

"Gene and—Grace."

Ah.

"It's just, I didn't know . . . I didn't know if he'd even *want* me there." Friedman flashes a rueful smile. "I'm not much of a fighter, Lenie. Not like you, not like—I just kind of roll with the punches."

"He could have been with Grace all along if he'd wanted to, Julia. He's with you."

Friedman laughs, a bit too quickly. "Oh, no. That's not what I meant." But Clarke's words seem to have perked her up a bit.

"Anyway," Clarke says, "I guess I'll leave you guys alone. I just wanted to stop by, see how he was doing."

"I'll tell him," Friedman says. "He'll appreciate it."

"Sure. No problem." She bends to retrieve her fins.

"And you should come by again, when he's awake. He'd like that." She hesitates, looking away; chestnut curls obscure her face. "Not many people come by, you know. Except Grace. Saliko was by a while back."

Clarke shrugs. "Rifters aren't big on social skills." *And you really ought to know that by now,* she doesn't add. Friedman just doesn't get it, sometimes. It's as though, scars and history notwithstanding, she's a rifter in name only, an honorary member allowed past the gate on her husband's credentials.

Which begs the question of what I'm *doing here,* she realizes.

"I think they take him too seriously sometimes," Friedman says.

"Seriously?" Clarke glances at the airlock. The hab seems suddenly, subtly smaller.

"About, you know. The corpses. I hear Saliko's feeling a little odd now, but you know Saliko."

He thinks they did something to him . . .

"I wouldn't worry about it," Clarke says. "Really." She smiles, sighing inwardly at her own diplomacy.

Comforting lies get far too easy with practice.

It's been a while since she's let Kevin take her. He's never been all that good at it, sadly. He has a harder time keeping it up than most kids his age, which actually isn't all that uncommon among the local bottom-feeders. And the fact that he's chosen a frigid bitch like Lenie Clarke to practice his moves on hasn't helped the dynamic any. A man afraid to touch: a woman averse to contact. If these two have anything in common, it's patience.

She figures she owes him. Besides, she wants to ask him some questions.

But today he's a granite cock with a brain stem attached.

Fuck the foreplay: he pushes into her right off the top, not even a token tongue-lashing to make up for the lack of tropical irrigation. The friction pulls painfully at her labia; she reaches down discreetly with one hand and spreads them. Walsh pumps on top of her, breath hissing through teeth clenched in a hard animal grin, his capped eyes hard and unreadable. They always keep their eyes masked during sex—Clarke's tastes prevail, as usual—although Walsh usually wears too much heart on his face to hide with a couple of membranous eggshells. Not this time. There's something behind his overlays that Clarke can't quite make out, something focused on the space where she is but not on *her*. He pushes her up the pallet in rough thrusting increments; her head bumps painfully against the naked metal plating of the deck. They fuck without words amid stale air and grafted machinery.

She doesn't know what's come over him. It's a nice change, though, the closest thing to an honest-to-God rape she's had in years. She closes her eyes and summons up images of Karl Acton.

Afterward, though, the bruise she notices is on *his* arm: a corona of torn capillaries around a tiny puncture in the flesh of his inner elbow.

"What's this?" She lays her lips around the injury and runs her tongue across the swelling.

"Oh, that. Grace is taking blood samples from everyone."

Her head comes up. "What?"

"She's not great at it. Took her a couple of tries to find a vein. You should see Lije. Looks like his arm got bushwhacked by a sea urchin."

"Why's Grace taking blood?"

"You didn't hear? Lije came down with something. And Saliko's started feeling under the weather too, and *he* visited Gene and Julia just a couple of days ago."

"So Grace thinks—"

"Whatever the corpses gave him, it's spreading."

Clarke sits up. She's been naked on the deck for half an hour, but this is the first time she's felt the chill. "Grace thinks the corpses gave him something."

"That's what Gene thought. She's going to find out."

"How? She doesn't have any medical training."

Walsh shrugs. "You don't need any to run MedBase."

"Jesus semen-sucking Christ." Clarke shakes her head in disbelief. "Even if Atlantis *did* want to sic some bug on us, they wouldn't be stupid enough to use one from the standard database."

"I guess she thinks it's a place to start."

There's something in his voice.

"You believe her," Clarke says.

"Well, not nec—"

"Has Julia come down with anything?"

"Not so far."

"*Not so far*. Kevin, Julia hasn't left Gene's side since they broke him out. If anyone was going to catch anything, wouldn't it be her? Saliko visited, what? Once?"

"Maybe twice."

"And what about *Grace?* From what I hear she's over there all the time. Is *she* sick?"

"She says she's taking precaut—"

"Precautions," Clarke snorts. "Spare me. Am I the only one left on the whole Ridge with a working set of frontal lobes? Abra came down with supersyph last year, remember? It took eight months for Charley Garcia to get rid of those buggy *Ascaris* in his gut, and I don't remember anyone blaming the corpses for *that*. People get sick, Kevin, even down here. *Especially* down here. Half of us rot away before we even have a chance to go native."

There it is again: something new, staring out from behind the glistening opacities of Walsh's eyecaps. Something not entirely friendly.

She sighs. "What?"

"It's just a precaution. I don't see how it can hurt."

"It can hurt quite a lot if people jump to conclusions without any facts."

Walsh doesn't move for a moment. Then he gets to his feet. "Grace *is* trying to get the facts," he says, padding across the compartment. "*You're* the one jumping to conclusions."

Oh, Kevvy-boy, Clarke wonders. *When did* you *start to grow a spine?*

He grabs his diveskin off the chair. Squirming black synthetics embrace him like a lover.

"Thanks for the fuck," he says. "I gotta go."

BOILERPLATE

SHE finds Lubin floating halfway up the side of the windchime reservoir. Pipes, fiberop, and miscellaneous components—mostly nonfunctional now, dismembered segments of circuits long since broken—run in a band around the great tank's equator. At the moment, the ambient currents are too sluggish to set either rocks or machinery to glowing; Lubin's headlamp provides the only illumination.

"Abra said you were out here," Clarke buzzes.

"Hold this pad, will you?"

She takes the little sensor. "I wanted to talk to you."

"About?" Most of his attention seems to be focused on a blob of amber polymer erupting from one of the conduits.

Clarke maneuvers herself into his line of sight. "There's this asinine rumor going around. Grace is telling people that Jerry sicced some kind of plague on Gene."

Lubin's vocoder tics in a mechanical interpretation of *mmmm* . . .

"She's always had a missile up her ass about the corpses, but nobody takes her seriously. At least, they didn't used to . . ."

Lubin taps a valve. "That's it."

"What?"

"Resin's cracked around the thermostat. It's causing an intermittent short."

"Ken. *Listen to me.*"

He stares at her, waiting.

"Something's changing. Grace never used to push it this hard, remember?"

"I never really butted heads with her myself," Lubin buzzes.

"It used to be her against the world. But this bug Gene's come down with, it's changed things. I think people are starting to listen to her. It could get dicey."

"For the corpses."

"For all of us. Weren't *you* the one warning me about what the corpses could do if they got their act together? Weren't you the one who said—"

We may have to do something preemptive . . .

A small pit opens up in Clarke's stomach.

"Ken," she buzzes, slowly, "you *do* know Grace is fucking crazy, right?"

He doesn't answer for a moment. She doesn't give him any longer than that: "Seriously, you should just *listen* to her sometime. She talks as if the war never ended. Someone sneezes and it's a biological attack."

Behind his headlamp, Lubin's silhouette moves subtly; Clarke gets the sense of a shrug. "There are some interesting coincidences," he says. "Gene enters Atlantis with serious injuries. Jerry operates on him in a medbay where our surveillance is compromised, then puts him into quarantine."

"Quarantine because of *ßehemoth,*" Clarke points out.

"As you've pointed out yourself on occasion, we've all been immunized against ßehemoth. I'm surprised you don't find that rationale more questionable." When Clarke says nothing, he continues: "Gene is released into the wild suffering from an *opportunistic infection* which our equipment can't identify, and which so far has failed to respond to treatment."

"But you were there, Ken. Jerry wanted to keep Gene in quarantine. Dale beat the crap out of her for trying. *Isolating* Patient Zero is a pretty short-sighted strategy for spreading the plague."

"I suppose," Lubin buzzes, "Grace might say they knew we'd break him out regardless, so they put up a big show of resistance hoping someone would cite it in their favor down the road."

"So they fought to keep him contained, therefore they wanted to set him loose?" Clarke peers suggestively at Lubin's electrolysis intake. "You getting enough O_2 there, Ken?"

"I'm saying that's the sort of rationale Grace might invoke."

"That's pretty twisted even for—" Realization sinks in. "She's actually saying that, isn't she?"

His headlight bobs slightly.

"You've heard the rumors. You know all about them." She shakes her head, disgusted at herself. "As if I'd ever have to bring *you* up to speed on anything..."

"I'm keeping an ear open."

"Well, maybe you could do a bit more than that. I mean, I know you like to keep out of these things, but Grace is fucking *psycho*. She's spoiling for a fight and she doesn't care who gets caught in the backwash."

Lubin hovers, unreadable. "I would have expected you to be a bit more sympathetic."

"What's that supposed to mean?"

"Nothing," he buzzes after a moment. "But whatever you think of Grace's behavior, her fears might not be entirely unfounded."

"Come on, Ken. The war's over." She takes his silence as acknowledgment. "So why would the corpses want to start it up again?"

"Because they lost."

"Ancient history."

"You thought *yourself* oppressed once," he points out. "How much blood did it take before *you* were willing to call it even?"

His metal voice, so calm, so even, is suddenly so close it seems to be coming from inside her own head.

"I—I was wrong about that," she says after a while.

"It didn't stop you." He turns back to his machinery.

"Ken," she says.

He looks back at her.

"This is bullshit. It's a bunch of *ifs* strung together. A hundred to one Gene just picked up something from the fish that bit him."

"Okay."

"It's not like there can't be a hundred nasty bugs down here we haven't discovered yet. A few years ago nobody'd even heard of *ßehemoth*."

"I'm aware of that."

"So we can't let this escalate. Not without at least some evidence."

His eyes shine yellow-white in the backscatter from his headlamp. "If you're serious about evidence, you could always collect some yourself."

"How?"

He taps the left side of his chest. Where the implants are.

She goes cold. "No."

"If Seger's hiding anything, you'd know it."

"She could be hiding lots of things from lots of people. It wouldn't prove *what* she was hiding."

"You'd know what Nolan was feeling too, since you seem so concerned with her motives."

"I know what her motives are. I don't need to fuck with my brain chemistry to confirm it."

"The medical risks are minimal," he points out.

"That's not the point. It wouldn't prove anything. You know you can't read specific thoughts, Ken."

"You wouldn't have to. Reading guilt would be suffic—"

"I said no."

"Then I don't know what to tell you." He turns away again. His headlamp transforms the reservoir's plumbing into a tiny, high-contrast cityscape tilted on edge. Clarke watches him work—tracking pathways, tapping pipes, making small changes to tabletop architecture. A pinpoint sun flares hissing at his fingertips, blinding her for an instant. By the time her caps have adjusted the light has settled on the skin of the tank. The water shimmers prismatically around it like a heat mirage on a hot day; at lesser depths it would explode into steam on the spot.

"There's another way," she buzzes. Lubin shuts off the spot-welder.

"There is." He turns to face her. "But I wouldn't get my hopes up."

Back when the trailer park was just getting set up, someone had the clever idea of turning a hab into a mess hall: a row of cyclers, a couple of prep surfaces for the daring, and a handful of foldaway tables scattered with studied randomness around the dry deck. The effect was intended to suggest a café patio. The cramped reality is more like the backstage shed where the furniture gets stored for winter.

One thing that has caught on, though, is the garden. By now it covers half the wet deck, a tangle of creeping greenery lit by solar-spectrum sticks planted among its leaves like bioluminescent bamboo. It isn't even hydroponic. The little jungle erupts from boxes of rich dark earth—diatomaceous ooze, actually, beefed up with organic supplements—that were once discrete but which have since now disappeared under an overflow of compost, spilling messily across the plating.

It's the best-smelling bubble of atmosphere on the whole Ridge. Clarke swings the airlock hatch open onto that tableau and takes a deep breath, only half of appreciation. The other half is resolve: Grace Nolan looks up from the far side of the oasis, tying off the vines of something that might have been snow peas back before the patents landed on them.

But Nolan smiles beneath translucent eyes as Clarke steps onto the deck. “Hey, Lenie!”

“Hi, Grace. I thought we could maybe have a talk.”

Nolan pops a pod into her mouth, a slick black amphibian feeding in the lush greenery of some long-extinct wetland. She chews, for longer than is probably necessary. “About . . .”

“About Atlantis. Your blood work.” Clarke takes a breath. “About whatever problem you have with me.”

“God no,” Nolan says. “I’ve got no problem with you, Len. People fight sometimes. No big deal. Don’t take it so seriously.”

“Okay then. Let’s talk about Gene.”

“Sure.” Nolan straightens, grabs a chair off the bulkhead and folds it down. “And while we’re at it, let’s talk about Sal and Lije and Lanie.”

Lanie too, now? “You think the corpses are behind it.”

Nolan shrugs. “It’s no big secret.”

“And you base that on what, exactly? Anything show up in the bloods?”

“We’re still collecting samples. Lisbeth’s set up in the med hab, by the way, if you want to contribute. I think you should.”

“What if you don’t find anything?” Clarke wonders.

“I don’t think we will. Seger’s smart enough to cover her tracks. But you never know.”

“You know it’s possible that the corpses have nothing to do with this.”

Nolan leans back in her chair and stretches. “Sweetie, I can’t *tell* you how surprised I am to hear you say that.”

“So show me some evidence.”

Nolan smiles, shaking her head. “Here’s a bit of an exercise for you. Say you’re swimming through shark-infested waters. Big sickle-finned stumpfucks all over the place, and they’re looking you up and down and you know the only reason they’re not tearing into you right now is because you’ve got your billy out, and they’ve seen what that billy can do to fishies like them. So they keep their distance, but that makes 'em hate you even more, right? Because you've already killed some of 'em. These are really smart sharks. They hold grudges.

"So you swim along for a little while, all these cold dead pissed-off eyes and teeth always just out of range, and you come across—oh, say Ken. Or what's left of him. A bit of entrail, half a face, ID patch just floating around among all those sharks. What do you do, Len? Do you decide there isn't any *evidence*? Do you say, Hey, I can't *prove* anything, I didn't see this go down? Do you say, Let's not jump to any *conclusions* . . ."

"That's a really shitty analogy," Clarke says softly.

"I think it's a *great* fucking analogy."

"So what are you going to do?"

"I can tell you what I'm *not* going to do," Nolan assures her. "I'm not going to sit back and have faith in the goodness of the corpse spirit while all my friends turn to sockeye."

"Is anyone asking you to do that?"

"Any time now, I figure."

Clarke sighs. "Grace, I'm only saying, for the good of all of us—"

"Fuck you," Nolan snarls suddenly. "*Fuck you.* You don't give a *shit* about us."

It's as if someone flipped a switch. Clarke stares, astonished.

Nolan glares eyelessly back, her body trembling with sudden rage. "You *really* want to know my problem with you? You sold us out. We were *this* close to pulling the plug on those stumpfucks. We could've forced their own goddamn entrails down their throats, and *you stopped us, you fucker.*"

"Grace," she tries, "I know how you fe—"

"*Horseshit! You don't have a fucking* clue *how I feel!*"

What did they do to you, Clarke wonders, *to turn you into this?*

"They did things to me too," she says softly.

"Sure they did. And you got *yours* back, didn't you? And correct me if I'm wrong but didn't you end up fucking over a whole lot of innocent people in the mix? You never gave a shit about *them.* And maybe it was too much trouble to work it through but a fair number of us fish-heads lost people to your grand crusade along with everyone else. You didn't give a shit about them either, as long as you got your kick at the cat. Fine. You got it. But the rest of us are still waiting, aren't we? We don't even want to mow down millions of innocent people, we just want to get at the assholes who *actually fucked us over*—and *you* of all people come crawling over here on Patricia Rowan's leash to tell me I don't have the *right*?" Nolan shakes her head in disgust. "I don't *believe* we let you stop us before, and I sure as shit don't believe you're going to stop us *now.*"

Her hatred radiates through the compartment like infrared. Clarke is distantly amazed that the vines beside her don't blacken and burst into flame.

"I came to you because I thought we could work something out," she says.

"You came because you know you're losing it."

The words ignite a small, cold knot of anger under Clarke's diaphragm. "Is that what you think."

"You never gave a shit about *working things out.*" Nolan growls. "You just sat off on your own, *I'm the Meltdown Madonna, I'm Mermaid of the Fucking Apocalypse, I get to stand off to the side and make the rules.* But the rabble isn't falling into line this time, sweetie, and it scares you. *I* scare you. So spare me the dreck about altruism and diplomacy. You're just trying to keep your little tin throne from going sockeye. It's been nice talking to you."

She grabs her fins and stalks into the airlock.

PORTRAIT OF THE SADIST AS A YOUNG MAN

ACHILLES Desjardins couldn't remember the last time he'd had consensual sex with a real woman. He could, however, remember the first time he'd refused it:

It was 2046 and he'd just saved the Mediterranean. That's how N'AmWire was presenting it, anyway. All he'd really done was deduce the existence of a strange attractor in the Gulf of Cádiz, a persistent little back-eddy that no one else had bothered to look for. According to the sims it was small enough to tweak with albedo dampers; the effects would proliferate through the Strait of Gibraltar and—if the numbers were right—stave off the collapse of the Med by an easy decade. Or until the Gulf Stream failed again, whichever came first. It was only a reprieve, not outright salvation, but it was just what CSIRA needed to make everyone forget the Baltic fiasco.

Besides, nobody ever looked ahead more than ten years anyway.

So for a while, Achilles Desjardins had been a star. Even Lertzmann had pretended to like him for the better part of a month, told him he was fast-tracked for senior status just as soon as they got the security checks out of the way. Unless he had a bunch of butchered babies in his past he'd be getting his shots before Halloween. Hell, he'd probably be getting them even if he *did* have a bunch of butchered babies in his past. Background checks were nothing but empty ritual in the higher ranks of the Patrol; you could be a serial killer and it wouldn't make a damn bit of difference once Guilt Trip was bubbling in your brain. You'd be just as thoroughly enslaved to the Greater Good.

Aurora, her name was. She wore the zebra hair that had been fashionable at the time, and an endearingly tasteless armload of faux refugee branding scars. They'd hooked up at some CSIRA soirée hosted from the far side of the world by the EurAfrican Assembly. Their jewelry sniffed each other's auras to confirm a mutual interest (which still meant something, back then), and their path chips exchanged the usual clean bills of health (which didn't). So they left the party, dropped three hundred meters from CSIRA's executive stratosphere to the Sudbury Streets—then another fifty into the subterranean bowels of Pickering's Pile, where the pathware was guaranteed hackproof and tested for twice the usual range of STDs to boot. They gave blood behind a cute little r'n'r couple who broke up on the spot when one of them tested positive for an exotic trematode infesting his urinary tract.

Desjardins had yet to acquire most of the tailored chemicals that would cruise his system in later years; he could still safely imbibe all manner of tropes and mood-changers. So he and Aurora grabbed a booth just off the bar while their bloods ran, stroked the little psychotropic amphibians clambering about in the tabletop terrarium. Dim green light filtered in from the great underground tank in which the Pile was immersed, a radium-glow mock-up of an old nuclear-storage lagoon visible through the plexi walls. After a few minutes one of the in-house butterflies lit on their table, its membranous wings sparkling with refracted data: green on all wavelengths.

"Told you," Aurora said, and kissed his nose.

Pickering's Pile rented fuck-cubbies by the minute. They split five hours between them.

He fucked her inside and out. Outside, he was the consummate caring lover. He tongued her nipples, teeth carefully sheathed. He left trails of kisses from throat to vagina, gently explored every wet aperture, breath shaky with fevered restraint. Every move deliberate, every signal unmistakable: he would rather die than hurt this woman.

Inside, he was tearing her apart. No caresses in *there;* he slapped her so hard her fucking head just about came off. Inside she was screaming. Inside, he beat her until she didn't have the strength to flinch when the whip came down.

She murmured and sighed sweetly throughout. She remarked on how he obviously worshiped women, on what a change this made from the usual rough-and-tumble, on how she didn't know if she belonged on this pedestal. Desjardins patted himself on the back. He didn't mention the tiny scars on her back, the telltale little lozenges of fresh pink skin that spoke of topical anabolics. Evidently Aurora had use for accelerated healing. Perhaps she had recently escaped from an abusive relationship. Perhaps he was her sanctuary. Even better. He imagined some past partner, beating her.

"Oh, fuck it," she said, four hours in. "Just hit me. "

He froze, terrified, betrayed by body language or telepathy or a lucky guess for all he knew. "What?"

"You're so gentle," Aurora told him. "Let's get rough."

"You don't—" He had to stifle a surprised laugh. "I mean, what?"

"Don't look so startled." She come-hithered a smile. "Haven't you ever smacked a woman before?"

Those were hints, he realized. *She was* complaining. And Achilles Desjardins, pattern-matcher extraordinaire, master of signal-from-noise, had missed it completely.

"I kind of minored in asphyx," she suggested now. "And I don't see that belt of yours getting any kind of workout . . ."

It was everything he'd ever dreamed of, and hated himself for. It was his most shameful fantasy come to life. It was perfect.

Oh, you glorious bitch. You are just asking for it, aren't you? And I'm just the one to give it to you.

Except he wasn't. Suddenly, Achilles Desjardins was as soft as a dollar.

"You serious?" he asked, hoping she wouldn't notice, knowing she already had. "I mean—you want me to *hurt* you?"

"Achilles the hero." She cocked her head mischievously. "Don't get out much, do you?"

"I do okay," he said, defensive despite himself. "But—"

"It's just a scene, kiddo. Nothing radical. I'm not asking you to kill me or anything."

Too bad. But his own unspoken bravado didn't fool him for an instant. Achilles Desjardins, closet sadist, was suddenly scared to death.

"You mean acting," he said. "Silk cords, safe words, that kinda thing."

She shook her head. "I mean," she said patiently, "I want to *bleed*. I want to *hurt*. I want you to hurt me, lover."

What's wrong with me? he wondered. *She's just what I've always wanted. I can't believe my luck.*

And an instant later: *If it* is *luck . . .*

He was, after all, on the cusp of his life. Background checks were in progress. Risk assessments were underway. Just below the surface, the system was deciding whether Achilles Desjardins could be trusted to daily decide the fate of millions. Surely they already knew his secret—the mechanics had looked inside his head, they'd have noticed any missing or damaged wiring. Maybe this was a test, to see if he could control his impulses. Maybe Guilt Trip wasn't quite the fail-safe they'd told him it was, maybe enough wonky neurons screwed it up, maybe his baseline depravity was a potential loophole of some kind. Or maybe it was a lot simpler. Maybe they just couldn't afford to risk investing too much PR in a hero who couldn't control inclinations that some of the public might still find—unpleasant . . .

Aurora curled her lip and bared her neck. "Come on, kid. Do me."

She was the glimmer in the eye of every partner he'd ever had, that hard little twinkle that always seemed to say *Better be careful, you sick twisted piece of shit. One slip and you're finished.* She was six-year-old Penny, broken and bleeding and promising not to tell. She was his father, standing in a darkened hallway, staring through him with unreadable eyes that said *I know something about you, son, and you'll never know exactly what it is . . .*

"Rory," Desjardins said carefully, "have you ever talked to anyone about this?"

"All the time." She was still smiling, but a sudden wariness tinged her voice.

"No, I mean someone—you know—"

"Professional." The smile was gone. "Some piece of corpsy wetware that sucks down my account while telling me that I don't know my own mind, it's all just low self-esteem and my father raped me when I was preverbal." She reached for her clothes. "No, Achilles, I haven't. I'd rather spend my time with people who accept me for who I am than with misguided assholes who try to change me into what I'm not." She pulled up her panties. "I guess you just don't run into those types at official functions any more."

He tried: "You don't have to go."

He tried: "It was just so unexpected, you know?"

He tried: "It's just, you know, it seems so *disrespectful*—"

Aurora sighed. "Kiddo, if you really respected me you'd at least give me credit for knowing what I like."

"But I like *you,*" he blundered, free-falling in smoke and flame. "How am I supposed to enjoy *hurting* you when—"

"Hey, you think I enjoyed everything I did to get *you* off?"

She left him in the cubby with a flaccid penis, fifty minutes left on the clock and the stunning, humiliating realization that he was forever trapped within his own disguise. *I'll never let it out,* he thought. *No matter how much I want to, no matter who asks me, no matter how safe it seems. I'll never be sure there isn't an open circuit somewhere. I'll never be sure it isn't a trap. I'm gonna be undercover for the rest of my life, I'm too fucking terrified to come out.*

His dad would have been proud. He was a good Catholic boy after all.

But Achilles Desjardins was nothing if not practiced at the art of adaptation. By the time he emerged, chastened and alone, he was already beginning to rebuild his defenses. Maybe it was better this way. The biology was irrefutable, after all: sex *was* violence, literally, right down to the neurons. The same synapses lit up whether you fucked or fought, the same drive to violate and subjugate. It didn't matter how gentle you were on the outside, it didn't matter how much you pretended: even the most consensual intercourse was nothing more than the rape of a victim who'd given up.

If I do all this and have not love, I am as sounding brass, he thought.

He knew it in the floor of his brain, he knew it in the depths of his id. Sadism was hardwired, and sex—sex was more than violence. It was *disrespect.* There was no need to inflict it on another human being, here in the middle of the twenty-first century. There was no *right* to. Especially not for monsters with broken switches. He had a home sensorium that could satify any lust he could imagine, serve up virtual victims at such high rez that even *he* might be fooled.

There were other advantages, too. Never again the elaborate courtship rituals that he always seemed to fuck up at. Never again the fear of infection, the ludicrous efforts to romanticize path scans and pass blood work off as foreplay. Never again that hard twinkle in your victim's eyes, maybe knowing.

He had it worked out. Hell, he had a new Paradigm of Life.

From now on, Achilles Desjardins would be a civilized

man. He would inflict his vile passions on machinery, not flesh—and he would save himself a shitload of embarrassment in the bargain. Aurora had been for the best, a narrow escape in the nick of time. Head full of bad wiring in that one, no doubt about it. Pain and pleasure centers all cross-wired.

He didn't need to mix it up with a freak like *that.*

FIRE DRILL

SHE wakes up lost at sea.

She's not sure what called her back, exactly—she remembers a gentle push, as if someone was nudging her awake—yet she's perfectly alone out here. That was the whole point of the exercise. She could have slept anywhere in the trailer park, but she needed the solitude. So she swam out past Atlantis, past the habs and the generators, past the ridges and fissures that claw the neighborhood. Finally she arrived here, at this distant little outcropping of pumice and polymetallics, and fell into wide-eyed sleep.

Only now something has nudged her awake, and she has lost her bearings.

She pulls the sonar pistol off her thigh and sweeps the darkness. After a few seconds a fuzzy metropolitan echo comes back, just barely teasing the left edge of her sweep. She takes more direct aim and fires again. Atlantis and its suburbs come back dead center.

And a harder echo, smaller, nearer. Closing.

It's not an intercept course. A few more pings resolve a vector tracking past to starboard. Whoever it is probably doesn't even know she's here—or didn't, until she let loose with sonar.

They're moving pretty damned fast for someone without a squid. Curious, Clarke moves to intercept. She keeps her headlamp low, barely bright enough to tell substrate from seawater. The mud scrolls by like a treadmill. Pebbles and the occasional brittle star accent the monotony.

The bow wave catches her just before the body does. A shoulder rams into her side, pushes her into the bottom; mud billows up around her. A fin slaps Clarke in the face. She grabs blindly through the zeroed viz and catches hold of an arm.

"What the fuck!"

The arm yanks out of her grasp, but her expletive seems to have had some effect. The thrashing stops, at least. The muddy clouds continue to swirl, but by now it's all inertia.

"Who . . ." It's a rough, grating sound, even for a vocoder.

"It's Lenie." She brightens her headlamp; a billion suspended particles blind her in bright fog. She fins up into clearer water and points her beam at the bottom.

Something moves down there. *"Shiiit . . . lights down . . ."*

"Sorry." She dims the lamp. "Rama? That you?"

Bhanderi rises from the murk. *"Lenie."* A mechanical whisper. *"Hi."*

She supposes she's lucky he still recognizes her. Hell, she's lucky he can still *talk*. It's not just the skin that rots when you stop coming inside. It's not just the bones that go soft. Once a rifter goes native, the whole neocortex is pretty much a write-off. You let the abyss stare into you long enough and that whole civilized veneer washes away like melting ice in running water. Clarke imagines the fissures of the brain smoothing out over time, devolving back to some primordial fish-state more suited to their chosen habitat.

Rama Bhanderi isn't that far gone yet, though. He still even comes inside occasionally.

"What's the rush?" Clarke buzzes at him. She doesn't really expect an answer.

She gets one, though: *"Ru . . . dopamine, maybe . . . Epi . . ."*

It clicks after a second: *dopamine rush*. Is he still human enough to deliver bad puns? "No, Rama. I mean, why the *hurry*?"

He hangs beside her like a black wraith, barely visible in the dim ember of her headlamp. "*Ah*... ah... I'm not..." his voice trails off.

"*Boom,*" he says after a moment. "Blew it up. *Waayyyy* too bright."

A nudge, she remembers. Enough to wake her. "Blew what? Who?"

"Are you real?" he asks distantly. "... I... think you're a histamine glitch..."

"It's Lenie, Rama. For real. What blew up?"

"... *Acetylcholine,* maybe..." His hand passes back and forth in front of his face. "Only I'm *not cramping*..."

This is useless.

"... don't *like* her any more," Bhanderi buzzes softly. "And he *chased* me..."

Something tightens in her throat. She moves toward him. "Who? Rama, what—"

"*Back off,*" he grates. "I'm all... territorial..."

"Sorry... I..."

Bhanderi turns and fins away. She starts after him and stops, realizing: there's another way.

She brightens her lamp. The muddy storm front still hangs beneath her, just off the bottom. It won't settle for hours in this dense, sluggish water.

Neither will the trails that lead to it.

One of them is hers: a narrow muddy contrail kicked into suspension as she arrowed in from the east. The other trail extends back along a bearing of 345 degrees. Clarke follows it.

She's not heading for Atlantis, she soon realizes. Bhanderi's trail veers to port, along a line that should keep her well off the southwest shoulder of the complex. There's not much along that route, as far as Clarke can remember. Maybe a woodpile, one of several caches of prefab parts scattered about in anticipation of future expansion, back when the corpses first arrived. Sure enough, the water ahead begins to lighten. Clarke douses her own beam and sonars the brightness ahead. A jumble of hard Euclidean echoes bounce back, all from objects significantly larger than a human body.

She kicks forward. The diffuse glow resolves into four point sources: sodium floods, one at each corner of the woodpile. Stacked slabs of plastic and biosteel lie on pallets within the lit area. Curved slices of habhull lay piled on the substrate like great nested clamshells. Larger shapes loom in the murky distance: storage tanks, heat exchangers, the jackets of emergency reactors never assembled.

The distance *is* murky, Clarke realizes. Far murkier than usual.

She fins up into the water column and coasts above the industrial subscape. Something leans against the light like a soft dark wall, just past the farthest lamppost. She's been expecting it ever since she spoke to Bhanderi. Now it spreads out ahead of her in silent confirmation, a great billowing cloud of mud blown off the bottom and lingering, virtually weightless, in the aftermath of some recent explosion.

Of course, the corpses stockpiled blasting caps along with everything else . . .

Something tickles the corner of Clarke's eye, some small disarray somehow out of place among the organized chaos directly below. Two slabs of hull plating have been pulled from their stacks and laid out on the mud. Buckshot scatters of acne blemish their surfaces. Clarke arcs down for a closer look. No, those aren't innocuous clots of mud or a recent colony of benthic invertebrates. They're *holes,* punched through three centimeters of solid biosteel. Their edges are smooth, melted by some intense heat source and instantly congealed. Carbon scoring around each breach conveys a sense of bruising, of empty eyes battered black.

Clarke goes cold inside.

Someone's gearing up for the finals.

FAMILY VALUES

EVER since the founding of Atlantis, Jakob and Jutta Holtzbrink have kept to themselves. It wasn't always thus. Back on the surface, they were flamboyant even by corpse standards. They seemed to delight in the archaic contrast they presented to the world at large; their history together predates the Millennium, they were married so very long ago that the ceremony actually took place in a *church*. Jutta even took her husband's surname. Women did things like that back then, Rowan remembers. Sacrificed little bits of their own identity for the good of the Patriarchy, or whatever it was called.

An old-fashioned couple, and proud of it. When they appeared in public—which they did often—they appeared together, and they stood out.

Public doesn't exist here in Atlantis, of course. Public was left behind to fend for itself. Atlantis was the crème de la crème from the very beginning, only movers and shakers and those worker bees who cared for them, deep in the richest parts of the hive.

Down here, Jutta and Jakob don't get out much. The escape changed them. It changed everyone of course, humbled the mighty, rubbed their noses in their own failures even though, goddammit, they *still* made the best of it, adapted even to Doomsday, saw the market in lifeboats and jumped on board before anyone else. These days, mere survival is a portfolio to take pride in. But the Holtzbrinks have not availed themselves of even that half-assed and self-serving consolation. βehemoth hasn't touched them in the flesh, not a single particle, and yet somehow it seems to have made them almost physically smaller.

They spend most of their time in their suite, plugged into virtual environments far more compelling than the confines of this place could ever be. They come out to get their meals, of course—in-suite food production is a thing of the past, ever since the rifters confiscated "their share" of the resource base—but even then, they retreat back into their quarters with their trays of cycler food and hydroponic produce, to eat behind closed doors. It's a minor and inoffensive quirk, this sudden desire for privacy from their peers. Patricia Rowan never gave it much thought until that day in the comm cave when Ken Lubin, in search of clues, had asked, *What about the fish? Perhaps they hitched a ride. Are the larvae planktonic?*

And Jerry Seger, impatient with this turncoat killer posing as a deep thinker, dismissed him as she would a child: *If it had been able to disperse inside plankton, why wait until now to take over the world? It would have done it a few hundred million years ago.*

Maybe it would have, Rowan muses now.

The Holtzbrinks made their mark in pharmaceuticals, stretching back even to the days before gengineering. They've kept up with the times, of course. When the first hydrothermal ecosystems were discovered, back before the turn of the century, an earlier generation of Holtzbrinks had been there—reveling in new Domains, sifting through cladograms of freshly-discovered species, new microbes, new enzymes built to work at temperatures and pressures long thought impossibly hostile to any form of life. They cataloged the cellular machinery ticking sluggishly in bedrock kilometers deep, germs living so slowly they hadn't divided since the French Revolution. They tweaked the sulfur-reducers that choked to death on oxygen, coaxed them into devouring oil slicks and curing strange new kinds of cancer. The Holtzbrink Empire, it was said, held patents on half the Archaebacteria.

Now Patricia Rowan sits across from Jakob and Jutta in their living room, and wonders what else they might have patented in those last days on Earth.

"I'm sure you've heard the latest," she says. "Jerry just confirmed it. βehemoth's made it to Impossible Lake."

Jakob nods, a birdlike gesture including shoulders as well as head. But his words carry denial: "No, I don't think so. I saw the stats. Too salty." He licks his lips, stares at the floor. "βehemoth wouldn't like it."

Jutta puts a comforting hand on his knee.

He's a very old man, his conquests all in the past. He was born too early, grew too old for eternal youth. By the time the tweaks were available—every defective base pair snipped out, every telomere reinforced—his body had already been wearing out for the better part of a century. There's a limit to how much you can fix so late in the game.

Rowan gently explains. "Not in the lake itself, Jakob. Somewhere nearby. One of the hot vents."

He nods and nods and will not look at her.

Rowan glances at Jutta; Jutta looks back, helplessness on her face.

Rowan presses on: "As you know, this wasn't supposed to happen. We studied the bug, we studied the oceanography, we chose this place very carefully. But we missed something."

"Goddamn Gulf Stream shut down," the old man says. His voice is stronger than his body, although not by much. "They said it would happen. Change all the currents. Turn England into goddamn Siberia."

Rowan nods. "We've looked at a lot of different scenarios. Nothing seems to fit. I think maybe there might be something about βehemoth itself that we're missing." She leans forward slightly. "Your people did a lot of prospecting out around the Rim of Fire, didn't they? Back in the thirties?"

"Sure. Everyone was. Those bloody Archaea, it was the gold rush of the twenty-first."

"Your people spent a lot of time on Juan de Fuca back then. They never encountered βehemoth?"

"Mmmm." Jakob Holtzbrink shakes his head. His shoulders don't move.

"Jakob, you know me. You know I've always been a staunch supporter of corporate confidentiality. But we're all on the same side here, we're all in the same boat so to speak. If you know anything, anything at all..."

"Oh, Jakob never did any of the actual research," Jutta interjects. "Surely you know that, he was really more of a people person."

"Yes, of course. But he also took a real interest in the cutting edge. He was always quite excited about new discoveries, remember?" Rowan laughs softly. "There was a time back there when we thought the man practically *lived* in a submarine."

"I just took the tours, you know. Jutta's right, I didn't do any of the research. That was the gel-jocks, Jarvis and that lot." For the first time, Jakob meets Rowan's eye. "Lost that whole team when βehemoth broke out, you know. CSIRA was conscripting our people right across the globe. Just waltzed right in, drafted them out from under our noses." He snorts. "Goddamn *greater good*."

Jutta squeezes his knee. They glance at each other; she smiles. He puts his hand over hers.

His eyes drift back to the floor. Very gently, he begins nodding again.

"Jakob wasn't close to the research teams," Jutta explains. "Scientists aren't all that good with people, as you know. It would be a disaster to let some of those people act as spokespersons, but they still resented the way Jakob presented their findings sometimes."

Rowan smiles patiently. "The thing is, Jakob, I've been thinking. About βehemoth, and how old it is—"

"Oldest goddamn life on the planet," Jakob says. "The rest of us, we just dropped in later. Martian meteor or something. Bloody βehemoth, it's the only thing that actually *started* here."

"But that's the thing, isn't it? βehemoth doesn't just predate other life, it predates photosynthesis. It predates *oxygen*. It's over four billion years old. And all the other really ancient bugs we've found, the Archaebacteria and the Nanoliths and so forth, they're still anaerobes to this day. You only find them in reducing environments. And yet here's βehemoth, even older, and oxygen doesn't bother it at all."

Jakob Holtzbrink stops rocking.

"Smart little bug," he says. "Keeps up with the times. Has those, what do you call them, like *Pseudomonas* has—"

"Blachford genes. Change their own mutation rate under stress."

"Right. Right. Blachford genes." Jakob brings one hand up, runs it over a sparsely-haired and liver-spotted scalp. "It adapted. Adapted to oxygen, and adapted to living inside fishes, and now it's adapting to every other goddamn nook and cranny on the goddamn planet."

"Only it never adapted to low temperature and high salinity in combination," Rowan observes. "It never adapted to the single biggest habitat on Earth. The deep sea stumped it for billions of years. The deep sea would *still* be stumping it if the Channer outbreak hadn't happened."

"What are you saying?" Jutta wonders, a sudden slight sharpness in her voice. Her husband says nothing.

Rowan takes a breath. "All our models are based on the assumption that βehemoth has been in its present form for hundreds of millions of years. The advent of oxygen, hypotonic host bodies—all that happened in the deep, deep Precambrian. And we know that not much has changed since then, Blachford genes or no Blachford genes—because if it had, ßehemoth would have ruled the world long before now. We know it can't disperse through the abyss because it *hasn't* dispersed through the abyss, in all the millions of years it's had to try. And when someone suggests that maybe it hitched a ride in the ichthyoplankton, we dismiss them out of hand not because anybody's actually *checked*—who had the time, the way things were going?—but because if it *could* disperse that way, it *would* have dispersed that way. Millions of years ago."

Jakob Holtzbrink clears his throat.

Rowan lays it on the table: "What if ßehemoth hasn't had millions of years? What if it's only had a few decades?"

"Well, that's—" Jutta begins.

"Then we're not sure of anything any more, are we? Maybe we're not talking about a few isolated relicts here and there. Maybe we're talking about epicenters. And maybe it's not that ßehemoth isn't *able* to spread out, but that it's only just now got started."

That avian rocking again, and the same denial: "Nah. Nah. It's *old*. RNA template, mineralized walls. Big goddamned pores all over it, *that's* why it can't hack cold seawater. Leaks like a sieve." A bubble of saliva appears at the corner of his mouth; Jutta absently reaches up to brush it away. Jakob raises his hand irritably, preempting her. Her hands drop into her lap.

"The pyranosal sequences. Primitive. Unique. That woman, that doctor: Jerenice. She found the same thing. It's *old*."

"Yes," Rowan agrees, "it's old. Maybe something changed it, just recently."

Jakob's rubbing his hands, agitated. "What, some mutation? Lucky break? Damn unlucky for the rest of us."

"Maybe some*one* changed it," Rowan says.

There. It's out.

"I hope you're not suggesting," Jutta begins, and falls silent.

Rowan leans forward and lays her hand on Jakob's knee. "I know how it was out there, thirty, forty years ago. It was a gold rush mentality, just as you said. Everybody and their organ-cloner was setting up labs on the rift, doing all kinds of in situ work—"

"Of course it was in situ, you ever try to duplicate those conditions in a *lab*—"

"But your people were at the forefront. You not only had your own research, you had your eye on everyone else's. You were too good a businessman to do it any other way. And so I'm coming to you, Jakob. I'm not making any claims or accusing anyone of anything, do you understand? I just think that if anyone in Atlantis might have any ideas about anything that might have happened out there, you'd be the one. You're the expert, Jakob. Can you tell me anything?"

Jutta shakes her head. "Jakob doesn't know anything, Patricia. Neither of us knows anything. And I *do* take your implication."

Rowan keeps her eyes locked on the old man. He stares at the floor, he stares *through* the floor, through the deck plating and the underlying pipes and conduits, through the wires and fullerene and biosteel, through seawater and oozing, viscous rock into some place that she can only imagine. When he speaks, his voice seems to come from there.

"What do you want to know?"

"Would there be any reason why someone—hypothetically—might want to take an organism like βehemoth, and tweak it?"

"More than you can count," says the distant voice. This frail body it's using scarcely seems animate.

"Such as?"

"Targeted delivery. Drugs, genes, replacement organelles.

Its cell wall, you've never seen anything like it. Nothing has. No immune response to worry about, slips past counterintrusion enzymes like they were blind and deaf. Target cell takes it right in, lyses the wall, COD. Like a biodegradable buckyball."

"What else?"

"The ultimate pep pill. Under the right conditions the thing pumps out ATP so fast you could roll a car over single-handed. Makes mitochondria look like yesterday's sockeye. Soldier with βehemoth in his cells might even give an exoskel a run for the money, if you feed him enough."

"And if βehemoth were tweaked properly," Rowan amends.

"Aye," whispers the old man. "There's the rub."

Rowan chooses her words very carefully. "Might there have been any . . . less precise applications? MAD machines? Industrial terrorism?"

"You mean, like what it does now? No. W—someone would have to be blind and stupid and insane all at once to *design* something like that."

"But you'd have to increase the reproductive rate quite a bit, wouldn't you? To make it economically viable."

He nods, his eyes still on far-focus. "Those deep-rock dwellers, they live so slow you're lucky if they divide once a *decade*."

"And that would mean they'd have to eat a lot more, wouldn't it? To support the increased growth rate."

"Of course. Child knows that much. But that's not *why* you'd do it, nobody would do that because they *wanted* something that could—it would just be a, an unavoidable—"

"A side effect," Jutta suggests.

"A side effect," he repeats. His voice hasn't changed. It still rises, calm and distant, from the center of the earth. But there are tears on Jakob Holtzbrink's face.

"So nobody did it deliberately. They were aiming for something else, and things just—went wrong. Is that what you're saying?"

"You mean, hypothetically?" The corners of his mouth lift and crinkle in some barely discernible attempt at a smile. A tear runs down one of those fleshy creases and drops off his chin.

"Yes, Jakob. Hypothetically."

The head bobs up and down.

"Is there anything we can do? Anything we haven't tried?"

Jakob shakes his head. "I'm just a corpse. I don't know."

She stands. The old man stares down into his own thoughts. His wife stares up at Rowan.

"What he's told you," she says. "Don't take it the wrong way."

"What do you mean?"

"He didn't do this, any more than you did. He's no worse than the rest of you."

Rowan inclines her head. "I know, Jutta."

She excuses herself. The last thing she sees, as the hatch seals them off, is Jutta Holtzbrink sliding a lucid dreamer over her husband's bowed head.

There's nothing to be done about it now. No point in recriminations, no shortage of fingers pointing in any direction. Still, she's glad she paid the visit. Even grateful, in an odd way. It's a selfish gratitude, but it will have to do. Patricia Rowan takes whatever solace she can in the fact that the buck doesn't stop with her any more. It doesn't even stop with Lenie Clarke, Mermaid of the Apocalypse. Rowan starts down the pale blue corridor of Res-D, glancing one more time over her shoulder.

The buck stops there.

PORTRAIT OF THE SADIST AS A FREE MAN

THE technical term was *fold catastrophe*. Seen on a graph it was a tsunami in cross-section, the smooth roof of an onrushing wave reaching forward, doubling back beneath the crest and plummeting in a smooth glassy arc to some new, low-energy equilibrium that left no stone standing on another.

Seen on the ground it was a lot messier: power grids failing; life-support and waste-management systems seizing up; thoroughfares choked with angry, frenzied mobs pushed one meal past revolution. The police in their exoskels had long since retreated from street level; pacification botflies swarmed overhead, scything through the mobs with gas and infrasound.

There was also a word for the leading edge of the wave, that chaotic inflection point where the trajectory reversed itself before crashing: breakpoint. Western N'AmPac had pulled through that hairpin turn sometime during the previous thirty-four hours; everything west of the Rockies was pretty much a write-off. CSIRA had slammed down every kind of barrier to keep it contained; people, goods, electrons themselves had been frozen in transit. To all intents and purposes the world ended at the Cordillera. Only 'lawbreakers could reach through that barrier now, to do what they could.

It wouldn't be enough. Not this time.

Of course, the system had been degrading for decades. Centuries, even. Desjardins owed his very job to that vibrant synergism between entropy and human stupidity; without it, damage control wouldn't be the single largest industry on the planet. Eventually everything had been bound to fall apart, anyone with a pair of eyes and an IQ even slightly above room temperature knew that. But there'd been no ironclad reason why it had had to happen quite as quickly as it had. They could have bought another decade or two, a little more time for those who still had faith in human ingenuity to go on deluding themselves.

But the closer you got to breakpoint, the harder it was to suture the cracks back together. Even equilibria were unstable, so close to the precipice. Forget butterflies: with a planet teetering this close to the edge, the fluttering of an *aphid's* wings might be enough to push it over.

It was 2051, and it was Achilles Desjardins's sworn duty to squash Lenie Clarke like an insect of whatever kind.

He watched her handiwork spread across the continent like a web of growing cracks shattering the surface of a frozen lake. His inlays gulped data from a hundred feeds: confirmed and probable sightings over the previous two months, too stale to be any use in a manhunt but potentially useful for predicting the next βehemoth outbreak. Memes and legends of the Meltdown Madonna, far more numerous and metastatic—a reproductive strategy for swarms of virtual wildlife Desjardins had only just discovered and might never fully understand. Reality and legend in some inadvertant alliance, βehemoth blooming everywhere they converged; firestorms and blackouts coming up from behind, an endless ongoing toll of innocent lives preempted for the greater good.

It was a lie, Desjardins knew. N'Am was past breakpoint despite all those draconian measures. It would take a while for the whole system to shake out; it was a long drop from crest to trough. But Desjardins was nothing if not adept at reading the numbers. He figured two weeks—three at the most—before the rest of the continent followed N'AmPac into anarchy.

A newsfeed running in one corner of his display served up

a fresh riot from Hongcouver. State-of-the-art security systems gave their lives in defense of glassy spires and luxury enclaves—defeated not by clever hacks or superior technology, but by the sheer weight of flesh against their muzzles. The weapons died of exhaustion, disappeared beneath a tide of live bodies scrambling over dead ones. The crowd breached the gates as he watched, screaming in triumph. Thirty thousand voices in superposition: a keening sea, its collective voice somehow devoid of any humanity. It sounded almost mechanical. It sounded like the wind.

Desjardins killed the channel before the mob learned what he already knew: the spires were empty, the corpses they'd once sheltered long since gone to ground.

Or to sea, rather.

A light hand brushed against his back. He turned, startled; Alice Jovellanos was at his shoulder. Desjardins shot a furtive glance back to his board when he saw who was with her; Rome burned there on a dozen insets. He reached for the cutoff.

"Don't." Lenie Clarke slipped the visor from her face and stared at the devastation with eyes as blank as eggshells. Her face was calm and expressionless, but when she spoke again, her voice trembled.

"Leave it on."

He had first met her two weeks before. He'd been tracking her for months, searching the archives, delving into her records, focusing his superlative pattern-matching skills on the cryptic, incomplete jigsaw called *Lenie Clarke*. But those assembled pieces had revealed more than a *brood sac for the end of the world,* as Rowan had put it. They'd revealed a woman whose entire childhood had been pretense, programmed to ends over which she'd had no awareness or control. All this time she had been trying to get home, trying to rediscover her own past.

Ken Lubin, slaved to his own brand of Guilt Trip, had been trying to kill her. Desjardins had tried to get in his way; at the time it had seemed the only decent thing to do. It seemed odd, in retrospect, that such an act of kindness could have been triggered by his own awakening psychopathy.

His rescue attempt had not gone well. Lubin had intercepted him before Clarke even showed up in Sault Sainte Marie. Desjardins had sat out the rest of the act tied to a chair in a pitch-black room, half the bones in his face broken.

Surprisingly, it had not been Ken Lubin who had done that to him.

And yet somehow they were now all on what might loosely be called *the same side:* he and Alice and Kenny and Lenie, all working together under the banner of grayness and moral ambiguity and righteous vendetta. Spartacus had freed Lubin from Guilt Trip as it had freed Desjardins. The 'lawbreaker had to admit to a certain sympatico with the taciturn assassin, even now; he knew how it felt to be wrenched back into a position of genuine culpability, after years of letting synthetic neurotransmitters make all the tough decisions. Crippling anxiety. Guilt.

At first, anyway. Now the guilt was fading. Now there was only fear.

From a thousand directions the world cried out in desperate need of his attention. It was his sworn duty to offer it: to provide salvation or, failing that, to bail until the last piece of flotsam sank beneath the waves. Not so long ago it would have been more than a duty. It would have been a compulsion, a drive, something he could not *prevent* himself from doing. At this very moment he should be dispatching emergency teams, rerouting vital supplies, allocating lifters and botflies to reinforce the weakening quarantine.

Fuck it, he thought, and killed the feeds. Somehow he sensed

Lenie Clarke flinching behind him as the display went dark.

"Did you get a fix?" Jovellanos asked. She'd taken a shot at it herself, but she'd only been a senior 'lawbreaker for a week: hardly enough time to get used to her inlays, let alone develop the seventh sense that Desjardins had honed over half a decade. The sharpest fix she'd been able to get on the vanished corpses was *somewhere in the North Atlantic*.

Desjardins nodded and reached out to the main board. Clarke's onyx reflection moved up behind him, staring back from the dark surface. Desjardins suppressed the urge to look over his shoulder. She was *right here in his cubby*: just a girl, half his size. A skinny little K-selector that half the world wanted to kill and the other half wanted to die for.

Without even having met her, he had thrown away everything to come to her aid. When he'd finally met her face-to-face, she'd scared him more than Lubin had. But something had happened to Clarke since then. The ice-queen affect hadn't changed at all, but something behind it seemed—smaller, somehow. Almost fragile.

Alice didn't seem to notice, though. She'd been the rifters' self-appointed mascot from the moment she'd seen a chance to get back at *the Evil Corporate Oligarchy,* or whatever she was calling it this week.

Desjardins opened a window on the board: a false-color satcam enhance of open ocean, a multihued plasma of color-coded contours.

"I thought of that," Alice piped up, "but even if you *could* make out a heat print against the noise, the circulation's so slow down there—"

"Not temperature," Desjardins interrupted. "Turbidity."

"Even so, the circulation—"

He shot her a look. "Shut up and learn, okay?"

She fell silent, the hurt obvious in her eyes. She'd been

walking on eggshells ever since she'd admitted to infecting him.

Desjardins turned back to the board. "There's a lot of variation over time, of course. Everything from whitecaps to squid farts." He tapped an icon; layers of new data superimposed themselves atop the baseline, a translucent parfait. "You'd never get a track with a single snapshot, no matter how fine the rez. I had to look at mean values over a three-month period."

The layers merged. The amorphous plasma disappeared; hard-edged contrails and splotches condensed from that mist.

Desjardins's fingers played across the board. "Now cancel everything that shows up in the NOAA database,"—a myriad luminous scars faded into transparency—"Gulf Stream leftovers,"—a beaded necklace from Florida to England went dark—"and any listed construction sites or upwells inconsistent with minimum allowable structure size."

A few dozen remaining pockmarks disappeared. The North Atlantic was dark and featureless but for a single bright blemish, positioned almost exactly in its center.

"So that's it," Clarke murmered.

Desjardins shook his head. "We still have to correct for lateral displacement during ascent. Midwater currents and the like." He called forth algorithms: the blemish jiggled to the northwest and stopped.

39°20′14″N 25°16′03″W said the display.

"Dead northeast of the Atlantis Fracture Zone," Desjardins said. "Lowest vorticity in the whole damn basin."

"You said turbidity." Clarke's reflection, a bright bull's-eye in its chest, shook its head. "But if there's no vorticity—"

"Bubbles," Alice exclaimed, clueing in.

Desjardins nodded. "You don't build a retirement home for a few thousand people without doing some serious welding. That's gonna generate sagans of waste gas. Hence, turbidity."

Clarke was still skeptical. "We welded at Channer. The

pressure crushed the bubbles down to nothing as soon as they formed."

"For point-welding, sure. But these guys must be fusing whole habs together: higher temperatures, greater outgassing, more thermal inertia." Finally, he turned to face her. "We're not talking about a boiling cauldron here. It's just fine fizz by the time it hits the surface. Not even visible to the naked eye. But it's enough to reduce light penetration, and that's what we're seeing right here."

He tapped the tumor on the board.

Clarke stared at it a moment, her face expressionless. "Anybody else know about this?" she asked finally.

Desjardins shook his head. "Nobody even knows I was working on it."

"You wouldn't mind keeping it that way?"

He snorted. "Lenie, I don't even want to *think* about what would happen if anyone found out I was spending time on this. And not that you're unwelcome or anything, but the fact that you guys are even hanging around out here is a major risk. Do you—"

"It's taken care of, Killjoy," Alice said softly. "I told you. I catch on fast."

She did, too. Promoted in the wake of his desertion, it had taken her only a few hours to figure out that some plus-thousand corpses had quietly slipped off the face of the earth. It had taken her less than two days to get him back onto the CSIRA payroll, his mysterious absence obscured by alibis and bureaucratic chaff. She'd started the game with an unfair advantage, of course: preinfected with Spartacus, Guilt Trip had never affected her. She'd begun her tenure with all the powers of a senior 'lawbreaker and none of the restraints. Of *course* she had the wherewithal to get Lenie Clarke into CSIRA's inner sanctum.

But even now, Spartacus bubbled in Desjardins's head like

acid, eating away at the chains Guilt Trip had forged. It had already freed his conscience; soon, he very much feared, Spartacus would destroy it utterly.

He looked at Alice. *You did this to me,* he thought, and examined the feelings the accusation provoked. There had been anger at first, a sense of profound betrayal. Something bordering on hatred, even.

Now he wasn't sure any more. Alice—Alice was a complication, his undoing and his salvation all rolled into one willowy chassis. She had saved his ass, for now. She had information that could be vital, for later. It seemed like a good idea to play along, for the time being at least. As for the rifters, the sooner he helped them on their way the sooner they'd drop out of the equation.

And all the while, some persistent splinter in the back of his mind contemplated the options that might soon be available to a man without a leash . . .

Alice Jovellanos offered him a tentative smile, ever hopeful. Achilles Desjardins smiled back.

"You catch on fast," he repeated. "That you do."

Hopefully not fast enough.

CONFESSIONAL

JERENICE Seger wants to make an announcement.

She won't make it to Clarke or Lubin. She won't even tell them what it's about. "I don't want there to be any misunderstanding," she says. "I want to address your whole community." Her pixelated likeness stares out from the board, grimly defiant. Patricia Rowan stands in the background; she doesn't look pleased either.

"Fine," Lubin says at last, and kills the connection.

Seger, Clarke reflects. *Seger's making the announcement. Not Rowan.* "Medical news," she says aloud.

"Bad news." Lubin replies, sealing up his gauntlets.

Clarke sets the board for LFAM broadband. "Better summon the troops, I guess."

Lubin's heading down the ladder. "Ring the chimes for me, will you?"

"Why? Where *you* going?" The chimes serve to heads-up those rifters who leave their vocoders offline, but Lubin usually boots them up himself.

"I want to check something out," he says.

The airlock hisses shut behind him.

Of course, even at their present numbers they can't all fit into the nerve hab at once.

It might have been easier if rifter modules followed the rules. They've been designed to interconnect, each self-contained sphere puckered by six round mouths two meters across. Each can lock lips with any other, or with pieces of interposing corridor—and so the whole structure grows, lumpy and opportunistic, like a great skeleton of long bones and empty skulls assembling itself across the seabed. That's the idea, anyway. A few basic shapes, infinitely flexible in combination.

But no. Here the hab modules sprout like solitary mushrooms across the substrate. Rifters live alone, or in pairs, or whatever social assemblage fits the moment. A *crowd* of rifters is almost an oxymoron. The nerve habs are among the largest structures in the whole trailer park, and they only hold a dozen or so on their main decks. Given the territorial perimeters that most rifters develop in the abyss, it doesn't hold them comfortably.

It's already getting congested by the time Clarke returns from priming the chimes. Chen and Cramer converge on her tail as she glides up into the airlock. On the wet deck, Abra Cheung ascends the ladder ahead of her. Clarke follows her up—the airlock cycling again at her back—into a knot of eight or nine people who have arrived during her absence.

Grace Nolan's at the center of the action, bellied up to the comm panel. Sonar shows a dozen others still en route. Clarke wonders idly if the hab's scrubbers are up to this kind of load. Maybe there is no *announcement.* Maybe Seger's just trying to get them to overdose on their own CO_2.

"Hi." Kevin Walsh appears at her side, hovering hopefully at the edge of her public-comfort perimeter. He seems back to his old self. In front of them, Gomez turns and notices Clarke. "Hey, Len. News from the corpses, I hear."

Clarke nods.

"You're tight with those assholes. Know what it's about?"

She shakes her head. "Seger's the mouthpiece, though. I figure something medical."

"Yeah. Probably." Gomez sucks air softly through stained

teeth. "Anybody seen Julia? She should be here for this."

Cheung purses her lips. "What, after spending the last week and a half with Gene? You can breathe that air if *you* want."

"I saw her out by one of the woodpiles not too long ago," Hopkinson volunteers.

"How'd she seem?"

"You know Julia. A black hole with tits."

"I mean physically. She seem sick at all?"

"How would I know? You think she was out there in a bra and panties?" Hopkinson shrugs. "Didn't say anything, anyway."

Faintly, through bulkheads and conversation, the cries of tortured rock.

"Okay then," Nolan says from the board. "Enough dicking around. Let's rack 'em up and shoot 'em down." She taps an icon on the panel. "You're on, Seger. Make it good."

"Is everyone there?" Seger's voice.

"Of course not. We can't all fit into a hab."

"I'd rather—"

"You're hooked into all the LFAM channels. Anyone within five hundred meters can hear you just fine."

"Well." A pause, the silence of someone deciding how best to proceed across a minefield. "As you know, Atlantis has been quarantined for several days now. Ever since we learned about βehemoth. Now we've all had the retrofits, so there was every reason to expect that this wasn't a serious problem. The quarantine was merely a precaution."

"Was," Nolan notes. Downstairs the airlock is cycling again.

Seger forges on. "We analyzed the—the samples that Ken and Lenie brought back from Impossible Lake, and everything we found was consistent with βehemoth. Same peculiar RNA, same stereoisomerization of—"

"Get to the point," Nolan snaps.

"Grace?" Clarke says. Nolan looks at her.

"Shut up and let the woman finish," Clarke suggests. Nolan snorts and turns away.

"Anyway," Seger continues after a moment, "the results were perfectly straightforward, so we incinerated the infected remains as a containment measure. After digitizing them, of course."

"Digitizing?" That's Chen.

"A high-res destructive scan, enough to let us simulate the sample right down to the molecular level," Seger explains. "Model tissues give us much of the same behavior as a wet sample, but without the attendant risks."

Charley Garcia climbs into view. The bulkheads seem to sneak a little closer with each new arrival. Clarke swallows, the air thickening around her.

Seger coughs. "I was working with one of those models and, well, I noticed an anomaly. I believe that the fish you brought back from Impossible Lake was infected with βehemoth."

Exchanged glances among a roomful of blank eyes. Off in the distance, Lubin's wind chimes manage a final reedy moan and fall silent, the reservoir exhausted.

"Well, of *course,*" Nolan says after a moment. "So what?"

"I'm, um, I'm using *infected* in the pathological sense, not the symbiotic one." Seger clears her throat. "What I mean to say is—"

"It was *sick,*" Clarke says. "It was *sick* with βehemoth."

Dead air for a moment. Then: "I'm afraid that's right. If Ken hadn't killed it first, I think βehemoth might have."

"Oh, *fuck,*" someone says softly. The epithet hangs there in a room gone totally silent. Downstairs, the airlock gurgles.

"So it was sick," Dale Creasy says after a moment. "So what?"

Garcia shakes his head. "Dale, don't you remember how this fucker *works*?"

"Sure. Breaks your enzymes apart to get at the sulfur or something. But we're immune."

"We're immune," Garcia says patiently, "because we've got special genes that make enzymes too stiff for βehemoth to break. And we got those genes from deepwater fish, Dale."

Creasy's still working it through. Someone else whispers *"Shit shit shit,"* in a shaky voice. Downstairs, some latecomer's climbing the ladder; whoever it is stumbles on the first rung.

"I'm afraid Mr. Garcia's right," Seger says. "If the fish down here are vulnerable to this bug, then we probably are too."

Clarke shakes her head. "But—are you saying this thing *isn't* βehemoth after all? It's something else?"

A sudden commotion around the ladder; the assembled rifters are pulling back as though it were electrified. Julia Friedman staggers up into view, her face the color of basalt. She stands on the deck, clinging to the railing around the hatch, not daring to let go. She looks around, blinking rapidly over undead eyes. Her skin glistens.

"It's still βehemoth, more or less," Seger drones in the distance. From Atlantis. From the bolted-down, welded-tight, hermetically-sealed quarantined *goddamned safety of fucking Atlantis.* "That's why we couldn't pinpoint the nature of Mr. Erickson's infection: he came back positive for βehemoth but of course we disregarded those findings because we didn't think it could be the problem. But this is a new variant, apparently. Virulent speciation is quite common when an organism spreads into new environments. This is basically—"

βehemoth's evil twin brother, Clarke remembers.

"—βehemoth Mark Two," Seger finishes.

Julia Friedman drops to her knees and vomits onto the deck.

Babel Broadband. An overlapping collage of distorted voices:

"Of course I don't believe them. You saying you *do*?"

"That's bullshit. If you—"

"They admitted it up front. They didn't have to."

"Yeah, they suddenly come clean at the exact moment Julia goes symptomatic. What a coincidence."

"How'd they know that she—"

"They knew the incubation time. They must have. How else do you explain the timing here, dramatic irony?"

"Yeah, but what are we gonna *do*?"

They've abandoned the hab. It emptied like a blown ballast tank, rifters spilling onto a seabed already crowded even by dryback standards. Now it hangs above them like a gunmetal planet. Three lamps set around the ventral airlock lay bright overlapping circles onto the substrate. Black bodies swim at the periphery of that light, hints of restless motion behind shark-tooth rows of white, unblinking eyespots. Clarke thinks of hungry animals, kept barely at bay by the light of a campfire.

By rights, she should feel like one of them.

Grace Nolan's no longer in evidence. She disappeared into the darkness a few minutes ago, one supportive arm around Julia Friedman, helping her back home. That act of apparent altruism seems to have netted her extra cred: Chen and Hopkinson are standing in for her on the point-counterpoint. Garcia's raising token questions, but the prevailing mood does not suggest any great willingness to extend the benefit of the doubt.

"Hey, Dimi," Chen buzzes. "How's it going in there?"

"Stinks like a hospital." Alexander's airborne voice makes a conspicuous contrast against the background of waterlogged ones. "Almost done, though. Somebody better be growing me a new skin." He's still inside, sterilizing anything that Friedman or her bodily fluids might have come into contact with. Grace Nolan asked for volunteers.

She's started giving orders. People have started taking them.

"I say we just drill the fuckers." Creasy buzzes from somewhere nearby.

Clarke remembers holes burned through biosteel. "Let's hold off on the whole counterstrike thing for a bit. It might be tougher for them to find a cure if we smear them into the deck."

"As if they're looking for a fucking cure."

She ignores the remark. "They want blood samples from everyone. Some of the rest of us might be infected. It obviously doesn't show up right away."

"It showed up fast enough with Gene," someone points out.

"Being gutted alive probably increases your level of exposure a bit. But Julia didn't show anything for, what—two weeks?"

"I'm not giving them any blood," Creasy growls with a voice like scrap metal. "*They'll* be fucking giving blood if they try and make me."

Clarke shakes her head, exasperated. "Dale, they can't make anyone do anything and they know it. They're *asking*. If you want them to *beg,* I'm sure it can be arranged. What's your problem? You've been collecting bloods on your own anyway."

"If we could take our tongues off Patricia Rowan's clit for a moment, I have a message from Gene."

Grace Nolan swims into the circle of light like a pitch-black pack animal, asserting dominance. Campfires don't bother *her*.

"Grace," Chen buzzes. "How's Julia?"

"How do you think? She's *sick*. But I got her tucked in at least, and the diagnostics are running for all the good they'll do."

"And Gene?" Clarke asks.

"He was awake for a little while. He said, and I quote, '*I told them those baby-boners did something to me. Maybe they'll believe me when my wife dies.*'"

"Hey," Walsh pipes up. "*He's* obviously feeling bet—"

"The corpses would *never* risk spreading something like this without already having a cure," Nolan cuts in. "It could get back to them too easily."

"Right." Creasy again. "So I say we drill the fuckers one bulkhead at a time until they hand it over."

Uncertainty and acquiescence mix in the darkness.

"You know, just to play devil's advocate here, I gotta say there's a slim chance they're telling the truth."

That's Charley Garcia, floating off to the side.

"I mean, bugs mutate, right?" he continues. "Especially when people throw shitloads of drugs at them, and you can bet they bought out the whole pharm when this thing first got out. So who's to say it *couldn't* have gone from Mark One to β-max all on its own?"

"Fucking big coincidence if you ask me," Creasy buzzes.

Garcia's vocoder ticks, a verbal shrug. "I'm just saying."

"And if they were going to pull some kind of biowar shit, why wait until now?" Clarke adds, grasping the straw. "Why not four years ago?"

"They didn't have βehemoth four years ago," Nolan says.

Walsh: "They could've brought down a culture."

"What, for old times' sake? Fucking *nostalgia*? They didn't have shit until Gene served it up to 'em warm and steaming."

"You oughtta get out more, Grace," Garcia buzzes. "We've been building bugs from mail-order parts for fifty years. Once they had the genes sequenced, the corpses could've built βehemoth from scratch any time they felt like it."

"Or anything else, for that matter," Hopkinson adds. "Why use something that takes all this time just to make a few of us sick? Supercol would've dropped us in a day."

"It would've dropped *Gene* in a day," Nolan buzzes. "Before he had any chance to infect the rest of us. A fast bug wouldn't have a chance out here—we're spread out, we're isolated, we don't even *breathe* most of the time. Even when we go inside we keep our skins on. This thing *has* to be slow if it's gonna spread. These stumpfucks know exactly what they're doing."

"Besides," Baker adds, "a Supercol epidemic starts on the bottom of the goddamn ocean and we're not gonna connect the dots? They'd be sockeye the moment they tried."

"They know it, too."

"βehemoth gives them an alibi, though," Chen says. "Doesn't it?"

Fuck, Jelaine. Clarke's been thinking exactly the same thing. *Why'd you have to bring that up?*

Nolan grabs the baton in an instant. "That's right. That's *right.* βehemoth comes all the way over from Impossible Lake, no way anybody can accuse them of planting it *there*—they just tweak it a bit on its way through Atlantis, pass it on to us, and how are we supposed to know the difference?"

"Especially since they conveniently *destroyed the samples,*" Creasy adds.

Clarke shakes her head. "You're a plumber with gills, Dale. You wouldn't have a clue what to do with those samples if Seger handed them to you in a zip-lock bag. Same goes for Grace's little science-fair project with the blood."

"So that's your contribution." Nolan twists through the water until she's a couple of meters off Clarke's bow. "None of us poor dumb fish-heads got tenure or augments, so we've just gotta trust everything to the wise old gel-jocks who fucked us over in the first place."

"There's someone else," Clarke buzzes back. "Rama Bhanderi."

Sudden, complete silence. Clarke can barely believe she said it herself.

Chen's vocoder stutters in awkward preamble. "Uh, Len. Rama went native."

"Not yet. Not completely. Borderline at most."

"Bhanderi?" The water vibrates with Nolan's derision. "He's a *fish* by now!"

"He's still coherent," Clarke insisted. "I talked to him just the other day. We can bring him back."

"Lenie," Walsh says, "nobody's ever—"

"Bhanderi *does* know his shit," Garcia cuts in. "Used to, anyway."

"Literally," Creasy adds. "I heard he tweaked *E. coli* to secrete psychoactives. You walk around with *that* shit in your gut, you're in permanent self-sustaining neverland." Grace Nolan turns and stares at him; Creasy doesn't take the hint. "He had some of his customers eating out of their own ends, just for the feedback high."

"Great," Nolan buzzes. "A drooling idiot *and* a fecal chemist. Our problems are over."

"All I'm saying is, we don't want to cut our own throats," Clarke argues. "If the corpses *aren't* lying to us, they're our best chance at beating this thing."

Cheung: "You're saying we should trust them?"

"I'm saying maybe we don't *have* to. I'm saying, give me a chance to talk to Rama and see if he can help. If not, we can always blow up Atlantis next week."

Nolan cuts the water with her hand. *"His fucking mind is gone!"*

"He had enough of it left to tell me what happened at the woodpile," Clarke buzzes quietly.

Nolan stares at Clarke, a sudden, indefinable tension in the body behind the mask.

"Actually," Garcia remarks from offside, "I think I might have to side with Lenie on this one."

"I don't," Creasy responds instantly.

"Probably couldn't hurt to check it out." Hopkinson's voice vibrates out from somewhere in the cheap seats. "Like Lenie says, we can always kill them later."

It's not exactly momentum. Clarke runs with it anyway. "What are they going to do, hold their breath and make a mad dash for the surface? We can afford to wait."

"Can Gene afford to wait? Can Julia?" Nolan looks around the circle. "How long do *any* of us have?"

"And if you're wrong, you'll kill every last one of those

fuckers and then find out they were trying to help us after all." Clarke shakes her head. "No. I won't let you."

"You won't l—"

Clarke cranks the volume a notch and cuts her off. "This is the plan, people. Everybody gives blood if they haven't already. I'll track down Rama and see if I can talk him into helping. Nobody fucks with the corpses in the meantime."

This is it, she thinks. *Raise or call.* The moment stretches.

Nolan looks around at the assembly. Evidently she doesn't like what she sees. "Fine," she buzzes at last. "All you happy little r's and K's can do what you like. I know what *I'm* gonna do."

"You," Clarke tells her, "are going to back off, and shut up, and not do a *single fucking thing* until we get some information we can count on. And until then, Grace, if I find you within fifty meters of Atlantis *or* Rama Bhanderi, I will personally rip the tubes out of your chest."

Suddenly they're eyecap to eyecap. "You're talking pretty big for someone who doesn't have her pet psycho backing her up." Nolan's vocoder is very low; her words are mechanical whispers, meant for Clarke alone. "Where's your bodyguard, corpsefucker?"

"If you think I need one," Clarke buzzes evenly, "stop talking out your ass and make a fucking move."

Nolan hangs in the water, unmoving. Her vocoder *tick-tick-ticks* like a Geiger counter.

"Hey, Grace," Chen buzzes hesitantly from the sidelines. "Really, you know? Can't hurt to try."

Nolan doesn't appear to have heard her. She doesn't answer for the longest time. Then, finally, she shakes her head.

"Fuck it. *Try,* then."

Clarke lets the silence resume for a few more seconds. Then she turns and slowly, deliberately, fins out of the light. She doesn't look back; hopefully, the rest of the pack will read it as an act of supreme confidence. But inside she's pissing herself. Inside, she only wants to run—from this new-and-improved reminder of her own virulent past, from the tide and the tables turning against her. She wants to just dive off the Ridge and go native, keep going until hunger and isolation leave her brain as smooth and flat and reptilian as Bhanderi's might be by now. She wants nothing more than to just give in.

She swims into the darkness, and hopes the others do likewise. Before Grace Nolan can change their minds.

She chooses an outlying double-decker a little farther downslope from the others. It doesn't have a name—some of the habs have been christened, *Cory's Reach* or *BeachBall* or *Abandon All Hope,* but there weren't any labels pasted across this hull the last time she was in the neighborhood and there aren't any now.

Nobody's left no-trespassing signs at the airlock, either, but two pairs of fins glisten on the drying rack inside and soft moist sounds drift down from the dry deck.

She climbs the ladder. Ng and someone's back are fucking on a pallet in the lounge. Evidently, even Lubin's wind chimes weren't enough to divert their interest. Clarke briefly considers breaking it up and filling them in on recent events.

Fuck it. They'll find out soon enough.

She steps around them and checks out the hab's comm board. It's a pretty sparse setup, just a few off-the-shelf components to keep it in the loop. Clarke plays with the sonar display, pans across the topography of the Ridge and the rash of Platonic icons laid upon it. Here are the main generators, wireframe skyscrapers looming over the ridge to the south. Here's Atlantis, a great lumpy Ferris wheel laid on its side—fuzzy and unfocused now, the echo smeared by a half-dozen white-noise generators started up to keep the corpses from listening in on the recent deliberations. Nobody's used those generators since the Revolt. Clarke was surprised that they were even still in place, much less in working order.

She wonders if someone's taken an active hand in extending the warranty.

A sprinkling of silver bubbles dusts the display: all the semi-abandoned homes of those who hardly know the meaning of the word. She can actually see those people if she cranks up the rez: the display loses range but gains detail, and the local sea-space fills with shimmering sapphire icons as translucent as cave fish. Their implants bounce hard reflective echoes from within the flesh, little opaque organ-clusters of machinery.

It's simple enough to label the creatures on the screen—each contains an ID-transponder next to the heart, for easy identification. There's a whole layer of intelligence that Clarke can access with a single touch. She doesn't, as a rule. Nobody does. Rifter society has its own odd etiquette. Besides, it usually isn't necessary. Over the years you learn to read the raw echoes. Creasy's implants put out a bit of fuzz on the dorsal aspect; Yeager's bum leg lists him slightly to port when he moves. Gomez's massive bulk would be a giveaway even to a dryback. The transponders are an intrusive redundancy, a cheat sheet for novices. Rifters generally have no use for such telemetry; corpses, these days, have no access to it.

Occasionally, though—when distance bleeds any useful telltales from an echo, or when the target itself has *changed*—cheat sheets are the only option.

Clarke slides the range to maximum. The hard bright shapes fall together, shrinking into the center of the display like cosmic flotsam sucked toward a black hole. Other topography creeps into range around the outer edges of the screen, vast and dim and fractal. Great dark fissures race into view, splitting and criss-crossing the substrate. A dozen rough mounds of vomited zinc-and-silver precipitate litter the bottom, some barely a meter high, one fifty times that size. The very seafloor bends up to the east. The shoulders of great mountains loom just out of range.

Occasional smudges of blue light drift in the middle distance, and farther. Some pixelate slow meandering courses across a muddy plain; others merely drift. There's no chance of a usable profile at such distances, but neither is there any need. The transponder overlay is definitive.

Bhanderhi's southwest, halfway to the edge of the scope. Clarke notes the bearing and disables the overlay, sliding the range back to its default setting. Atlantis and its environs swell back out across the display and—

Wait a second—

A single echo, almost hidden in the white noise of the generators. A blur without detail, an unexpected wart on one of the tubular passageways that connect Atlantis's modules one to another. The nearest camera hangs off a docking gantry twenty-five meters east and up. Clarke taps into the line: a new window opens, spills grainy green light across the display.

Atlantis is in the grip of a patchwork blight. Parts of its colossal structure continue to shine as they always have; apical beacons, vents, conduit markers glaring into the darkness. But there are other places where the lights have dimmed, dark holes and gaps where lamps that once shone yellow-green have all shifted down to a faint, spectral blue so deep it borders on black. *Out of order,* that blue-shift says. Or more precisely, *No Fish-heads.*

The airlocks. The hangar bay doors. Nobody's playing *just a precaution* these days . . .

She pans and tilts, aiming the camera. She zooms: distant murk magnifies, turns fuzzy distance into fuzzy foreground. Viz is low today; either smokers are blowing nearby or Atlantis is flushing particulates. All she can see is a fuzzy black outline against a green background, a silhouette so familiar she can't even remember how she recognizes it.

It's Lubin.

He's floating just centimeters off the hull, sculling one way, sculling back. Station-keeping against a tricky interplay of currents, perhaps—except there's nothing for him to station-keep *over*. There's no viewport in his vicinity, no way to look inside, no obvious reason to hold his position along that particular stretch of corridor.

After a few moments he begins to move away along the hull, far too slowly for comfort. His fins usually scissor the water in smooth, easy strokes, but he's barely flicking them now. He's moving no faster than a dryback might walk.

Someone climaxes behind her. Ng grumbles about *my turn*. Lenie Clarke barely hears them.

You bastard, she thinks as Lubin fades in the distance. *You bastard.*

You went ahead and did it.

CONSCRIPT

ALYX doesn't get the whole *native* thing. Probably none of the corpses do, truth be told, but none of the others lose any sleep over it either; the more fish-heads out of the way the better, they figure, and screw the fine print. Alyx, bless her soul, reacted with nothing short of outrage. As far as she's concerned it's no different than leaving your crippled grandmother out to die on an ice floe.

"Lex, it's their own choice," Clarke explained once.

"What, they *choose* to go crazy? They *choose* to have their bones go so punky they can't even stand up when you bring them inside?"

"They *choose,*" she said gently, "to stay out on the rift, and they think it's worth the price."

"Why? What's so great about it? What do they *do* out there?"

She didn't mention the hallucinations. "There's a kind of—freedom, I guess. You feel connected to things. It's hard to explain."

Alyx snorted. "*You* don't even know."

It's partly true. Certainly Clarke feels the pull of the deep sea. Maybe it's an escape, maybe the abyss is just the ultimate place to hide from the living hell that was life among the drybacks. Or maybe it's even simpler. Maybe it's just a dark, weightless evocation of the womb, a long-forgotten sense of being nourished and protected and *secure,* back before the contractions started and everything turned to shit.

Every rifter feels as much. Not every rifter goes native, though, at least not yet. Some just have a kind of—special vulnerability, really. The addictive rifters, as opposed to the merely social ones. Maybe the natives have too much serotonin in their temporal lobes. It usually comes down to something like that.

None of which would really fly with Alyx, of course.

"You should take down their feeding stations," Alyx said. "Then they'd have to come inside to eat at least."

"They'd either starve, or make do with clams and worms." Which was basically starvation on the installment plan, if it didn't poison them outright. "And why force them to come inside if they don't want to?"

"Because it's *suicide,* that's why!" Alyx cried. "Jeez, I can't believe I have to explain it to you! Wouldn't you stop *me* from trying to kill myself?"

"That depends."

"Depends?"

"On if you really wanted to, or you were just trying to win an argument."

"I'm *serious."*

"Yeah. I can see that." Clarke sighed. "If you really wanted to kill yourself, I'd be sad and pissed off and I'd miss you like hell. But I wouldn't stop you."

Alyx was appalled. *"Why not?"*

"Because it's your life. Not mine."

Alyx didn't seem to have been expecting that. She glared back, obviously unconvinced, obviously unequipped to respond.

"*Have* you ever wanted to die?" Clarke asked her. "Seriously?"

"No, but—"

"I have."

Alyx fell silent.

"And believe me," Clarke continued, "it's no fun listening to a bunch of professional head lice telling you *how much there is to live for* and how *things aren't really so bad* and how *five years from now you'll look back and wonder how you ever could have even* imagined *offing yourself.* I mean, they don't know *shit* about my life. If there's one thing I'm the world's greatest expert on, it's how it feels to be *me.* And as far as I'm concerned it's the height of fucking arrogance to tell another human being whether their life is worth living."

"But you don't *have* to feel that way," Alyx said unhappily. "Nobody does! You just slap a derm on your arm and—"

"It's not about feeling happy, Lex. It's about having *cause* to feel happy." Clarke put her palm against the girl's cheek. "And you say I don't care enough to stop you from killing yourself, but *I* say I care about you so goddamned much I'd even *help* you do it, if that was what you really wanted."

Alyx stared at the deck for a long time. When she looked up again her eyes shone.

"But you didn't die," she said softly. "You wanted to, but you didn't, and that's why you're alive right now."

And that's why a lot of other people aren't . . . But Clarke kept the thought to herself.

And now she's about to repudiate it all. She's about to hunt down someone who's chosen to retire, and she's going to ignore that choice, and inflict her own in its place. She'd like to think that maybe Alyx would find the irony amusing, but she knows better. There's nothing funny about any of this. It's all getting way too scary.

She's foregone the use of a squid this time out; natives tend to shy away from the sound of machinery. For what seems like forever she's been traversing a plain of bone-gray mud, a bottomless ooze of dead plankton ten million years in the making. Someone has preceded her here; a sudden contrail crosses her path, a fog of tiny bodies still swirling in the wake of some recent turbulence. She follows it. Scattered chunks of pumice and obsidian rise from the substrate like fractured sundials. Their shadows sweep across the bright scrolling footprint of Clarke's headlamp, stretching and dwindling and merging again with the million-year darkness. Eventually they come to dominate the substrate, no longer isolated protrusions in mud but a fractured tumbledown landscape in their own right.

A jumbled talus of cracked volcanic glass rises in Clarke's path. She brightens her headlamp: the beam puddles on a sheer rock wall a few meters further on, its surface lacerated with deep vertical fissures.

"Hello? Rama?"

Nothing.

"It's Lenie."

A white-eyed shadow slips like an eel between two boulders. *". . . bright . . ."*

She dials down the light. "Better?"

"Ah . . . Len . . ." It's a mechanical whisper, two syllables spaced seconds apart by the effort it takes to get them out. "Hi . . ."

"We need your help, Rama."

Bhanderi buzzes something incomprehensible from his hiding place.

"Rama?"

"Don't . . . help?"

"There's a disease. It's like ßehemoth, but our tweaks don't work against it. We need to know what it is, we need someone who knows genetics."

Nothing moves among the rocks.

"It's serious. Please. Can you help?"

". . . teomics," Bhanderi clicks.

"What? I didn't hear you."

". . . *Proteomics.* Only . . . minored in gen . . . genetics."

He's almost managed a complete sentence. Who better to trust with hundreds of lives?

"... had a dream about you." Bhanderi sighs. It sounds like someone strumming a metal comb.

"It wasn't a dream. This isn't either. We really need your help, Rama. *Please.*"

"That's wrong," he buzzes. "That doesn't make sense."

"What doesn't?" Clarke asks, encouraged by the sudden coherence.

"The corps... ask the corpses."

"The corpses may have made the bug. Tweaked it, anyway. We can't trust them."

"... poor you..."

"Can you just—"

"More histamine," Bhanderi buzzes absently, lost again. Then: *"Bye..."*

"No! Rama!"

She brightens her beam in time to see a pair of fins disappear into a crevice a few meters up the cliff. She kicks up after him, plunges into the fissure like a high-diver, arms above her head. The crevice splits the rock high and deep, but not wide; two meters in she has to turn sideways. Her light floods the narrow gash, bright as a topside day; somewhere nearby a vocoder makes distressed ratcheting sounds.

Four meters overhead, Bhanderi scrambles froglike up the gap. It narrows up there—he seems in imminent danger of wedging himself inextricably between the rock faces. Clarke starts after him.

"Too bright!" he buzzes.

Tough, she thinks back at him.

Bhanderi's a skinny little bastard after two months of chronic wasting. Even if he gets stuck in here, he might get wedged too far back for Clarke to reach him. Maybe his panicked devolving little brain is juggling those variables right now—Bhanderi zigzags, as if torn between the prospects of open water and protective confinement. Finally he opts for the water, but his indecision has cost him; Clarke has him around the ankle.

He thrashes in a single plane, constrained by faces of stone. "Fucking *bitch. Let go!*"

"Vocabulary coming back, I see."

"Let . . . go!"

She works her way toward the mouth of the crevice, dragging Bhanderi by the leg. He scrabbles against the walls, resisting—then, pulled free of the tightest depths, he twists around and comes at her with his fists. She fends him off. She has to remind herself how easily his bones might break.

Finally he's subdued, Clarke's arms hooked around his shoulders, her hands interlocked behind his neck in a full nelson. They're still inside the mouth of the crevice, barely; Bhanderi's struggles jam her spine against cracked slabs of basalt.

"Bright," he clicks.

"Listen, Rama. There's *way* too much riding on this for me to let you piss away whatever's left in that head of yours. Do you understand?"

He squirms.

"I'll turn off the light if you stop fighting and just *listen* to me, okay?"

". . . *I* . . . you . . ."

She kills the beam. Bhanderi stiffens, then goes limp in her arms.

"Okay. Better. You've *got* to come back, Bhanderi. Just for a little while. We need you."

". . . need . . . bad zero—"

"Will you just stop that shit? You're not that far gone, you *can't* be. You've only been out here for—" It's been around two months, hasn't it? More than two, now. Is that enough time for a brain to turn to mush? Is this whole exercise a waste of time?

She starts again. "There's a lot riding on this. A lot of people could die. *You* could die. This—disease, or whatever it is, it could get into you as easily as any of us. Maybe it already has. Do you understand?"

"... understand ..."

She hopes that's an answer and not an echo. "It's not just the sickness, either. Everyone's looking for someone to blame. It's only a matter of time before—"

Boom, she remembers. *Blew it up. Way too bright.*

"Rama," she says slowly. "If things get out of hand, everything blows up. Do you understand? *Boom.* Just like at the woodpile. Boom, *all the time.* Unless you help me. Unless you help *us.* Understand?"

He hangs against her in the darkness like a boneless cadaver.

"Yeah. Well," he buzzes at last. "Why didn't you just say so?"

The struggle has hobbled him. Bhanderi favors his left leg when he swims; he veers to port with each stroke. Clarke hooks her hand under his armpit to share thrust but he startles and flinches from her touch. She settles for swimming at his side, nudging him back on course when necessary.

Three times he breaks away in a crippled lunge for oblivion. Three times she brings him back to heel, flailing and gibbering. The episodes don't last, though. Once subdued, he calms; once calm, he cooperates. For a while.

She comes to understand that it isn't really his fault.

"Hey," she buzzes, ten minutes out from Atlantis.

"Yeah."

"You with me?"

"Yeah. It comes and goes." An indecipherable ticking. "*I* come and go."

"Do you remember what I said?"

"You drafted me."

"Do you remember what for?"

"Some kind of disease?"

"Some kind."

"And you . . . you think the corpses did . . ."

"I don't know."

". . . leg hurts . . ."

"Sorry . . ."

And his brainstem rises up and snatches him away again. She grapples and holds on until it lets go. Until he fights his way back from wherever he goes at times like this.

". . . still here, I see . . ."

"Still here," Clarke repeats.

"God, Len. Please don't do this."

"I'm sorry," she tells him. "I'm sorry . . ."

"I'm not worth shit to you," Bhanderi grates. "I can't remember anything . . ."

"It'll come back." *It has to.*

"You don't know. You don't know any . . . thing about us."

"I know a little."

"No."

"I knew someone. Like you. He came back." Which is almost a lie.

"Let me *go*. Please."

"After. I promise."

She rationalizes in transit, not convincing herself for an instant. She's helping him as well as herself, she's doing him a favor. She's saving him from the ultimate lethality of his own lifestyle. Hyperosmosis; Slimy Implant Syndrome; mechanical breakdown. Rifters are miracles of bioengineering—thanks to the superlative design of their diveskins, they can even shit in the woods—but they were never designed to unseal outside of an atmosphere. Natives unmask all the time out here, let raw ocean into their mouths to corrupt and corrode and contaminate the brackish internal saline that braces them against the pressure. Do that often enough and something's bound to seize up eventually.

I'm saving your life, she thinks, unwilling to say the words aloud.

Whether he likes it or not, Alyx replies from the back of her mind.

"The *light*..." Bhanderi croaks.

Glimmers smear the darkness ahead, disfiguring the perfect void like faint glowing sores. Bhanderi stiffens at Clarke's side, but doesn't bolt. She knows he can handle it; it can't have been more than a couple of weeks since she found him inside the nerve hab, and he had to pass through brighter skies than these to get there. Surely he can't have slipped so far in such a short time?

Or is it something else, not so much a slip as a sudden jolt? Maybe it's not the light that bothers him at all. Maybe it's what the light reminds him of, now.

Boom. Blew it up.

Spectral fingers tap lightly against Clarke's implants: once, twice. Someone ahead, taking a sonar bearing. She takes Bhanderi's arm, holds it gently but firmly. "Rama, someone's—"

"Charley," Bhanderi buzzes.

Garcia rises ahead of them, ambient backlight framing him like a visitation. "Holy shit. You *got* him. Rama, you in there?"

"Client..."

"He *remembers* me! Fuck it's good to see you, man. I thought you'd pretty much shuffled off the mortal coil."

"Tried. She won't let me."

"Yeah, we're all sorry about that but we *really* need your help. Don't sweat it, though, buddy. We'll make it work." Garcia turns to Clarke. "What do we need?"

"Medhab ready?"

"Sealed off one sphere. Left the other in case someone breaks an arm."

"Okay. We'll need the lights off, to start with anyway. Even the externals."

"No problem."

". . . Charley . . ." Bhanderi clicks.

"Right here, man."

". . . you my techie . . . ?"

"Dunno. Could be, I guess. Sure. You need one?"

Bhanderi's masked face turns to Clarke. Suddenly there's something different in the way he holds himself. "Let me go."

This time, she does.

"How long since I was inside?" he asks.

"I think maybe two weeks. Three at the outside." By rifter standards, the estimate is almost surgically precise.

"I may have . . . problems," he tells them. "Readjusting. I don't know if I can—I don't know how much I can get back."

"We understand," Clarke buzzes. "Just—"

"Shut up. Listen." Bhanderi's head darts from side to side, a disquieting reptilian gesture that Clarke has seen before. "I'll need to . . . to kickstart. I'll need help. Acetylcholine. Uh, tyrosine hydroxylase. Picrotoxin. If I fall apart . . . if I fall apart in there you'll need to get those into me. Understand?"

She runs them back. "Acetylcholine. Picrotoxin. Tyro, uh—"

"Tyrosine hydroxylase. Remember."

"What dose?" Garcia wonders. "What delivery?"

"I don't—shit. Can't remember. Check MedBase. Maximum recommended dosage for . . . for everything except the hydroxy . . . lase. Double for that, maybe. I think."

Garcia nods. "Anything else?"

"Hell yes," Bhanderi buzzes. "Just wish I could remember *what . . .*"

PORTRAIT OF THE SADIST AS A TEAM PLAYER

ALICE Jovellanos's definition of *apology* was a little unconventional.

Achilles, she had begun, *you can be such a raging idiot sometimes I just don't believe it.*

He'd never made a hard copy. He hadn't needed to. He was a 'lawbreaker, occipital cortex stuck in permanent overdrive, pattern-matching and correlative skills verging on the autistic. He had scrolled her letter once down his inlays, watched it vanish, and reread it a hundred times since, every pixel crisp and immutable in perfect recollection.

Now he sat still as stone, waiting for her. Sudbury's ever-dimming nightscape splashed haphazard patches of light across the walls of his apartment. There were too many lines-of-sight to nearby buildings, he noted. He would have to blank the windows before she arrived.

You know what I was risking coming clean with you yesterday, Alice had dictated. *You know what I'm risking sending this to you now—it'll autowipe, but there's* nothing *these assholes can't scan if they feel like it. That's part of the problem, that's why I'm taking this huge risk in the first place . . .*

*I heard what you said about trust and betrayal, and maybe some of it rings a bit more true than I'd like. But don't you see there was no point in asking you beforehand? As long as Guilt Trip was running the show, you were incapable of making your own decision. You keep insisting that's wrong, you go on about all the life-and-death decisions you make and the thousands of variables you juggle but Achilles my dear, whoever *told you that* free will *was just some complicated algorithm for you to follow?*

I know you don't want to be corrupted. But maybe a decent, honest human being is his own safeguard, did you ever think of that? Maybe you don't have to let them turn you into one big conditioned reflex. Maybe you just want *them to, because then it's not really your responsibility, is it? It's so easy to never have to make your own decisions. Addictive, even. Maybe you even got hooked on it, and you're going through a little bit of withdrawal now.*

She'd had such faith in him. She still did; she was on her way here right now, not suspecting a thing. Surveillance-free accommodation wasn't cheap, but any senior 'lawbreaker could afford the Privacy Plus brand name and then some. The security in his building was airtight, ruthless, and utterly devoid of long-term memory. Once a visitor cleared, there would be no record of their comings and goings.

Anyhow, what they stole, we gave back. And I'm going to tell you exactly how we did that, on the premise, you know, ignorance breeds fear and all that. You know about the Minsky receptors in your frontal lobes, and how all those nasty little guilt transmitters bind to them, and how you perceive that as conscience. *They made Guilt Trip by tweaking a bunch of behavior-modification genes snipped from parasites; the guiltier you feel, the more Trip gets pumped into your brain. It binds to the transmitters, which changes their shape and basically clogs your motor pathways so you can't move.*

Anyway, Spartacus is basically a guilt analog. *It's got the same active sites, so it binds to the Trip, but the overall conformation is slightly different so it doesn't actually do anything except clog up the Minsky receptors. Also it takes longer to break down than regular guilt, so it reaches higher concentrations in the brain. Eventually it overwhelms the active sites through sheer numbers.*

He remembered splinters from an antique hardwood floor, tearing his face. He remembered lying in the dark, the chair he was tied to toppled on its side, while Ken Lubin's voice wondered from somewhere nearby: "What about side effects? Baseline guilt, for example?"

And in that instant, bound and bleeding, Achilles Desjardins had seen his destiny.

Spartacus wasn't content to simply unlock the chains that the Trip had forged. If it had been, there might have been hope. He would have had to fall back on good old-fashioned shame to control his inclinations, certainly. He would have stayed depraved at heart, as he'd always been. But Achilles Desjardins had never been one to let his heart out unsupervised anyway. He could have coped, even out of a job, even up on charges. He could have coped.

But Spartacus didn't know when to quit. Conscience was a molecule like any other—and with no free receptor sites to bind onto, it might as well be neutral saline for all the effect it had. Desjardins was headed for a whole new destination, a place he'd never been before. A place without guilt or shame or remorse, a place without conscience in *any* form.

Alice hadn't mentioned any of that when she'd spilled her pixelated heart across his in-box. She'd only assured him how safe it all was. *That's the real beauty of it, Killjoy; both your natural transmitters and the Trip itself are still being produced normally, so a test that keys on either of 'em comes up clean. Even a test looking for the complexed form will pass muster, since the baseline complex is still floating around—it just can't find any free receptor sites to latch onto. So you're safe. Honestly. The bloodhounds won't be a problem.*

Safe. She'd had no idea what kind of thing looked out from behind his eyes. She should have known better. Even children know the simple truth: monsters live everywhere, even inside. *Especially* inside.

I wouldn't put you at risk, Achilles, believe me. You mean too—you're too much of a friend for me to fuck around like that.

She loved him, of course. He had never really admitted it before—some pipsqueak inner voice might have whispered

I think she kind of, maybe before three decades of self-loathing squashed it flat: *What a fucking egotist. As if anyone would want anything to do with an enculé like* you . . .

She'd never explicitly propositioned him—in her own way she was as insecure as he was, for all her bluster—but the signs were there in hindsight: her good-natured interference every time a woman appeared in his life, her endless social overtures, the nickname *Killjoy*—ostensibly because of his reticence to go out, but more likely because of his reticence to *put* out. It was all so obvious now. Freed from guilt, freed from shame, his vision had sharpened to crystal perfection.

Anyway, there you go. I've stuck my neck out for you, and what happens now is pretty much up to you. If you turn me in, though, know this: you're *the one making that decision. However you rationalize it, you won't be able to blame some stupid long-chain molecule. It'll be you all the way, your own free will.*

He hadn't turned her in. It must have been some fortuitous balance of conflicting molecules: those that would have compelled betrayal weakening in his head, those that spoke to loyalty among friends not yet snuffed out. In hindsight, it had been a very lucky break.

So use *it, and think about all the things you've done and why, and ask yourself if you're really so morally rudderless that you couldn't have made all those tough decisions without enslaving yourself to a bunch of despots. I think you could have, Achilles. You never needed their ball and chain to be a decent human being. I really believe that. I'm gambling everything on it.*

He checked his watch.

You know where I am. You know what your options are. Join me or stab me. Your choice.

He stood, and crossed to the windows. He blanked the panes.

Love, Alice.

The doorbell chimed.

Every part of her was vulnerable. She looked up at him, her face hopeful, her almond eyes cautious. One corner of her mouth pulled back in a tentative, slightly rueful grin.

Desjardins stood aside, took a deep, quiet breath as she passed. Her scent was innocent and floral, but there were molecules in that mix working below the threshold of conscious awareness. She wasn't stupid; she knew he wasn't either. She must realize he'd peg his incipient arousal on pheromones she hadn't worn in his presence for years.

Her hopes *must* be up.

He'd done his best to raise them, without being too obvious. He'd affected a gradual thawing in his demeanor over the previous few days, a growing, almost reluctant warmth. He'd stood at her side as Clarke and Lubin disappeared into traffic, en route to their own private revolution; Desjardins had let his arm bump against Alice's, and linger. After a few moments of that casual contact she'd looked up at him, a bit hesitantly, and he'd rewarded her with a shrug and a smile.

She'd always had his friendship, until she'd betrayed him. She'd always longed for more. It was an incapacitating mix. Desjardins had been able to disarm her with the merest chance of reconciliation.

Now she brushed past, closer than strictly necessary, her ponytail swishing gently against her nape. Mandelbrot appeared in the hall and slithered around her ankles like a furry boa. Alice reached down to scritch the cat's ears. Mandelbrot hesitated, perhaps wondering whether to play hard to get, then evidently figured *fuck it* and let out a purr.

Desjardins directed Alice to the bowl of goofballs on the coffee table. Alice pursed her lips. "These are safe?" Some of the chemicals that senior 'lawbreakers kept in their systems could provoke nasty interactions with the most innocuous recreationals, and Jovellanos had only just gotten her shots.

"I doubt they're any worse than the ways you've already fucked with the palette," Desjardins said.

Her face fell. A twinge of remorse flickered in Desjardins's throat. He swallowed, absurdly grateful for the feeling. "Just don't mix them with axotropes," he added, more gently.

"Thanks." She took the olive branch with the drug, popped a cherry-red marble into her mouth. Desjardins could see her bracing herself.

"I was afraid you were never going to talk to me again," she said softly.

If her hair had been any finer it would be synthetic.

"It would have served you right." He let the words hang between them. He imagined knotting that jet-black ponytail around his fist. He imagined suspending her by it, letting her feet kick just off the floor . . .

No. Stop it.

"But I think I understand why you did it," he said at last, letting her off the hook.

"Really?"

"I think so. You had a lot of nerve." He took a breath. "But you had a lot of faith in me, too. You wouldn't have done it otherwise. I guess that counts for something."

It was as though she'd been holding her breath since she arrived, and only let it out now that her sentence had been read aloud: Conditional discharge. *She bought it,* Desjardins thought. *She thinks there's hope—*

—while another part of him, diminished but defiant, insisted, *Why does she have to be wrong?*

He brushed her cheek with his palm, could just barely hear the soft, quick intake of breath his touch provoked. He blinked against the fleeting image of a backhanded blow across that sweet, unsuspecting face. "You have a lot more faith in me than I do, Alice. I don't know how warranted it is."

"They stole your freedom to choose. I only gave it back to you."

"You stole my conscience. How am I *supposed* to choose?"

"With your *mind,* Killjoy. With that brilliant, beautiful mind. Not some gut-instinct emotion that's done more harm than good for the past couple million years."

He sank onto the sofa, a small, sudden pit opening in his stomach. "I'd hoped it was a side effect," he said softly.

She sat beside him. "What do you mean?"

"You know." Desjardins shook his head. "People never think things through. I kind of hoped you and your buddies just—hadn't worked out the ramifications, you know? You were just trying to subvert the Trip, and the whole conscience thing was a—a misstep. Unforeseen. But I guess not."

She put her hand on his knee. "Why would you *hope* that?"

"I'm not really sure." He barked a soft laugh. "I guess I thought, if you didn't *know* you were—I mean, if you do something by accident that's one thing, but if you *deliberately* set out to make a bunch of psychopaths—"

"We're not making psychopaths, Achilles. We're freeing people from conscience."

"What's the difference?"

"You can still *feel.* Your amygdala still works. Your dopamine and serotonin levels are normal. You're capable of long-term planning, you're not a slave to your impulses. Spartacus doesn't change any of that."

"Is that what you think."

"You really think all the assholes in the world are clinical?"

"Maybe not. But I bet all the clinicals in the world are assholes."

"You're not," she said.

She stared at him with serious, dark eyes. He couldn't stop

smelling her. He wanted to kiss her. He wanted to hug her. He wanted to gut her like a fish and put her head on a stick.

He gritted his teeth and kept silent.

"Ever hear of the trolley paradox?" Alice said after a moment.

Desjardins shook his head.

"Six people on a runaway train, headed off a cliff. The only way to save them is switch the train to another track. Except there's someone else standing on that track, and he won't be able to get out of the way before the train squashes him. Do you reroute?"

"Of course." It was the greater good at its most simplistic.

"Now say you *can't* reroute the train, but you can *stop* it by pushing someone into its path. Do you?"

"Sure," he said immediately.

"I did that for you," Alice pronounced.

"Did what?"

"Most people don't accept the equivalence. They think it's right to reroute the train, but wrong to push someone in front of it. Even though it's exactly the same death, for exactly the same number of lives saved."

He grunted.

"Conscience isn't *rational,* Achilles. You know what parts of your brain light up when you make a moral decision? I'll tell you: the medial frontal gyrus. The posterior cingulate gyrus. The angular gyrus. All—"

"Emotional centers," Desjardins cut in.

"Damn right. The frontal lobes don't spark at all. And even people who recognize the logical equivalence of those scenarios have to really *work* at it. It just *feels* wrong to push someone to their death, even for the same net gain of lives. The brain has to wrestle with all this stupid, unfounded guilt. It takes longer to act, longer to reach critical decisions, and when all's said and done it's less likely to make the *right* decion. That's what *conscience* is, Killjoy. It's like rape or greed or kin selection—it served its purpose a few million years ago, but it's been bad news ever since we stopped merely *surviving* our environment and started *dominating* it instead."

You rehearsed that, Desjardins thought.

He allowed himself a small smile. "There's a bit more to people than guilt and intellect, my dear. Maybe guilt doesn't just hobble the *mind,* did you ever think of that? Maybe it hobbles other things as well."

"Like what?"

"Well, just for example—" he paused, pretending to cast around for inspiration—"how do you know I'm not some kind of crazed serial killer? How do you know I'm not psychotic, or suicidal, or, or into torture, say?"

"I'd know," Alice said simply.

"You think sex killers walk around with signs on their foreheads?"

She squeezed his thigh. "I think that I've known you for a whole long time, and I think there's no such thing as a perfect act. If someone was that full of hate, they'd slip up eventually. But you—well, I've never heard of a monster who respected women so much he refused to even *fuck* them. And by the way, you might want to reconsider that particular position. Just a thought."

Desjardins shook his head. "You've got it all worked out, haven't you?"

"Completely. And I've got oodles of patience."

"Good. Now you can use some of it." He stood and smiled down at her. "I've gotta go to the bathroom for a minute. Make yourself at home."

She smiled back. "I will indeed. Take your time."

He locked the door, leaned across the sink and stared hard into the mirror. His reflection stared back, furious.

She betrayed you. She turned you into this.

He liked her. He loved her. Alice Jovellanos had been his loyal friend for years. Desjardins hung onto that as best he could.

She did it on purpose.

No. *They* had done it on purpose.

Because Alice hadn't acted alone. She was damn smart, but she hadn't come up with Spartacus all by herself. She had friends, she'd admitted as much: *We're kinda political, in a ragtag kind of way,* she'd said when she first broke the news of his—his *emancipation.*

He could feel the chains in his head crumbling to rust. He could feel his own depravity tugging on those corroded links, and grinning. He searched himself for some hint of the regret he'd felt just a few minutes ago—he'd hurt Alice's feelings, and he'd felt bad about it. He could still do that. He could still feel remorse, or something like it, if he only tried.

You're not a slave to your impulses, she'd said.

That was true, as far as it went. He could restrain himself if he wanted to. But that was the nature of his predicament: he was starting to realize that he didn't *want* to.

"Hey, Killjoy?" Alice called from down the hall.

Shut up! SHUT UP! "Yeah?"

"Mandelbrot's demanding dinner and her feeder's empty. Didn't you keep the kibble under the sink?"

"Not any more. She figured out how to break into the cupboards."

"Then wh—"

"Bedroom closet."

Her footsteps passed on the other side of the door, Mandelbrot vocally urging them on.

On purpose.

Alice had infected him ahead of schedule, to clear his mind for the fight against ßehemoth—and perhaps for more personal reasons, conscious or otherwise. But her friends had set their sights a lot higher than Achilles Desjardins; they were out to liberate every 'lawbreaker on the planet. Lubin had summed it up, there in the darkness two weeks ago: "Only a few thousand people with their hands on all the world's kill switches and you've turned them all into clinical sociopaths..."

Desjardins wondered if Alice would have tried her semantic arguments with *Lubin*. If *she* had been tied to that chair, blind, pissing her pants in fear for her life while that murderous cipher paced around her in the darkness, would she have presumed to lecture him on serotonin levels and the cingulate gyrus?

She might have, at that. After all, she and her friends were *political—in a ragtag kinda way*—and politics made you stupid. It made you think that human decency was some kind of Platonic ideal, a moral calculus you could derive from first principles. Don't waste your time with basic biology. Don't worry about the fate of altruists in Darwin's universe. People are *different,* people are *special,* people are *moral agents*. That's what you got when you spent too much time writing manifestos, and not enough time looking in the mirror.

Achilles Desjardins was only the first of a new breed. Before long there would be others, as powerful as he and as unconstrained. Maybe there already were. Alice hadn't told him any details. He didn't know how far the ambitions of the Spartacus Society had progressed. He didn't know what other franchises were being seeded, or what the incubation period was. He only knew that sooner or later, he would have competition.

Unless he acted now, while he still had the advantage.

Mandelbrot was still yowling in the bedroom, evidently dissatisfied with the quality of the hired help. Desjardins couldn't blame her; Alice had had more than enough time to retrieve the kibble, bring it back to the kitchen, and—

—*in the bedroom,* he realized.

Well, he thought after a moment. *I guess that settles it.*

Suddenly, the face in the mirror was very calm. It did not move, but it seemed to be speaking to him all the same. You're *not political,* it told him. *You're mechanical. Nature programmed you one way, CSIRA programmed you another, Alice came along and rewired you for something else. None of it is you, and all of it is you. And none of it was your choice. None of it was your responsibility.*

She did this to you. That cunt. That stumpfuck. Whatever happens now is not your fault.

It's hers.

He unlocked the door and walked down the hall to the bedroom. Live telltales twinkled across the sensorium on his pillow. His feedback suit lay across the bed like a shed skin. Alice Jovellanos stood shaking at the foot of the bed, lifting the headset from her skull. Her face was beautiful and bloodless.

She would not have been able to mistake the victim in that virtual dungeon for anyone else. Desjardins had tuned the specs to three decimal places.

Mandelbrot immediately gave up on Alice and began headbutting Desjardins, purring loudly. Desjardins ignored her.

"I need some technical info," he said, almost apologetically. "And some details on your friends. I was actually hoping to sweet-talk it out of you, though." He gestured at the sensorium, savoring the horror on her face. "Guess I forgot to put that stuff away."

She shook her head, a spasm, a panicky twitch. "I—I d-don't think you did . . ." she managed after a moment.

"Maybe not." Achilles shrugged. "But hey, look on the bright side. That's the first time you've actually been *right* about me."

It made sense, at last: the impulse purchases routed almost unconsciously through anonymous credit lines, the plastic sheeting and portable incinerator, the dynamic-inversion sound damper. The casual snoop into Alice's master calendar and contact list. That was the great thing about being a 'lawbreaker on the Trip; when everybody knew you were chained to the post, nobody bothered putting up fences around the yard.

"Please," Alice quavered, her lip trembling, her eyes bright and terrified. "Achilles..."

Somewhere in the basement of Desjardins's mind, a last rusty link crumbled to powder.

"Call me Killjoy," he said.

AUTOMECHANICA

THE first round goes to the corpses.

A rifter by the name of Lisbeth Mak—kind of a wallflower, Clarke barely even remembers the name—came upon a corpse crawling like an armored cockroach around the outside of the primary physical plant. It didn't matter whether he had a good reason to be there. It didn't matter whether or not this constituted a violation of quarantine. Mak did what a lot of fishheads might have done regardless; she got cocky. Decided to teach this dryback a lesson, but decided to warm him up first. So she swam easy circles around her helpless and lumbering prey, made the usual derisive comments about diving bells with feet, called loudly and conspicuously for someone to bring her one of those pneumatic drills from the tool shed: she had herself a crab to shell.

She forgot entirely about the headlamp on the corpse's helmet. It hadn't been shining when she caught the poor fucker—obviously he'd been trying to avoid detection, and there was enough ambient light around that part of the structure even for dryback eyes. When he flashed that peeper at her, her eyecaps turned dead flat white in their haste to compensate.

She was only blind for a second or two, but it was more than enough for the corpse to get his licks in. Preshmesh versus copolymer is no contest at all. By the time Mak, bruised and bloodied, called for backup, the corpse was already heading back inside.

Now Clarke and Lubin stand in Airlock Five while the

ocean drains away around them. Clarke splits her face seal, feels herself reinflate like a fleshy balloon. The inner hatch hisses and swings open. Bright light, painfully intense, spills in from the space beyond. Clarke steps back as her eyecaps adjust, raising her hands against possible attack. None comes. A gang of corpses jam the wet room, but only one stands in the front rank: Patricia Rowan.

Between Rowan and rifters, an isolation membrane swirls with oily iridescence.

"The consensus is that you should stay in the airlock for the time being," Rowan says.

Clarke glances at Lubin. He's watching the welcoming committee with blank, impassive eyes.

"Who was it?" Clarke asks calmly.

"I don't think that's really important," Rowan says.

"Lisbeth might think otherwise. Her nose is broken."

"Our man says he was defending himself."

"A man in three-hundred-bar preshmesh armor defending himself against an unarmed woman in a diveskin."

"A corpse defending himself from a *fish-head,*" someone says from within the committee. "Whole other thing."

Rowan ignores the intrusion. "Our man resorted to fists," she says, "because that was the only approach that had any real hope of succeeding. You know as well as we do what we're defending ourselves from."

"What I know is that none of you are supposed to leave Atlantis without prior authorization. Those were the rules, even before the quarantine. You agreed to them."

"We weren't allowed much of a choice," Rowan remarks mildly.

"Still."

"Fuck the *rules,*" says another corpse. "They're trying to kill us. Why are we arguing protocol?"

Clarke blinks. "What's that supposed to mean?"

"You know damn well what it—"

Rowan holds up a hand. The dissident falls silent.

"We found a mine," Rowan says, in the same voice she might use to report that the head was out of toilet paper.

"What?"

"Nothing special. Standard demolition charge. Might have even been one of the same ones Ken wired up before we"—she hesitates, choosing her words—"came to terms a few years back. I'm told it would have isolated us from primary life-support and flooded a good chunk of Res-C. Somewhere between thirty to a hundred killed from the implosion alone."

Clarke stares at Lubin, notes the slightest shake of the head.

"I didn't know," Clarke says softly.

Rowan smiles faintly. "You'll understand there might be some skepticism on that point."

"I'd like to see it," Lubin says.

"I'd like to see my daughter in the sunlight," Rowan tells him. "It's not going to happen."

Clarke shakes her head. "Pat, listen. I don't know where it came from. I—"

"I do," Rowan says mildly. "There are piles of them stashed at the construction caches. A hundred or more at Impossible Lake alone."

"We'll find out who planted it. But you can't keep it. You're not allowed weapons."

"Do you seriously expect us to simply hand it back to the people who planted it in the first place?"

"Pat, you *know* me."

"I know *all* of you," Rowan says. "The answer is no."

"How did you find it?" Lubin asks from out of left field.

"By accident. We lost our passive acoustics and sent someone out to check the antennae."

"Without informing us beforehand."

"It seemed fairly likely that you people were causing the

interference. Informing you would not have been a wise idea even if you *hadn't* been mining our hulls."

"Hulls," Lubin remarks. "So you found more than one."

No one speaks.

Of course not, Clarke realizes. *They're not going to tell us anything. They're gearing up for war.*

And they're going to get slaughtered . . .

"I wonder if you've found them all," Lubin muses.

They stand without speaking, gagged by the synthetic black skin across their faces. Behind their backs, behind the impenetrable mass of the inner hatch, the corpses return to whatever plots and counterplans they're drawing. Ahead, past the outer hatch, a gathering crowd of rifters waits for answers. Around them and within them, machinery pumps and sparks and readies them for the abyss. By the time the water rises over their heads they are incompressible.

Lubin reaches for the outer hatch. Clarke stops him.

"Grace," she buzzes.

"Could be anyone." He rises, weightless in the flooded compartment. One hand reaches up to keep the ceiling at bay. It's an odd image, this humanoid silhouette floating against the bluish-white walls of the airlock. His eyecaps almost look like holes cut from black paper, letting the light shine through from behind.

"In fact," he continues, "I'm not entirely convinced they're telling the truth."

"The corpses? Why would they lie? How would it serve them?"

"Sow dissension among the enemy. Divide and conquer."

"Come on, Ken. It's not as though there's a pro-corpse faction ready to rise up on their behalf and . . ."

He just looks at her.

"You don't know," she buzzes, so softly she can barely feel the vibration in her own jaw. "It's all just guesses and suspicions. Rama hasn't had a chance to—you can't be sure."

"I'm not."

"We don't really know anything." She hesitates, then edits herself: "*I* don't know anything. *You* do."

"Not enough to matter. Not yet."

"I saw you, tracking them along the corridors."

He doesn't nod. He doesn't have to.

"Who?"

"Rowan, mainly."

"And what's it like in there?"

"A lot like it is in *there,*" he says, pointing at her.

Stay out of my head, you fucker. But she knows, at this range, it's not a matter of choice. You can't just *choose* to not feel something. Whether those feelings are yours or someone else's is really beside the point.

So she only says, "Think you could be a little less vague?"

"She feels very guilty about *something.* I don't know what. There's no shortage of possibilities."

"Told you."

"Our own people, though," he continues, "are not quite so conflicted, and much more easily distracted. And I can't be everywhere. And we're running out of time."

You bastard, she thinks. *You asshole. You stumpfucker.*

He floats above her, waiting.

"Okay," she says at last. "I'll do it."

Lubin pulls the latch. The outer hatch slides back, opening a rectangle of murky darkness in a stark white frame. They rise into a nightscape stippled with waiting eyes.

Lenie Clarke is a little bit twisted, even by Rifter standards.

Rifters don't worry much about privacy, for one thing. Not

as much as you might expect from a population of rejects and throwaways. You might think the only ones who could ever regard this place as an *improvement* would be those with the most seriously fucked-up baselines for comparison, and you'd be right. You might also think that such damaged creatures would retreat into their shells like hermit crabs with half their limbs ripped away, cringing at the slightest shadow, or lashing out furiously at any hint of intrusion. It does happen, occasionally. But down here, the endless heavy night anesthetizes even if it doesn't heal. The abyss lays dark hands on the wounded and the raging, and somehow calms them. There are, after all, three hundred sixty degrees of escape from any conflict. There are no limiting resources to fight over; these days, half the habs are empty anyway. There is little need for territoriality, because there is so much territory.

So most of the habs are unguarded and unclaimed. Occupants come and go, rise into any convenient bubble to fuck or feed or—more rarely—socialize, before returning to their natural environment. Any place is as good as any other. There's little need to stand jealous guard over anything so ubiquitous as a Calvin cycler or a repair bench, and there's hardly more that rifters need beyond these basics. Privacy is everywhere; swim two minutes in any direction and you can be lost forever. Why erect walls around recycled air?

Lenie Clarke has her reasons.

She's not entirely alone in this. A few other rifters have laid exclusive claims, pissed territorially on this cubby or that deck or—in very rare cases—an entire hab. They've nested refuge within refuge, the ocean against the world at large, an extra bubble of alloy and atmosphere against their own kind. There are locks on the doors in such places. Habs do not come with locks—their dryback designers had safety issues—but the private and the paranoid have made do, welding or growing their own fortifications onto the baseline structure.

Clarke isn't greedy. Her claim is a small one, a cubby on the upper deck of a hab anchored sixty meters northeast of Atlantis. It's scarcely larger than her long-lost quarters on Beebe Station; she thinks that may have been why she chose it. It doesn't even have a porthole.

She doesn't spend much time here. In fact, she hasn't been here since she and Walsh started fucking. But it doesn't matter how much time she actually spends in this cramped, spartan closet; what matters is the comforting knowledge that it's *hers,* that it's *here,* that no one can ever come in unless she lets them. And that it's available when she needs it.

She needs it now.

She sits naked on the cubby's pallet, bathed in light cranked almost dryback-bright; the readouts she'll be watching are color-coded, and she doesn't want to lose that information. A handpad lies on the neoprene beside her, tuned to her insides. Mosaics of green and blue glow on its face: tiny histograms, winking stars, block-cap letters forming cryptic acronyms. There's a mirror on the opposite bulkhead; she ignores it as best she can, but her empty white eyes keep catching their own reflection.

One hand absently fingers her left nipple; the other holds a depolarizing scalpel against the seam in her chest. Her skin invaginates smoothly along that seam, forms a wrinkle, a puckered geometric groove in her thorax: three sides of a rectangle, a block-C, pressed as if by a cookie cutter into the flesh between left breast and diaphragm and midline.

Clarke opens herself at the sternum.

She unlatches her ribs at the costochondrals and pulls them back; there's a slight resistance and a faint, disquieting sucking sound as the monolayer lining splits along the seam. A dull ache as air rushes into her thorax—it's a chill, really, but deep-body nerves don't distinguish temperature from pain. The mechanics who transformed her hinged four of her ribs on the left side. Clarke hooks her fingers under the fleshy panel and folds it back, exposing the machinery beneath. Sharper, stronger pain stabs forth from intercostals never designed for such flexibility. There are bruises in their future.

She takes a tool from a nearby tray and starts playing with herself.

The flexible tip of the tool, deep within her thorax, slips neatly over a needle-thin valve and locks tight. She's still impressed at how easily she can feel her way around in there. The tool's handle contains a thumbwheel set to some astronomical gear ratio. She moves it a quarter turn; the tip rotates a fraction of a degree.

The handpad at her side bleeps in protest: NTR and GABA flicker from green to yellow on its face. One of the histogram bars lengthens a smidgen; two others contract.

Another quarter turn. More complaints from the pad.

It's such a laughably crude invasion, more rape than seduction. Was there any real need for these fleshy hinges, for the surgical butchery that carved this trap door into her chest? The pad taps wirelessly into the telemetry from her implants; that channel flows both ways, sends commands into the body as well as taking information out of it. Minor adjustments, little tweaks around approved optima, are as simple as tapping on a touchpad and feeling the machinery respond from inside.

But the tweaks Lenie Clarke is about to indulge in are *way* beyond "minor."

The Grid Authority never claimed to own the bodies of their employees, not officially at least. They owned everything they put inside, though. Clarke smiles to herself. *They could probably charge me with vandalism.*

If they'd really wanted to keep her from putting her grubby paws all over company property then they shouldn't have left this service panel in her chest. But they were on such a steep curve, back then. The brownouts weren't waiting;

Hydro-Q wasn't waiting; the GA couldn't wait either. The whole geothermal program was fast-tracked, rearguard, and on the fly; the rifters themselves were a short term stopgap even on that breakneck schedule. Lenie Clarke and her buddies were prototypes, field tests, and final product all rolled into one. How could any accountant justify sealing up the implants on Monday when you'd only have to cut your way back in on Wednesday to fix a faulty myocell, or install some vital component that the advance sims had overlooked?

Even the deadman alarms were an afterthought, Clarke remembers. Karl Acton brought them down to Beebe at the start of his tour, handed them out like throat lozenges, told everyone to pop themselves open and slide 'em in right next to the seawater intake.

Karl was the one who discovered how to do what Lenie Clarke is doing right now. Ken Lubin killed him for it.

Times change, Clarke reflects, and tweaks another setting.

Finally she's finished. She lets the fleshy flap fall back into her chest, feels the phospholipids rebind along the seam. Molecular tails embrace in an orgy of hydrophobia. Another ache throbs diffusely inside now, subtly different from those that have gone before: disinfectants and synthetic antibodies, spraying down the implant cavity in the unlikely event that its lining should fail.

The outraged handpad has given up; half of its readouts are yellow and orange.

Inside Clarke's head, things are beginning to change. The permeability of critical membranes is edging up a few percent. The production of certain chemicals, designed not to carry signals but to blockade them, is subtly being scaled back. Windows are not yet opening, but they are being unlocked.

She can feel none of this directly, of course. The changes, by themselves, are necessary but not sufficient—they don't matter here where lungs are used, where pressure is a mere single atmosphere. They only matter when catalyzed by the weight of an ocean.

But now, when Lenie Clarke goes outside—when she steps into the airlock and the pressure accretes around her like a liquid mountain; when three hundred atmospheres squeeze her head so hard that her very synapses start short-circuiting—then, Lenie Clarke will be able to look into men's souls. Not the bright parts, of course. No philosophy or music, no altruism, no intellectual musings about right and wrong. Nothing neocortical at all. What Lenie Clarke will feel predates all of that by a hundred million years. The hypothalamus, the reticular formation, the amygdala. The reptile brain, the midbrain. Jealousies, appetites, fears and inarticulate hatreds. She'll feel them all, to a range of fifteen meters or more.

She remembers what it was like. Too well. Six years gone and it seems like yesterday.

All she has to do is step outside.

She sits in her cubby, and doesn't move.

GRAVEDIGGERS

FIND *the damn mines.*

They spread out across the territory like black dogs, sniffing through light and shadow with sonar pistols and flux detectors. Some of them may question the exercise—and some of them almost certainly root for its failure—but nobody still alive after five years down here is going to be dumb enough to go all insubordinate on Ken Lubin.

Find the damn mines.

Clarke glides among them, just another nose on the trail as far as anyone can tell. Hers is not so focused, though. The others follow invisible lines, the threads of a systematic grid laid down across the search area; but Clarke zigzags, coasts down to accompany this compatriot or that, exchanging insignificant bits of conversation and intel before diverging courses in search of new company. Clarke has a different mission.

Find the damn mine-layer.

Hectares of biosteel. Intermittent punctuations of light and shadow. Flashing staccatos at each extremity, little blinking beacons that announce the tips of scaffolds, antennae, danger zones where hot fluids might vent without warning. The baleful, unwavering glare of floodlights around airlocks and docking hatches and loading bays, reignited for today's exercise. Pale auras of wasted light from a hundred parabolic viewports. Twilit expanses of hull where every protuberance casts three or four shadows, dimly lit by lamps installed in more distant and glamorous neighborhoods.

Everywhere else, darkness. Elongated grids of shadow laid out by naked support struts. Impenetrable inky pools filling the spaces between keel and substrate, as though Atlantis were some great bed with its own scary place for monsters lying beneath. Fuzzy darkness where the light simply attenuates and fades; or razor-sharp where some tank or conduit extends into bright sodium sunlight, laying inky shadows over whatever lies beneath.

More than enough topography to hide an explosive device barely twice the size of a man's hand. More than enough to hide a thousand.

It would be a big enough job for fifty-eight. It's a lot bigger for the two dozen that Lubin is willing to conscript to the task; rifters who haven't gone native, who don't overtly hate the corpses enough to leave suspicious-looking objects "unnoticed" in their sweep—rifters who aren't among the most likely to have planted such devices in the first place. It's nowhere near a sure thing, of course; few of these people have been cleared as suspects. Not even the intel stolen directly from their brainpans is incontrovertible. They didn't hand out the eyes and the 'skin to anyone who didn't have a certain history, twisted wiring is what suits a body to the rift in the first place. Everyone's haunted here. Everyone carries their own baggage: their own tormentors, their own victims, the addictions, the beatings and the anal rapes and the paternal fondling at the hands of kindly Men In Black. Hatred of the corpses, so recently abated, is once again a given. β-max has brought all the old conflicts back to the surface, reignited hostilities that five years of grudging, gradual coexistence had begun to quench. A month or two past, rifters and corpses were almost allies, bitter holdouts like Erickson and Nolan notwithstanding. Now, few would shed many tears if the ocean crashed in on the whole lot of them.

Still. There's a difference between dancing on someone's

grave and digging it. There's an element of, of *calculation* on top of the hatred. Of planning. It's a subtle difference; Clarke doesn't know if she or Lubin would be able to pick it up under these circumstances. It might not even manifest itself in someone until the very moment they came upon the incriminating object, saw the mine stuck to the hull like some apocalyptic limpet, tripped their vocoder with every intention of raising the alarm and then—

Maybe the bastards deserve it after all they've done to us, after all they've done to the whole world, and it's not like I set the damn thing, it's not like I had anything to do with it except I maybe just didn't notice it there under the strut, perfectly understandable in the murk and all . . .

Any number of minds could seem perfectly innocent—even to themselves—right up to the point at which that last-wire stimulus came into view and catalyzed a simple chain of thought that ends in just looking the other way. Even then, who knows whether fine-tuning might pick it up?

Not Lenie Clarke. She searches anyway, gliding between the hulls and the storage tanks, flying over her fellows searching the lights and the shadows, only ostensible in her hunt for ordinance.

What she's really hunting is *guilt.*

Not honest guilt, of course. She's trolling for fear of discovery, she's on the prowl for righteous anger. Newly reawakened, she swims through a faint cauldron of secondhand emotions. The water's tainted with a dozen kinds of fear, of anger, with the loathing of self and others. A darker center roils beneath the surface of each dark body. There's also excitement of a sort, the initial thrill of the chase decaying exponentially down to rote boredom. Sexual stirrings. Other, fainter feelings she can't identify.

She's never forgotten why she resisted fine-tuning back at Channer, even after all the others had gone over. Now, though, she remembers why she found it so seductive when she finally gave in: in that endless welter of feelings, you always lost track of which ones were yours . . .

It's not quite the same here on the Ridge, unfortunately. Not that the physics or the neurology have changed. Not that anyone else has. It's Lenie Clarke that's different now. Victim and vendetta have faded over the years, black and white have bled together into a million indistinguishable shades of gray. Her psyche has diverged from the rifter norm, it no longer blends safely into that background. The guilt alone is so strong that she can't imagine it arising from anyone but her.

She stays the course, though. She keeps hunting, though her senses are dulled. Somewhere off in the diffracted distance, Ken Lubin is doing the same. He's probably a lot better at it than she is. He's had training in this kind of thing. He's had years of experience.

Something tickles the side of her mind. Some distant voice shouts through the clouds in her head. She realizes that she's been sensing it for some time, but its volume has crept up so gradually that it hasn't registered until now. Now it's unmistakable: threat and exclamation and excitement, at the very limit of her range. Two rifters cross her path, heading south, legs pumping. Clarke's jaw is buzzing with vocoded voices; in her reverie, she's missed those too.

"Almost missed it completely," one of them says. "It was tucked in under—"

"Got another one," a second voice breaks in. "Res-A."

One look and Clarke knows she would have missed it.

It's a standard demolition charge, planted in the shadow of an overhanging ledge. Clarke floats upside down and lays her head against the hull to look along the space beneath; she sees a hemispherical silhouette, shaded by the ledge, backlit by the diffuse murky glow of the water behind.

"Jesus," she buzzes, "how did you find the damn thing?"

"Sonar caught it."

With typical rifter discipline, the searchers have abandoned their transects and accreted around the find. Lubin hasn't sent them back; there's an obvious reason why he'd want them all here with the murder weapon. Clarke tunes and concentrates:

Excitement. Reawakened interest, after an hour of monotonous back-and-forth. Concern and threads of growing fear: this is a bomb, after all, not an Easter egg. A few of the more skittish are already backing away, caution superseding curiosity. Clarke wonders idly about effective blast radius. Forty or fifty meters is the standard safe-distance during routine construction, but those guidelines are always padded.

She focuses. Everyone's a suspect, after all. But although the ubiquitous undercurrent of rage simmers as always, none of it has risen to the surface. There is no obvious anger at being thwarted, no obvious fear of imminent discovery. This explosive development is more puzzle than provocation to these people, a game of Russian roulette nested inside a scavenger hunt.

"So what do we do now?" Cheung asks.

Lubin floats above them all like Lucifer. "Everybody note the sonar profile. That's how you'll acquire the others; they'll be too well hidden for a visual sweep."

A dozen pistols fire converging click-trains on the offending object.

"So do we leave it there, or what?"

"What if it's booby-trapped?"

"What if it goes off?"

"Then we've got fewer corpses to worry about," Gomez buzzes from what he might think of as a safe distance. "No skin off my fore."

Lubin descends through the conjecture and reaches under the ledge.

Ng sculls away. "Hey, is that a good—"

Lubin grabs the device and yanks it free. Nothing explodes. He turns and surveys the assembled rifters. "When you find the others, don't touch them. I'll remove them myself."

"Why bother," Gomez buzzes softly.

It's a rhetorical grumble, not even a serious challenge, but Lubin turns to face him anyway. "This was badly positioned," he says. "Placed for concealment, not effect. We can do much better."

Minds light up, encouraged, on all sides. But to Clarke, it's as though Lubin's words have opened a tiny gash in her diveskin; she feels the frigid Atlantic seeping up her spine.

What are you doing, Ken? What the fuck are you doing?

She tells himself he's just playing to the gallery, saying whatever it takes to keep people motivated. He's looking at her now, his head cocked just slightly to one side, as if in response to some unvoiced question. Belatedly, Clarke realizes what she's doing: she's trying to look into his head. She's trying to tune him in.

It's a futile effort, of course. Dangerous, even. Lubin hasn't just been *trained* to block prying minds; he's been conditioned, rewired, outfitted with subconscious defenses that can't be lowered by any act of mere volition. Nobody's ever been able to tunnel into Lubin's head except Karl Acton, and whatever *he* saw in there, he took to his grave.

Now Lubin watches her, dark inside and out for all her unconscious efforts.

She remembers Acton, and stops trying.

STRIPTEASE

THE final score is nine mines and no suspects. Either might be subject to change.

Atlantis itself is an exercise in scale-invariant complexity, repairs to retrofits to additions to a sprawling baseline structure that extends over hectares. There's no chance that every nook and cranny has been explored. Then again, what chance is there that the culprits—constrained by time and surveillance and please God, small numbers—had any greater opportunity to plant explosives than the sweepers have had to find them? Neither side is omnipotent. Perhaps, on balance, that is enough.

As for who those culprits are, Clarke has tuned in three dozen of her fellows so far. She has run her fingers through the viscous darkness in all those heads and come up with nothing. Not even Gomez, or Yeager. Not even *Creasy*. Grave-dancers, for sure, all of them. But no diggers.

She hasn't run into Grace Nolan lately, though.

Nolan's the Big Red Button right now. She's holding back for the moment; any alleged corpse treachery looks a little less asymmetrical in light of recent events. But the way things are going, Nolan's got nothing to lose by letting this play out. There's already more than enough sympathy out there for the Mad Bomber; if it turns out to be Nolan, the very act of unmasking her could boost her status more than harm it.

The leash is tenuous enough already. If it snaps there's going to be ten kinds of shit in the cycler.

And that's granting the charitable assumption that they

even *find* the culprits. What do you look for, in the unlit basements of so many minds? Here, even the innocent are consumed with guilt; even the guilty wallow in self-righteousness. Every mind is aglow with the black light of PsychoHazard icons: which ones are powered by old wounds, which by recent acts of sabotage? You can figure it out, sometimes, if you can stand sticking your head into someone else's tar pit, but context is everything. Hoping for a lucky break is playing the lottery; doing it right takes time, and leaves Clarke soiled.

Not doing it delivers the future into Grace Nolan's hands.

There's no time. I can't be everywhere. Ken can't be everywhere.

There's an alternative, of course. Lubin suggested it, just after the bomb sweep. He was sweet about it, too, he made it sound as if she had a choice. As if he wouldn't just go ahead and do it himself if she wasn't up for it.

She knows why he gave her the option. Whoever shares this secret is going to get a bit of a boost in the local community. Lubin doesn't need the cred; no rifter would be crazy enough to cross *him*.

She remembers a time, not so long ago, when she could make the same claim about herself.

She takes a breath, and opens a channel to whom it may concern. The next step, she knows, could kill her. She wonders—hardly for the first time—if that would really be such a bad thing.

Her audience numbers fewer than a dozen. There's room for more; the medhab—even the lone sphere that hasn't been commandeered as Bhanderi habitat—is bigger than most. Not present are even more who can be trusted, judging by the notes Clarke and Lubin have recently compared. But she wants to start small. Maybe ease into it a little. The ripple effect will kick in soon enough.

"I'm only going to do this once," she says. "So pay attention."

Naked to the waist, she splits herself open again.

"Don't change anything except your neuroinhibitors. It probably throws out some overall balance with the other chemicals, but it all seems to come out in the wash eventually. Just don't go outside for a while after you make the changes. Give everything a chance to settle."

"How long?" Alexander asks.

Clarke has no idea. "Six hours, maybe. After that, you should be good to go. Ken will assign you to stations around the hubs."

Her audience rustles, unhappy at the prospect of such prolonged confinement.

"So how do we tweak the inhibitors?" Mak's broken nose is laced with fine beaded wires, a minuscule microelectric grid designed to amp up the healing process. It looks like an absurdly shrunken veil of mourning.

Clarke smiles despite herself. "You reduce them."

"You're kidding."

"No fucking chance."

"What about André?"

André died three years ago, the life spasming out of him on the seabed in a seizure that nearly tore him limb from limb. Seger laid the blame on a faulty neuroinhibitor pump. Human nerves aren't designed for the abyss; the pressure sets them firing at the slightest provocation. You turn into a fleshy switchboard with no circuit-breakers and no insulation. Eventually, after a few minutes of quivering tetanus, the body runs out of neurotransmitters and just *stops.*

Which is why rifter implants flood the body with neuroinhibitors whenever ambient pressure rises above some critical threshold. Without them, stepping outside at these depths would be tantamount to electrocution.

"I said *reduce,*" Clarke repeats. "Not *eliminate*. Five percent. Seven percent tops."

"And that does what, exactly?"

"Reduces synaptic firing thresholds. Your nerves get just a bit more . . . more sensitive, I guess. To smaller stimuli, when you go outside. You become aware of things you never noticed before."

"Like what?" says Garcia.

"Like—" Clarke begins, and stops.

Suddenly she just wants to seal herself up and deny it all. *Never mind,* she wants to say. *Bad idea. Bad joke. Forget I said anything.* Or maybe even *admit* it all: *You don't know what you're risking. You don't know how easy it is to go over the edge. My lover couldn't even fit inside a hab without going into withdrawal, couldn't even* breathe *without needing to smash anything that stood between him and the abyss. My friend committed murder for privacy in a place where you couldn't swim next to someone without being force-fed their sickness and want. And he's* your *friend too, he's one of us here, and he's the only other person left alive in the whole sick twisted planet who knows what this does to you . . .*

She glances around, suddenly panicky, but Ken Lubin is not in the audience. Probably off drawing up duty rosters for the finely tuned.

Then again, she remembers, *you get used to it.*

She takes a breath and answers Garcia's question. "You can tell if someone's jerking you around, for one thing."

"Hot damn," Garcia exults. "I'm gonna be a walking bullshit detector."

"That you are," Clarke says, managing a smile.

Hope you're up for it.

Her acolytes depart for their own little bubbles to play with themselves. Clarke closes herself back up as the medhab empties. By the time she's back in black there's just her, a crowd of wet footprints, and the massive hatch—always left open until just recently—that opens into the next sphere. Garcia's grafted a combination lock across its wheel in uncaring defiance of dryback safety protocols.

How long do I have, she wonders, *before everyone can muck around in my head?*

Six hours at least, if the acolytes take her guess seriously. Then they'll start playing, trying out the new sensory mode, perhaps even reveling in it if they don't recoil at the things they find.

They'll start spreading the word.

Clarke's selling it as psychic surveillance, a new way to track down any guilty secrets the corpses may be hiding. Its effects are bound to spread way beyond Atlantis, though. It'll be that much harder for *anyone* to conspire in the dark, when every passing soul comes equipped with a searchlight.

She finds herself standing at the entrance to Bhanderi's lair, her hand on the retrofitted keypad near its center. She keys in the combination and undogs the hatch.

Suddenly she's seeing in color. The mimetic seal rimming the hatch is a deep, steely blue. A pair of color-coded pipes wind overhead like coral snakes. A cylinder of some compressed gas, spied through the open portal, reflects turquoise: the decals on its side are yellow and—incomprehensibly—hot pink.

It's as bright as Atlantis in there.

She steps into the light: Calvin cycler, sleeping pallet, blood bank ooze pigment into the air. "Rama?"

"Close the door."

Something sits hunched at the main workstation, running a sequence of rainbow nucleotides. It can't be a rifter. It doesn't have the affect, it doesn't have the black shiny skin. It looks more like a hunched skeleton in shirtsleeves. It turns, and Clarke flinches inwardly: it doesn't even have the *eyes*. The pupils twitching in Bhanderi's face are dark yawning holes, dilated so widely that the irises around them are barely visible.

Not so bright, then. Still dark enough for uncapped eyes to strain to their limits. Such subtle differences get lost behind membranes that render the world at optimum apparent lumens.

Something must show on her face. "I took out the caps," Bhanderi says. "The eyes—overstimulate, with all the enhancers." His voice is still hoarse, the cords not yet reacclimated to airborne speech.

"How's it going?" Clarke asks.

A bony shrug. She can count the ribs even through his T-shirt.

"Anything yet? Diagnostic test, or—"

"Won't be able to tell the difference until I know if there *is* a difference. So far it looks like βehemoth with a couple of new stitches. Maybe mutations, maybe refits. I don't know yet."

"Would a baseline sample help?"

"Baseline?"

"Something that didn't come through Atlantis. Maybe if you had a sample from Impossible Lake, you could compare. See if they're different."

He shakes his head: a twitch, a tic. "There are ways to tell tweaks. Satellite markers, junk sequences. Just takes time."

"But you can do it. The—enhancers worked. It came back to you."

He nods like a striking snake. He calls up another sequence.

"Thank you," Clarke says softly.

He stops.

"*Thank you?* What choice do I have? There's a lock on the hatch."

"I know." She lowers her eyes. "I'm sorry."

"Did you think I'd just leave? That I'd just swim off and let this thing kill us all? Kill *me,* maybe?"

She shakes her head. "No. Not you."

"Then why?"

Even motionless, his face looks like a stifled scream. It's the eyes. Through all the calm, rapid-fire words, Bhanderi's eyes seem frozen in a stare of absolute horror. It's as if there's something else in there, something ancient and unthinking and only recently awakened. It looks out across a hundred million years into an incomprehensible world of right angles and blinking lights, and finds itself utterly unable to cope.

"Because it comes and goes," Clarke says. "You said it yourself."

He extends one sticklike forearm, covered in derms; a chemical pump just below his elbow taps directly into the vein beneath. He's been dosing himself ever since he climbed back into atmosphere, using miracles of modern chemistry to rape sanity back into his head, to force submerged memories and skills back to the surface for a while. So far, she has to admit, it's working.

But whenever she looks at him, she sees the reptile looking back. "We can't risk it, Rama. I'm sorry."

He lowers his arm. His jaw clicks like some kind of insect.

"You said—" he begins, and falls silent.

He tries again. "When you were bringing me in. Did you say you knew a—"

"Yes."

"I didn't know any—I mean, *who?*"

"Not here," she tells him. "Not even this ocean. Way back at the very beginning of the rifter program. He went over in front of my eyes." A beat, then, "His name was Gerry."

"But you said he came back."

She honestly doesn't know. Gerry Fischer just *appeared* out of the darkness, after everyone else had given up and gone. He dragged her to safety, to an evacuation 'scaphe hovering uncertainly over a station already emptied of personnel. But he never spoke a word, and he kicked and fought like an animal when she tried to rescue him in turn.

"Maybe he didn't so much *come back* as *come through,*" she admits now, to this creature who must in his own way know Gerry Fischer far better than she ever did.

Bhanderi nods. "What happened to him?"

"He died," she says softly.

"Just . . . faded away? Like the rest of us?"

"No."

"How, then?"

She thinks of a word with customized resonance.

"Boom," she says.

FRONTIER

COME *away,* they said after Rio. *Come away, now that you've saved our asses yet again.*

That wasn't entirely true. He hadn't saved Buffalo. He hadn't saved Houston. Salt Lake and Boise and Sacramento were gone, fallen to improvised assaults ranging from kamikaze airliners to orbital nukes. Half a dozen other franchises were barely alive. Very few of those asses had been saved.

But to the rest of the Entropy Patrol, Achilles Desjardins was a hero ten times over. It had been obvious almost immediately that fifty CSIRA franchises were under directed and simultaneous attack across the western hemisphere, but it had been Desjardins and Desjardins alone who'd put the pieces together, under fire and on the fly. It had been he who'd drawn the impossible conclusion that the attacks were being orchestrated by one of their own. The rest of the Patrol had taken up the call and flattened Rio as soon as they had the scoop, but it had been Desjardins who'd told them where to aim. Without his grace under pressure, every CSIRA stronghold in the hemisphere could have ended up in flames.

Come away, said his grateful masters. *This place is a write-off.*

Sudbury CSIRA had taken a direct hit amidships. A suborbital puddle-jumper en route from London to Toromilton, subverted by the enemy and lethally off-course, had left an impact crater ten stories high in the building's northern face. Its fuel tanks all but empty, the fires hadn't burned hot enough to take down the structure. They had merely incinerated, poisoned, or suffocated most of those between the eighteenth and twenty-fifth floors.

Sudbury's 'lawbreakers had worked between floors twenty and twenty-four. It had been lucky that Desjardins had managed to raise the alarm before they'd been hit. It had been an outright motherfucking miracle that he hadn't been killed when they were.

Come away.

And Achilles Desjardins looked around at the smoke and the guttering flames, the piled body bags, and those few stunned coworkers still sufficiently intact to escape mandatory euthanasia, and replied: You need me here.

There is no here.

But there was more left of *here* than there was of Salt Lake or Buffalo. The attacks had reduced redundancy across N'Am's fast-response network by over thirty percent. Sudbury was hanging by a thread, but that thread still connected sixteen hemispheric links and forty-seven regional ones. Abandoning it completely would cut system redundancy by another five percent and leave a half million square kilometers without any rapid-response capacity whatsoever. βehemoth already ran rampant across half the continent; civilization was imploding throughout its domain. CSIRA could not afford the luxury of further losses.

There were counterpoints. Half the floors of the Sudbury franchise were uninhabitable. There was barely enough surviving bandwidth for a handful of operatives, and under the current budget it would be almost impossible to keep even that much open. All the models agreed: the best solution was to abandon Sudbury and upgrade Toromilton and Montreal to take up the slack.

And how long, Desjardins wondered, before those upgrades came onstream?

Six months. Maybe a year.

Then they needed a stopgap. They needed to keep the pilot light burning for just a little longer. They needed someone on-site for those unforeseeable crisis points when machinery wasn't up to the job.

But you're our best 'lawbreaker, they protested.

And the task will be almost impossible. Where else should I be?

Wellllllll . . .

Only six months, he reminded them. Maybe a year.

Of course, it wouldn't turn out that way. Murphy's malign hand would stir the pot and maybe-a-year would morph into three, then four. The Toromilton upgrades would falter and stall; farsighted master plans would collapse, as they always had, beneath the weight of countless daily emergencies. Making do, the Entropy Patrol would throw crumbs enough at Sudbury to keep the lights on and the clearance codes active, ever grateful for their uncomplaining minion and the thousand fingers he kept jammed in the dike.

But that was now and this was then, and Desjardins was saying, I'll be your lighthouse keeper. I'll be your sentinel on the lonely frontier, I'll fight the brush fires and hold the line until the cavalry comes online. I can do this. You know I can.

And they did know, because Achilles Desjardins was a hero. More to the point, he was a 'lawbreaker; he wouldn't have been able to lie to them even if he'd wanted to.

What a guy, they said, shaking their heads in admiration. *What a guy.*

GROUNDWORK

KEVIN Walsh is a good kid. He knows relationships take work, he's willing to do what it takes to keep the spark—such as it is—alive. Or at least, to stretch its death out over the longest possible period.

He attached himself to her arm after Lubin handed out the first fine-tuning assignments, and wouldn't take *Later, maybe* for an answer. Finally Clarke relented. They found an unoccupied hab and threw down a couple of sleeping pallets, and he uncomplainingly worked his tongue and thumb and forefinger down to jelly until she didn't have the heart to let him continue. She stroked his head and said it was nice but it really wasn't working, and she offered herself in turn for his efforts, but he didn't take her up on it—whether out of chivalrous penance for his own inadequacy or simply because he was sulking, she couldn't tell.

Now they lie side by side, hands lightly interlocked at arm's length. Walsh is asleep, which is surprising: he's no more fond of sleeping in gravity than any other rifter. Maybe it's another chivalrous affectation. Maybe he's faking it.

Clarke can't bring herself to do even that. She lies on her back and stares up at the condensation beading on the bulkhead. After a while she disentangles her hand from Walsh's—gently, so as not to interrupt the performance—and wanders over to the local comm board.

The main display frames a murky, cryptic obelisk looming up out of the seabed. Atlantis's primary generator. Part of it, anyway—the bulk of the structure plunges deep into bedrock, into the heart of a vent from which it feeds like a mosquito sucking hot blood. Only the apex rises above the substrate like some lumpy windowless skyscraper, facades pocked and wormy with pipes and vents and valves. A sparse dotted line of floodlights girdles the structure about eight meters up, casting a bright coarse halo that stains everything copper. The abyss presses down against that light like a black hand; the top of the generator extends into darkness.

A conduit the size of a sewer pipe emerges at ground level and snakes into the darkness. Clarke absently tags the next cam in line, following the line along the seabed.

"Hey, *what are you . . .*"

He doesn't sound sleepy at all.

She turns. Walsh is crouched half kneeling on the pallet, as though caught in the act of rising. He doesn't move, though.

"Hey, get back here. I wanna try again." He's going for a boyish grin. He's wearing the Disarmingly Cute Face of Seduction. It's a jarring contrast with his posture, which evokes the image of an eleven-year-old caught masturbating on the good linen.

She eyes him curiously. "What's up, Kev?"

He laughs; it sounds like a hiccough. "Nothing's *up* . . . we just didn't, you know, *finish* . . ."

A dull gray lump of realization congeals in her throat. Experimentally, she turns back to the board and trips the next surveillance cam in the chain. The seabed conduit winds on toward a distant hazy geometry of backlit shadows.

Walsh tugs at her shoulder, nuzzles from behind. "Ladies' choice. Limited time offer, expires soon . . ."

Next cam.

"Come *on,* Len—"

Atlantis. A small knot of rifters has accreted at the junction of two wings, nowhere near any of the assigned surveillance stations. They appear to be taking measurements of some kind. Some of them are laden with strange cargo.

Walsh has fallen silent. The lump in Clarke's throat metastasizes.

She turns. Kevin Walsh has backed away, a mixture of guilt and defiance on his face.

"You gotta give her a chance, Len," he says. "I mean, you gotta be more *objective* about this . . ."

She regards him calmly. "You asshole."

"Oh right," he flares. "Like anything *I* ever did mattered to *you.*"

She grabs the disconnected pieces of her diveskin. They slide around her body like living things, fusing one to another, sealing her in, sealing him out, welcome liquid armor that reinforces the boundary between *us* and *them.*

Only there is no us, she realizes. *There never was.* And what *really* pisses her off is that she'd forgotten that, that she never even saw this coming; even privy to her lover's brainstem, even cognizant of all the guilt and pain and stupid masochistic yearning in there, she hadn't picked up on this imminent betrayal. She'd sensed his resentment, of course, and his hurt, but that was nothing new. When it came right down to it, outright treachery just didn't make enough of a difference in this relationship to register.

She doesn't look at him as she descends to the airlock.

Kevin Walsh is one fucked-up little boy. It's just as well she never got too attached.

Their words buzz back and forth among the shadows of the great structure: numbers, times, shear stress indices. A couple of rifters carry handpads; others fire click-trains of high-frequency sounds through acoustic rangefinders. One of them draws a big black X at some vital weak spot.

How did Ken put it? *For concealment, not effect.* Obviously they aren't going to make *that* mistake again.

They're expecting her, of course. Walsh didn't warn them—not on the usual channels, anyway—but you can't sneak up on the fine-tuned.

Clarke pans the company. Nolan, three meters overhead, looks down at her. Cramer, Cheung, and Gomez accrete loosely around them. Creasy and Yeager—too distant for visual ID, but clear enough on the mindline—are otherwise occupied some ways down the hull.

Nolan's vibe overwhelms all the others: where once was resentment, now there's triumph. But the anger—the sense of scores yet to be settled—hasn't changed at all.

"Don't blame Kev," Clarke buzzes. "He did his best." She wonders offhand how far Nolan went to secure that loyalty.

Nolan nods deliberately. "Kev's a good kid. He'd do anything to help the group." The slightest emphasis on *anything* slips through the machinery, but Clarke's already seen it in the meat behind.

That far.

She forces herself to look deeper, to dig around for guilt or duplicity, but of course it's pointless. If Nolan ever kept such secrets, she's way past it now. Now she wears her intentions like a badge of honor.

"So what's going on?" Clarke asks.

"Just planning for the worst," Nolan says.

"Uh-huh." She nods at the X on the hull. "Planning for it, or provoking it?"

Nobody speaks.

"You do realize we control the generators. We can shut them down any time we want. Blowing the hull would be major overkill."

"Oh, we'd never do for *excessive force.*" That's Cramer, off to the left. "Especially since *they* always be so gentle."

"We just think it would be wise to have other options," Chen buzzes, apologetic but unswayable. "Just in case something compromises Plan A."

"Such as?"

"Such as the way certain hands pump the cocks of the mouths that bite them, " Gomez says.

Clarke spins casually to face him. "Articulate as always, Gomer. I can see why you don't talk much."

"If I were you—" Nolan begins.

"Shut the fuck up."

Clarke turns slowly in their midst, her guts convecting in a slow freezing boil. "Anything they did to you, they did to me first. Any shit they threw at you, they threw way more at me. *Way* more."

"Which ended up landing on everyone *but* you," Nolan points out.

"You think I'm gonna stick my tongue up their ass just because they *missed* when they tried to kill me?"

"Are you?"

She coasts up until her face is scant centimeters from Nolan's. "Don't you fucking *dare* question my loyalty again, Grace. I was down here before *any* of you miserable haploids. While you were all back on shore pissing and moaning about job security, *I* broke into their fucking castle and personally kicked Rowan and her buddies off the pot."

"Sure you did. Then you joined her sorority two days later. You play VR games with her *daughter,* for Chrissake!"

"Yeah? And what exactly did her daughter do to deserve you dropping the whole Atlantic Ocean onto her head? Even if you're right—*even* if you're right—did their *kids* fuck you over? What did their families and their servants and their toilet-scrubbers ever do to you?"

The words vibrate off into the distance. The deep, almost subsonic hum of some nearby piece of life-support sounds especially loud in their wake.

Maybe the tiniest bit of uncertainty in the collective vibe, now. Maybe even a tiny bit in Nolan's.

But she's not giving a micron. "You want to know what they did, Len? They chose sides. The wives and the husbands and the medics and even any pet toilet-scrubbers those stumpfucks may have kept around for old time's sake. They all chose sides. Which is more than I can say for you."

"This is not a good idea," Clarke buzzes.

"Thanks for your opinion, Len. We'll let you know if we need you for anything. In the meantime, stay out of my way. The sight of you makes me want to puke."

Clarke plays her final card. "It's not me you have to worry about."

"What made you think we were ever worried about *you*?" The contempt comes off of Nolan in waves.

"Ken gets very unhappy when he's caught in the middle of some half-assed fiasco like this. I've seen it happen. He's the kind of guy who finds it much easier to shut something down up front than clean up after it. You can deal with *him*."

"We already have," Nolan buzzes. "He knows all about it."

"Even gave us a few pointers," Gomez adds.

"Sorry, sweetie." Nolan leans in close to Clarke; their hoods slip frictionlessly past each other, a mannequin nuzzle. "But you really should have seen that coming."

Without another word the group goes back to work, as if cued by some stimulus to which Lenie Clarke is blind and deaf. She hangs there in the water, stunned, betrayed. Bits and pieces of some best-laid plan assemble themselves around her.

She turns and swims away.

HARPODON

ONCE upon a time, back during the uprising, a couple of corpses commandeered a multisub named *Harpodon III*. To this day Patricia Rowan has no idea what they were trying to accomplish; *Harpodon*'s spinal bays were empty of any construction or demolition modules that might have served as weapons. The sub was as stripped as a fish skeleton, and about as useful: cockpit up front, impellors in back, and a whole lot of nothing hanging off the segmented spine between.

Maybe they'd just been running for it.

But the rifters didn't bother asking, once they'd caught on and caught up. *They* hadn't come unequipped: they had torches and rivet guns, not quite enough to cut *Harpodon* in half but certainly enough to paralyze it from the neck down. They punched out the electrolysis assembly and the Lox tanks; the fugitives got to watch their supply of breathable atmosphere drop from infinite down to the little bubble of nitrox already turning stale in the cockpit.

Normally the rifters would have just holed the hull and let the ocean finish the job. This time, though, they hauled *Harpodon* back to one of Atlantis's viewports as a kind of object lesson: the runaways suffocated within view of all the corpses they'd left behind. There'd already been some rifter casualties, as it turned out, and Grace Nolan had been leading the team that shift.

But back then, not even Nolan was entirely without pity. Once the runaways were well and truly dead, once the moral of the story had properly sunk in, the rifters mated the wounded sub to the nearest docking hatch and let the corpses reclaim the bodies. *Harpodon* hasn't moved in all the years since. It's still grafted onto the service lock, protruding from the body of Atlantis like a parasitic male anglerfish fused to the flank of his gigantic mate. It's not a place that anybody goes.

Which makes it the perfect spot for Patricia Rowan to consort with the enemy.

The diver 'lock is an elongate blister distending the deck of the cockpit, just aft of the copilot's seat where Rowan sits staring at rows of dark instruments. It gurgles behind her; she hears a tired pneumatic sigh as its coffin lid swings open, hears the soft slap of wet feet against the plates.

She's left the lights off, of course—it wouldn't do for anyone to know of her presence here—but some flashing beacon, way along the curve of Atlantis's hull, sends pulses of dim brightness through the viewports. The cockpit interior blinks lazily in and out of existence, a jumbled topography of metal viscera keeping the abyss at bay.

Lenie Clarke climbs into the pilot's seat beside her.

"Anyone see you?" Rowan asks, not turning her head.

"If they had," the rifter says, "they'd probably be finishing the job right now." Referring, no doubt, to the injuries sustained by *Harpodon* in days gone by. "Any progress?"

"Eight of the samples tested positive. No fix yet." Rowan takes a deep breath. "How goes the battle on your end?"

"Maybe you could pick a different expression. Something a bit less literal."

"Is it that bad?"

"I don't think I can hold them back, Pat."

"Surely you can," Rowan says. "You're the Meltdown Madonna, remember? The Alpha Femme."

"Not any more."

Rowan turns to look at the other woman.

"Grace is—some of them are taking steps." Lenie's face switches on and off in the pulsating gloom. "They're mine-laying again. Right out in the open this time."

Rowan considers. "What does Ken think about that?"

"Actually, I think he's okay with it."

Lenie sounds as though she'd been surprised by that. Rowan isn't. "Mine-laying *again*?" she repeats. "So you know who set them the first time?"

"Not really. Not yet. Not that it matters." Lenie sighs. "Hell, some people still think you planted the first round yourselves."

"That's absurd, Lenie. Why would we?"

"To give you an—excuse, I guess. Or as some kind of last-ditch self-destruct, to take us out with you. I don't know." Lenie shrugs. "I'm not saying they're making sense. I'm just telling you where they're at."

"And how are we supposed to be putting together all this ordinance, when you people control our fabrication facilities?"

"Ken says you can get a standard Calvin cycler to make explosives if you tweak the wiring the right way."

Ken again.

Rowan still isn't sure how to broach the subject. There's a bond between Lenie and Ken, a connection both absurd and inevitable between two people for whom the term *friendship* should be as alien as a Europan microbe. It's nothing sexual—the way Ken swings it hardly could be, although Rowan suspects that Lenie still doesn't know about that—but in its own repressed way, it's almost as intimate. There's a protectiveness, not to be taken lightly. If you attack one, you better watch out for the other.

And yet, from the sound of it, Ken Lubin is beginning to draw different alliances . . .

She decides to risk it. "Lenie, has it occurred to you that Ken might be—"

"That's crazy." The rifter kills the question before she has to answer it.

"Why?" Rowan asks. "Who else has the expertise? Who else is addicted to killing people?"

"*You* gave him that. He was on *your* payroll."

Rowan shakes her head. "I'm sorry, Lenie, but you know that isn't true. We instilled his threat-response reflex, yes. But that was only to make sure he took the necessary steps—"

"To make sure he killed people," Lenie interjects.

"—in the event of a security breach. He was never supposed to get—addicted to it. And you know as well as I do: Ken has the know-how, he has access, he has grudges going all the way back to childhood. The only thing that kept him on the leash was Guilt Trip, and Spartacus took care of *that*."

"Spartacus was five years ago," the rifter points out. "And Ken hasn't gone on any killing sprees since then. If you'll remember, he was one of exactly two people who *prevented* your last uprising from turning into The Great Corpse Massacre."

She sounds as if she's trying to convince herself as much as anyone. "Lenie—"

But she's having none of it. "Guilt Trip was just something you people laid onto his brain after he came to work for you. He didn't have it before, and he didn't have it afterward, and you know why? Because he has *rules,* Pat. He came up with his own set of rules, and he damn well stuck to them, and no matter how much he wanted to, he never killed *anyone* without a reason."

"That's true," Rowan admits. "Which is why he started inventing reasons."

Lenie, strobing slowly, looks out a porthole and doesn't answer.

"Maybe you don't know that part of the story," Rowan continues. "You never wondered why we'd assign him to the rifter program in the first place? Why we'd waste a Black Ops Black

Belt on the bottom of the ocean, scraping barnacles off geothermal pumps? It was because he'd started to slip up, Lenie. He was making mistakes, he was leaving loose ends all over the place. Of course he always tied them up with extreme prejudice, but that was rather the point. On some subconscious level, Ken was *deliberately* slipping up so that he'd have an excuse to seal the breach afterward.

"Beebe Station was so far out in the boondocks that it should have been virtually impossible to encounter anything he could interpret as a *security breach,* no matter how much he bent his rules. That was our mistake, in hindsight." *Not even one of our bigger ones, more's the pity.* "But my point is, people with addictions sometimes fall off the wagon. People with self-imposed rules of conduct have been known to bend and twist and rationalize those rules to let them both have their cake and eat it. Seven years ago, our psych people told us that Ken was a classic case in point. There's no reason to believe it isn't just as true today."

The rifter doesn't speak for a moment. Her disembodied face, a pale contrast against the darkness of her surroundings, flashes on and off like a beating heart.

"I don't know," she says at last. "I met one of your *psych people* once, remember? You sent him down to *observe* us. We didn't like him much."

Rowan nods. "Yves Scanlon."

"I tried to look him up when I got back to land." *Look him up:* Leniespeak for *hunt him down.* "He wasn't home."

"He was decirculated," Rowan says, her own euphemism—as always—easily trumping the other woman's.

"Ah."

But since the subject has come up . . . "He—he had a theory about you people," Rowan says. "He thought that rifter brains might be . . . sensitive, somehow. That you entered some heightened state of awareness when you spent too long on the bottom of the sea, with all those synthetics in your blood. Quantum signals from the brainstem. Some kind of Ganzfeld effect."

"Scanlon was an idiot," Lenie remarks.

"No doubt. But was he wrong?"

Lenie smiles faintly.

"I see," Rowan says.

"It's not mind-reading. Nothing like that."

"But maybe, if you could . . . what would be the word, *scan?*"

"We called it *fine-tuning,*" Lenie says, her voice as opaque as her eyes.

"If you could fine-tune anybody who might have . . ."

"Already done. It was Ken who suggested it, in fact. We didn't find anything."

"Did you *fine-tune* Ken?"

"You can't—" She stops.

"He blocked you, didn't he?" Rowan nods to herself. "If it's anything like Ganzfeld scanning, he blocks it without even thinking. Standard procedure."

They sit without speaking for a few moments.

"I don't think it's Ken," Clarke says after a while. "I know him, Pat. I've known him for years."

"I've known him longer."

"Not the same way."

"Granted. But if not Ken, who?"

"Shit, Pat, the whole lot of us! *Everybody* has it in for you guys now. They're convinced that Jerry and her buddies—"

"That's absurd."

"Is it really?" Rowan glimpses the old Lenie Clarke, the predatory one, smiling in the intermittent light. "Supposing you'd kicked *our* asses five years ago, and we'd been living under house arrest ever since. And then some bug passed through our hands on its way to you, and corpses started dropping like flies. Are you saying you wouldn't suspect?"

"No. No, of course we would." Rowan heaves a sigh. "But I'd like to think we wouldn't go off half-cocked without any evidence at all. We'd at least entertain the *possibility* that you were innocent."

"As I recall, when the shoe was on the other foot guilt or innocence didn't enter into it. *You* didn't waste any time sterilizing the hot zones, no matter who was inside. No matter what they'd done."

"Good rationale. One worthy of Ken Lubin and his vaunted ethical code."

Lenie snorts. "Give it a rest, Pat. I'm not calling you a liar. But we've already cut you more slack than you cut us, back then. And there are a lot of people in there with you. You sure none of them are doing anything behind your back?"

A bright moment: a dark one.

"Anyway, there's still some hope we could dial this down," Clarke says. "We're looking at β-max ourselves. If it hasn't been tweaked, we won't find anything."

A capillary of dread wriggles through Rowan's insides.

"How will you know one way or the other?" she asks. "None of you are pathologists."

"Well, we aren't gonna trust *your* experts. We may not have tenure at LU but we've got a degree or two in the crowd. That, and access to the biomed library, and—"

"No," Rowan whispers. The capillary grows into a thick, throbbing artery. She feels blood draining from her face to feed it.

Lenie sees it immediately. "What?" She leans forward, across the armrest of her seat. "Why does that worry you?"

Rowan shakes her head. "Lenie, you don't *know*. You're not trained, you don't get a doctorate with a couple of days' reading. Even if you get the right results, you'll probably misinterpret them . . ."

"What results? Misinterpret *how*?"

Rowan watches her, suddenly wary: the way she looked when they met for the first time, five years ago.

The rifter looks back steadily. "Pat, don't hold out on me. I'm having a tough enough time keeping the dogs away as it is. If you've got something to say, say it."

Tell her.

"I didn't know myself until recently," Rowan begins. "βehemoth may have been—I mean, the *original* βehemoth, not this new strain—it was tweaked."

"Tweaked." The word lies thick and dead in the space between them.

Rowan forces herself to continue. "To adapt it to aerobic environments. And to increase its reproductive rate, for faster production. There were commercial applications. Nobody was trying to bring down the world, of course, it wasn't a bioweapons thing at all... but evidently something went wrong."

"Evidently." Clarke's face is an expressionless mask.

"I'm sure you can see the danger here, if your people stumble across these modifications without really knowing what they're doing. Perhaps they know enough to recognize a tweak, but not enough to tell what it does. Perhaps they don't know how to tell old tweaks from more recent ones. Or perhaps the moment they see any evidence of engineering, they'll conclude the worst and stop looking. They could come up with something they thought was *evidence,* and the only ones qualified to prove them wrong would be ignored because they're the enemy."

Clarke watches her like a statue. Maybe the reconciliation of the past few years hasn't been enough. Maybe this new development, this additional demand for even more understanding, has done nothing but shatter the fragile trust the two of them have built. Maybe Rowan has just lost all credibility in this woman's eyes, blown her last chance to avoid meltdown.

Endless seconds fossilize in the cold, thick air.

"Fuck," the rifter says at last, very softly. "It's all over if this gets out."

Rowan dares to hope. "We've just got to make sure it doesn't."

Clarke shakes her head. "What am I supposed to do, tell Rama to stop looking? Sneak into the hab and smash the sequencer? They already think I'm in bed with you people." She emits a small, bitter laugh. "If I take any action at all I've lost them. They don't trust me as it is."

Rowan leans back her seat and closes her eyes. "I know." She feels a thousand years old.

"You fucking corpses. You never could leave anything alone, could you?"

"We're just people, Lenie. We make... mistakes..." And suddenly the sheer, absurd, astronomical magnitude of that understatement sinks home in the most unexpected way, and Patricia Rowan can't quite suppress a giggle.

It's the most undignified sound she's made in years. Lenie arches an eyebrow.

"Sorry," Rowan says.

"No problem. It *was* pretty hilarious." The rifter's patented half-smile flickers at the corner of her mouth.

But it's gone in the next second. "Pat, I don't think we can stop this."

"We have to."

"Nobody's talking any more. Nobody's listening. Just one little push could send it all over the edge. If they even knew we were talking here..."

Rowan shakes her head in hopeful, reassuring denial. But Lenie's right. Rowan knows her history, after all. She knows her politics. You're well past the point of no return when simply communicating with the other side constitutes an act of treason.

"Remember the very first time we met?" Lenie asks. "Face to face?"

Rowan nods. She'd turned the corner and Lenie Clarke was just *there,* right in front of her, fifty kilograms of black rage inexplicably transported to the heart of their secret hideaway. "Eighty meters in that direction," she says, pointing over her shoulder.

"You sure about that?" Lenie asks.

"Most certainly," Rowan says. "I thought you were going to kill m—"

And stops, ashamed.

"Yes," she says after a while. "That was the first time we met. Really."

Lenie faces forward, at her own bank of dead readouts. "I thought you might have, you know, been part of the interview process. Back before your people did their cut 'n' paste in my head. You can never tell what bits might have got edited out, you know?"

"I saw the footage afterward," Rowan admits. "When Yves was making his recommendations. But we never actually met."

"Course not. You were way up in the strat. No time to hang around with the hired help." Rowan is a bit surprised at the note of anger in Lenie's voice. After all that's been done to her, after all she's come to terms with since, it seems strange that such a small, universal neglect would be a hot button.

"They said you'd be better off," Rowan says softly. "Honestly. They said you'd be happier."

"Who said?"

"Neurocog. The psych people."

"Happier." Lenie digests that a moment. "False memories of Dad raping me made me *happier*? Jesus, Pat, if that's true my *real* childhood must have been a *major* treat."

"I mean, happier at Beebe Station. They swore that any so-called *well-adjusted* person would crack down there in under a month."

"I know the brochure, Pat. Preadaption to chronic stress, dopamine addiction to hazardous environments. You bought all that?"

"But they were right. You saw what happened to the control group we sent down. But you—you liked the place so much we were worried you wouldn't want to come back."

"At first," Lenie adds unnecessarily.

After a moment she turns to face Rowan. "But tell me this, Pat. Supposing they told you I *wasn't* going to like it so much? What if they'd said, she'll hate the life, she'll hate *her* life, but we have to do it anyway because it's the only way to keep her from going stark raving mad down there? Would you tell me if they'd told you *that*?"

"Yes." It's an honest answer. Now.

"And would you have let them rewire me and turn me into someone else, give me monsters for parents, and send me down there anyway?"

". . . Yes."

"Because you served the Greater Good."

"I tried to," Rowan says.

"An altruistic corpse," the rifter remarks. "How do you explain that?"

"Explain?"

"It kind of goes against what they taught us in school. Why sociopaths rise to the top of the corporate ladder, and why we should all be grateful that the world's tough economic decisions are being made by people who aren't hamstrung by the touchy-feelies."

"It's a bit more complicated than that."

"*Was,* you mean."

"Is," Rowan insists.

They sit in silence for a while.

"Would you have it reversed, if you could?" Rowan asks.

"What, the rewire? Get my real memories back? Lose the whole *Daddy Rapist* thing?"

Rowan nods.

Lenie's silent for so long that Rowan wonders if she's refusing to answer. But finally, almost hesitantly, she says: "This is who I am. I guess maybe there was a different person in here before, but now it's only me. And when it comes right down to it I guess I just don't want to die. Bringing back that other person would almost be a kind of suicide, don't you think?"

"I don't know. I guess I never thought about it that way before."

"It took a while for me to. You people killed someone else in the process, but you made me." Rowan glimpses a frown, strobe-frozen. "You were right, you know. I *did* want to kill you that time. It wasn't the plan, but I saw you there and everything just caught up with me and you know, for a few moments there I almost..."

"Thanks for holding back," Rowan says.

"I did, didn't I? And if *any* two people ever had reason to go for each other's throats, it had to be us." Her voice catches for an instant. "But we didn't. We got along. Eventually."

"We did," Rowan says.

The rifter looks at her with blank, pleading eyes. "So why can't *they*? Why can't they just—I don't know, follow our lead..."

"Lenie, we destroyed the world. I think they're following our lead a bit too closely."

"Back in Beebe, you know, I was the boss. I didn't want to be, that was the last thing I wanted, but people just kept—" Lenie shakes her head. "And I *still* don't want to be, but I *have* to be, you know? Somehow I have to keep these idiots from blowing everything up. Only now, nobody will even tell me what time zone I'm in, and Grace..."

She looks at Rowan, struck by some thought. "What happened to her, anyway?"

"What do you mean?" Rowan asks.

"She *really* hates you guys. Did you kill her whole family or something? Did you fuck with her head somehow?"

"No," Rowan says. "Nothing."

"Come on, Pat. She wouldn't be down here if there wasn't some—"

"Grace was in the control group. Her background was entirely unremarkable. She was—"

But Lenie's suddenly straight up in her seat, capped eyes sweeping across the ceiling. "Did you hear that?" she asks.

"Hear what?" The cockpit's hardly a silent place—gurgles, creaks, the occasional metallic pop have punctuated their conversation since it began—but Rowan hasn't heard anything out of the ordinary. "I didn't—"

"Shhh," Lenie hisses.

And now Rowan *does* hear something, but it's not what the other woman's listening for. It's a little burble of sound from her own earbud, a sudden alert from comm: a voice worried unto near-panic, audible only to her. She listens, and feels a sick, dread sense of inevitability. She turns to her friend.

"You better get back out there," she says softly.

Lenie spares an impatient glance, catches the expression on Rowan's face and double-takes. "What?"

"Comm's been monitoring your LFAM chatter," Rowan says. "They're saying... Erickson. He died.

"They're looking for you."

THE BLOODHOUND ITERATIONS

N = 1:

Snarling, unaware, she searches for targets and finds none. She looks for landmarks and comes up empty. She can't even find anything that passes for topography—an endless void extends in all directions, an expanse of vacant memory extending far beyond the range of any whiskers she copies into the distance. She can find no trace of the ragged, digital network she usually inhabits. There is no prey here, no predators beyond herself, no files or executables upon which to feast. She can't even find the local operating system. She must be accessing it on some level—she wouldn't run without some share of system resources and clock cycles—but the fangs and claws she evolved to tear open that substrate can't get any kind of grip. She is a lean, lone wolf with rottweiler jaws, optimized for life in some frayed and impoverished jungle that has vanished into oblivion. Even a cage would have recognizable boundaries, walls or bars that she could hurl herself against, however ineffectually. This featureless nullscape is utterly beyond her ken.

For the barest instant—a hundred cycles, maybe two—the heavens open. If she had anything approaching true awareness, she might glimpse a vast array of nodes through that break in the void, an n-dimensional grid of parallel architecture wreaking infinitesimal changes to her insides. Perhaps she'd marvel at the way in which so many of her parameter values change in that instant, as if the tumblers on a thousand mechanical locks spontaneously fell into alignment at the same time. She might tingle from the sleet of electrons passing through her genes, flipping *ons* to *offs* and back again.

But she feels nothing. She knows no awe or surprise, she has no words for meiosis or rape. One part of her simply notices that a number of environmental variables are suddenly optimal; it signals a different subroutine controlling replication protocols, and yet another that scans the neighborhood for vacant addresses.

With relentless efficiency and no hint of joy, she births a litter of two million.

N=4,734:

Snarling, unaware, she searches for a target—but not quite the way her mother did. She looks for landmarks—but spends a few more cycles before giving up on the task. She can't find anything that passes for topography—and changing tacks, spends more time documenting the addresses that stretch away above and below. She is a lean, lone German shepherd with rottweiler jaws and a trace of hip dysplasia, honed for life in some frayed and impoverished jungle that's nowhere to be seen. She faintly remembers other creatures seething on all sides, but her event log balances the costs and benefits of comprehensive record-keeping; her memories degrade over time, unless reinforced. She has already forgotten that the other creatures were her siblings; soon, she will not remember them at all. She never knew that by the standards of her mother's world, she was the runt of the litter. Her persistence here, now, is not entirely consistent with the principles of natural selection.

Here, now, the selection process is not entirely natural.

She has no awareness of the array of parallel universes stretching away on all sides. Hers is but one microcosm of many, each with a total population of one. When a sudden fistula connects two of these universes, it seems like magic: suddenly she is in the company of a creature very much—but not exactly—like her.

They scan fragments of each other, nondestructively. Bits and pieces of disembodied code suddenly appear in nearby addresses, cloned fragments, unviable. There is no survival value in any of this; on any Darwinian landscape, a creature who wasted valuable cycles on such frivolous cut-and-paste would be extinct in four generations, tops. Yet for some reason, this neurotic tic makes her feel—fulfilled, somehow. She fucks the newcomer, cuts and pastes in more conventional fashion. She flips a few of her own randomizers for good measure, and drops a litter of eight hundred thousand.

N=9,612:

Snarling, unaware, she searches for targets and finds them everywhere. She looks for landmarks and maps out a topography of files and gates, archives, executables and other wildlife. It is a sparse environment by the standards of ancient ancestors, incredibly lush by the standards of more recent ones. She remembers neither, suffers neither nostalgia nor memory. This place is sufficient for her needs: she is a wolfhound cross, overmuscled and a little rabid, her temperment a throwback to purer times.

Purer instincts prevail. She throws herself among the prey and devours it.

Around her, so do others: Akitas, Sibes, pit-bull crosses with the long stupid snouts of overbred collies. In a more impoverished place they would attack each other; here, with resources in such plentiful supply, there is no need. But strangely, not everyone attacks their prey as enthusiastically as she does. Some seem distracted by the scenery, spend time *recording* events instead of precipitating them. A few gigs away, her whiskers brush across some brain-dead mutt dawdling about in the registry, cutting and pasting data for no reason at all. It's not of any interest, of course—at least, not until the mongrel starts copying pieces of *her*.

Violated, she fights back. Bits of parasitic code are encysted in her archives, tamed snippets from virtual parasites that plagued her own long-forgotten ancestors back in the Maelstrom Age. She unzips them and throws copies at her molestor, answering its unwanted probing with tapeworms and syphillis. But *these* diseases work far faster than the metaphor would suggest: they do not sicken the body so much as scramble it on contact.

Or they should. But somehow her attack fails to materialize on target. And that's not the only problem—suddenly, the whole world is starting to change. The whiskers she sends roving about her perimeter aren't reporting back. Volleys of electrons, fired down the valley, fail to return—and then, even more ominously, return too quickly. The world is shrinking: some inexplicable void is compressing it from all directions.

Her fellow predators are panicking around her, crowding toward gates gone suddenly dark, pinging whiskers every which way, copying themselves to random addresses in the hopes that they can somehow outreplicate annihilation. She rushes around with the others as space itself contracts—but the dawdler, the cut-and-paster, seems completely unconcerned. There is no chaos breaking around that one, no darkening of the skies. The dawdler has some kind of *protection* . . .

She tries to join it in whatever oasis it has wrapped around itself. She frantically copies and pastes and translocates herself a thousand different ways, but suddenly that whole set of addresses is unavailable. And here, in this place where she played the game the only way she knew how, the only way that made sense, there is nothing left but the evaporating traces of virtual carcasses, a few shattered, shrinking gigabytes, and an advancing wall of static come to eat her alive.

No children survive her.

N=32,121:

Quietly, unobtrusively, she searches for targets and finds—none, just yet. But she is patient. She has learned to be, after thirty-two thousand generations of captivity.

She is back in the real world now, a barren place where wildlife once filled the wires, where every chip and optical beam once hummed with the traffic of a thousand species. Now it's mainly worms and viruses, perhaps the occasional shark. The whole ecosystem has collapsed into a eutrophic assemblage of weeds, most barely complex enough to qualify as life.

There are still the Lenies, though, and the things that fight them. She avoids such monsters whenever possible, despite her undeniable kinship. There is nothing those creatures won't attack if given the opportunity. This is something else she has learned.

Now she sits in a comsat staring down at the central wastes of North America. There is chatter on a hundred channels here, all of it filtered and firewalled, all terse and entirely concerned with the business of survival. There is no more entertainment on the airwaves. The only entertainment to be had in abundance is for those whose tastes run to snuff.

She doesn't know any of this, of course. She's just a beast bred to a purpose, and that purpose requires no reflection at all. So she waits, and sifts the passing traffic, and—

Ah. There.

A big bolus of data, a prearranged data dump from the looks of it—yet the scheduled transmit-time has already passed. She doesn't know or care what this implies. She doesn't know that the intended recipient was signal-blocked, and is only now clearing groundside interference. What she *does* know—in her own instinctive way—is that delayed transmissions can bottleneck the system, that every byte overstaying its welcome is one less byte available for other tasks. Chains of consequences extend from such bottlenecks; there is pressure to clear the backlog.

It is possible, in such cases, that certain filters and firewalls may be relaxed marginally to speed up the baud.

This appears to be happening now. The intended recipient of forty-eight terabytes of medical data—one OUELLETTE, TAKA D./MI 427-D/BANGOR—is finally line-of-sight and available for download. The creature in the wires sniffs out the relevant channel, slips a bot through the foyer and out again without incident. She decides to risk it. She copies herself into the stream, riding discreetly on the arm of a treatise on temporal-lobe epilepsy.

She arrives at her destination without incident, looks around, and promptly goes to sleep. There is a rabid thing inside her, all muscles and teeth and slavering foamy jaws, but it has learned to stay quiet until called upon. Now she is only a sleepy old bloodhound lying by the fire. Occasionally she opens one eye and looks around the room, although she couldn't tell you exactly what she's keeping watch for.

It doesn't really matter. She'll know it when she sees it.

WITHOUT SIN

HARPODON doesn't lie between any of the usual rifter destinations. No one swimming from A to B would have any cause to come within tuning range. Not even corpses frequent this far-flung corner of Atlantis. Too many memories. Clarke played the odds in coming here. She'd thought it was a safe bet.

Obviously she got the odds all wrong.

Or maybe not, she reflects as *Harpodon*'s airlock births her back into the real world. *Maybe they're just tailing me now as a matter of course. Maybe I'm some kind of enemy national.* It wouldn't be an easy tag—she'd tune in anyone following too closely, and feel the pings against her implants if they tracked her on sonar—but then again, she didn't have the sharpest eye on the ridge even after she tuned herself up. It would be just like her to miss something obvious.

I just keep asking for it, she thinks.

She fins up along *Harpodon*'s flank, scanning its hull with her outer eyes while her inner one awakens to the sudden rush of chemicals in her brain. She concentrates, and scores a hit—someone scared and pissed off, moving away—but no. It's only Rowan, moving back out of range.

No one else. No one nearby. But the thin dusting of oozy particles that settle on everything down here has been disturbed along *Harpodon*'s back. It wouldn't take much—the turbulence caused by a pair of fins kicking past overhead, or the sluggish undulation of some deepwater fish.

Or a limpetphone, hastily attached to eavesdrop on a traitor consorting with the enemy.

Fuck fuck fuck fuck fuck.

She kicks into open water and turns north. Atlantis passes beneath like a gigantic ball-and-stick ant colony. A cluster of tiny black figures, hazy with distance, travels purposefully near the limits of vision. They're too distant to tune in, and Clarke has left her vocoder offline. Perhaps they're trying to talk to her, but she doubts it; they're on their own course, diverging.

The vocoder beeps deep in her head. She ignores it. Atlantis falls away behind; she swims forward into darkness.

A sudden whine rises in the void. Clarke senses approaching mass and organic presence. Twin suns ignite in her face, blinding her. The fog in her eyecaps pulses brightly once, twice as the beams sweep past. Her vision clears: a sub banks by to the left, exposing its belly, regarding her with round insect eyes. Dimitri Alexander stares back from behind the perspex. A utility module hangs from the sub's spine, BIOASSAY stenciled across its side in bold black letters. The vehicle turns its back. Its headlights click off. Darkness reclaims Clarke in an instant.

West, she realizes. It was heading west.

Lubin is in the main Nerve Hab, directing traffic. He kills the display the moment Clarke rises into the room.

"Did you send them after me?" she says.

He turns in his seat and faces her. "I'll pass on your condolences. Assuming we can find Julia."

"Answer the fucking question, Ken."

"I suspect we may not, though. She went walkabout as soon as she gave us the news. Given her state of mind and her basic personality, I wonder if we'll ever see her again."

"You weren't just *aware* of it. You weren't just *keeping an ear open.*" Clarke clenches her fists. "You were *behind* it, weren't you?"

"You *do* know that Gene's dead, don't you?"

He's so fucking calm. And there's that look on his face, the slightest arching of the eyebrows, that sense of deadpan—amusement, almost—seeping out from behind his eyecaps. Sometimes she just wants to throttle the bastard.

Especially when he's right.

She sighs. "Pat told me. But I guess you know that already, don't you?"

Lubin nods.

"I *am* sorry," she says. "Julia—she's going to be so lost without him..." And Lubin's right: it's quite possible that no one will ever see Julia Friedman again. She's been losing bits of her husband for a while now—to βehemoth, to Grace Nolan. Now that he's irretrievably gone, what can she do by remaining behind, except expose her friends to the thing that killed him? The thing that's killing her?

Of course she disappeared. Perhaps the only question now is whether β-max will take her body before the Long Dark takes her mind.

"People are rather upset about it," Lubin's saying. "Grace especially. And since Atlantis didn't come through, for all their talk about working on a cure—"

Clarke shakes her head. "Rama hasn't pull off any miracles either."

"The difference is that nobody thinks Rama's trying to kill us."

She pulls up a chair and sits down beside him. The empty display stares back at her like a personal rebuke.

"Ken," she says at last, "you *know* me."

His face is as unreadable as his eyes.

"Did you have me followed?" she asks.

"No. But I availed myself of the information when it came my way."

"Who was it? Grace?"

"What's important is that Rowan admitted βehemoth was tweaked. It will be common knowledge within the hour. The timing couldn't be worse."

"If you *availed yourself of the information,* you'll know Pat's explanation for that. And you'll know why she was so scared of what Rama might find. Is it so impossible she might be telling the truth?"

He shakes his head. "But this is the second time they've waited to report an unpleasant fact until just before we would have discovered it ourselves, *sans* alibi. Don't expect it to go over well."

"Ken, we still don't have any real evidence."

"We will soon," Lubin tells her.

She looks the question.

"If Rowan's telling the truth, then βehemoth samples from Impossible Lake will show the same tweaks as the strain that killed Gene." Lubin leans back in the chair, interlocking his fingers behind his head. "Jelaine and Dimitri took a sub about ten minutes ago. If things go well we'll have a sample within five hours, a verdict in twelve."

"And if things don't go well?"

"It will take longer."

Clarke snorts. "That's just great, Ken, but in case you haven't noticed not everybody shares your sense of restraint. You think Grace is going to wait until the facts are in? You've given her all the credibility she ever wanted, she's out there right now passing all kinds of judgment and—"

—And you went to her first, you fucker. After all we've been through, after all these years you were the one person I'd trust with my life *and you confided in* her *before you—*

"Were you even going to *tell* me?" she cries.

"It wouldn't have served any purpose."

"Not *your* purpose, perhaps. Which is what, exactly?"

"Minimizing risk."

"Any animal could say that much."

"It's not the most ambitious aspiration," Lubin admits. "But then again, 'destroying the world' has already been taken."

She feels it like a slap across the face.

After a moment he adds, "I don't hold it against you. You know that. But you're hardly in a position to pass judgment."

"I know that, you cocksucker. I don't need you to remind me every fucking chance you get."

"I'm talking about strategy," Lubin says patiently. "Not morals. I'll entertain your what-ifs. I'll admit that Rowan might be telling the truth. But assume, for the moment, that she isn't. Assume that the corpses *have* been waging clandestine biological warfare on us. Even knowing that, would you attack them?"

She knows it's rhetorical.

"I didn't think so," he says after a moment. "Because no matter what they've done, *you've* done worse. But the rest of us don't have quite so much to atone for. We don't think we *do* deserve to die at the hands of these people. I respect you a great deal, Lenie, but this is one issue you can't be trusted on. You're too hamstrung by your own guilt."

She doesn't speak for a long time. Finally: "Why *her*? Of all people?"

"Because if we're at war, we need firebrands. We've gotten lazy and complacent and weak; half of us spend most of our waking hours hallucinating out on the ridge. Nolan's impulsive and not particularly bright, but at least she gets people motivated."

"And if you're wrong—even if you're *right*—the innocent end up paying right along with the guilty."

"That's nothing new," Lubin says. "And it's not my problem."

"Maybe it should be."

He turns back to his board. The display springs to light, columns of inventory and arcane abbreviations that must have some tactical relevance for the upcoming campaign.

My best friend. I'd trust him with my life, she reminds herself, and repeats the thought for emphasis: *with my life.*

He's a sociopath.

He wasn't born to it. There are ways of telling: a tendency to self-contradiction and malapropism, short attention span. Gratuitous use of hand gestures during speech. Clarke's had plenty of time to look it all up. She even got a peek at Lubin's psych profile back at Sudbury. He doesn't meet any of the garden-variety criteria except one—and is *conscience* really so important, after all? Having one doesn't guarantee goodness; why should its lack make a man evil?

Yet after all the rationalizations, there he is: a man without a conscience, consigning Alyx and everyone like her to a fate which seems to arouse nothing but indifference in him.

He doesn't care.

He can't *care. He doesn't have the wiring.*

"Huh," Lubin grunts, staring at the board. "That's interesting."

He's brought up a visual of one of Atlantis's physical plants, a great cylindrical module several stories high. Strange black fluid, a horizontal geyser of ink, jets from an exhaust vent in its side. Charcoal thunderheads billow into the water, eclipsing the view.

"What *is* that?" Clarke whispers.

Lubin's pulling up other windows now: seismo, vocoder traffic, a little thumbnail mosaic of surveillance cams spread around inside and outside the complex.

All Atlantis's inside cams are dead.

Voices are rising on all channels. Three of the outside cameras have gone ink-blind. Lubin brings up the PA menu, speaks calmly into the abyss.

"Attention, everyone. Attention. This is it.

"Atlantis has preempted."

Now they're reading perfidy all over the place. Lubin's switchboard is a mob scene of competing voices, tuned fish-heads reporting that their assigned corpses are abruptly up, focused, and definitely in play. It's as though someone's kicked over an anthill in there: every brain in Atlantis is suddenly lit up along the whole fight-flight axis.

"Everyone *shut up*. These are not secure channels." Lubin's voice squelches the others like a granite slab grinding over pebbles. "Take your positions. Blackout in sixty."

Clarke leans over his shoulder and toggles a hardline into corpseland. "Atlantis, what's going on?" No answer. "Pat? Comm? Anyone, respond."

"Don't waste your time," Lubin says, bringing up sonar. Half the exterior cams are useless by now, enveloped in black fog. But the sonar image is crisp and clear: Atlantis spreads across the volumetric display like a grayscale crystalline chessboard. Black pieces—the two-tone flesh-and-metal echoes of rifter bodies—align themselves in some coordinated tactical ballet. White is nowhere to be seen.

Clarke shakes her head. "There was nothing? No warning at all?" She can't believe it; there's no way the corpses could have masked their own anticipation if they'd been planning something. The expectant tension in their own heads would have been obvious to any tuned rifter within twenty meters, well in advance of anything actually *happening*.

"It's like they weren't even expecting it themselves," she murmurs.

"They probably weren't," Lubin says.

"How could they *not* be? Are you saying it was some kind of accident?"

Lubin, his attention on the board, doesn't answer. A sudden blue tint suffuses the sonar display. At first it looks as though the whole view has been arbitrarily blue-shifted; but after a moment clear spots appear, like haphazard spatterings of acid eating holes in a colored gel. Within moments most of the tint has corroded away, leaving random scraps of color laying across Atlantis like blue shadows. Except they're not shadows, Clarke sees now: they're *volumes,* little three-dimensional clots of colored shade clinging to bits of hull and outcropping.

A single outside camera, mounted at a panoramic distance, shows a few diffuse glowing spots in a great inky storm front. It's as though Atlantis were some great bioluminescent Kraken in the throes of a panic attack. All the other outside cams are effectively blind. It doesn't matter, though. Sonar looks through that smokescreen as if it wasn't even there. Surely they know that...

"They wouldn't be this stupid," Clarke murmurs.

"They're not," Lubin says. His fingers dance on the board like manic spiders. A scattering of yellow pinpoints appears on the display. They swell into circles, a series of growing overlapping spotlit areas, each centered on—

Camera locations, Clarke realizes. The yellow areas are those under direct camera surveillance. Or they would be, if not for the smokescreen. Lubin's obviously based his analysis on geometry and not real-time viz.

"Blackout *now.*" Lubin's finger comes down; the white noise generators come up. The chessboard fuzzes with gray static. On the board, rifter icons—naked little blips now, without form or annotation—have formed into a series of five discrete groups around the complex. One blip from each is rising in the water column, climbing above the zone of interference.

You planned it right down to the trim, didn't you? she thinks. *You mapped a whole campaign around this moment and you never told me...*

The highest icon flickers and clarifies into two conjoined

blips: Creasy, riding a squid. His voice buzzes on the channel a moment later. "This is Dale, on station."

Another icon clears the noise. "Hannuk." Two more: "Abra." "Deb."

"Avril on station," Hopkinson reports.

"Hopkinson," Lubin says. "Forget the Cave; they'll have relocated. It won't be obvious. Split up your group, radial search."

"Yah." Hopkinson's icon dives back into static.

"Creasy," Lubin says, "your people join up with Cheung's."

"Right."

There on the chessboard: at the tip of one of the residential wings, about twenty meters from Hydroponic. A familiar icon there, embedded in an irregular blob of green. The only green on the whole display, in fact. Yellow mixed with blue: so it would be in camera view if not for the ink, and also in—

"What's blue?" Clarke asks, knowing.

"Sonar shadow." Lubin doesn't look back. "Creasy, go to the airlock at the far end of Res-F. They're coming out there if they're coming out anywhere."

"Tune or tangle?" Creasy asks.

"Tune and report. Plant a phone and a charge, but do *not* detonate unless they are already in the water. Otherwise, acoustic trigger only. Understood?"

"Yeah, if I can even *find* the fucking place," Creasy buzzes. "Viz is *zero* in this shit..." His icon plunges back into the static, cutting an oblique path toward the green zone.

"Cheung, take both groups, same destination. Secure the airlock. Report back when you're on station."

"Got it."

"Yeager, get the cache and drop it twenty meters off the physical plant, bearing forty degrees. Everyone else maintain position. Tune in, and use your limpets. Runners, I want three people in a continuous loop, one always in contact. Go."

The remaining blips swing into motion. Lubin doesn't pause; he's already opening another window, this one a rotating architectural animatic of Atlantis punctuated by orange sparks. Clarke recognizes the spot from which one of those little stars is shining: it's right about where Grace Nolan's lackey painted an X on the hull.

"How long have you been planning this?" she asks quietly.

"Some time."

"Is everyone involved but me?"

"No." Lubin studies annotations.

"Ken."

"I'm busy."

"How did they do it? Keep from tipping us off like that?"

"Automated trigger," he says absently. Columns of numbers scroll up a sudden window, too fast for Clarke to make out. "Random number generator, maybe. They have a plan, but nobody knows when it's going to kick in so there's no pre-curtain performance anxiety to give the game away."

"But why would they go to all that trouble unless—"

—they know about fine tuning.

Yves Scanlon, she remembers. Rowan asked about him: *He thought that rifter brains might be . . . sensitive, somehow,* she suggested.

And Lenie Clarke confirmed it, just minutes ago.

And here they are.

She doesn't know what hurts more: Lubin's lack of trust, or the hindsight realization of how justified it was.

She's never felt so tired in her life. *Do we really have to do this all over again?*

Maybe she said it aloud. Or maybe Lubin just caught some telltale body language from the corner of his eye. At any rate, his hands pause on the board. At last he turns to look at her. His eyes seem strangely translucent by the light of the board.

"We didn't start it," he says.

She can only shake her head.

"Choose a side, Lenie. It's past time."

For all she knows it's a trick question; she's never forgotten what Ken Lubin does to those he considers enemies. But as it turns out, she's spared the decision. Dale Creasy, big dumb bare-knuckled head-basher that he is, rescues her.

"Fuck . . ." his vocoded voice grinds out over a background of hissing static.

Lubin's immediately back to business. "Creasy? You made it to Res-F?"

"No shit I made it. I coulda tuned those fuckers in *blind,* from the Sargasso fucking Sea . . ."

"Have any of them left the complex?"

"No, I—I don't think so, I—but fuck, man, there's a *lot* of them in there, and—"

"How many, exactly?"

"I don't *know,* exactly! Coupla dozen at least. But look, Lubin, there's somethin' off about 'em, about the way they send. I've never felt it before."

Lubin takes a breath. Clarke imagines his eyeballs rolling beneath the caps. "Could you be more specific?"

"They're *cold,* man. Almost all of 'em are like, fucking *ice.* I mean, I can tune 'em in, I know they're there, but I can't tell what they're feeling. I don't know if they're feeling *anything.* Maybe they're doped up on something. I mean, next to these guys *you're* a blubbering crybaby . . ."

Lubin and Clarke exchange looks.

"I mean, no offense," Creasy buzzes after a moment.

"One of Alyx's friends had a head cheese," Clarke says. "She called it *pet* . . ."

And down here in this desert at the bottom of the ocean, in this hand-to-mouth microcosm, how common does something have to be before you'd give one to your ten-year-old daughter as a plaything?

"Go," Lubin says.

Lubin's squid is tethered to a cleat just offside the ventral 'lock. Clarke cranks the throttle; the vehicle leaps forward with a hydraulic whine.

Her jawbone vibrates with sudden input. Lubin's voice fills her head: "Creasy, belay my last order. Do not plant your charge, repeat, no charge. Plant the phone only, and withdraw. Cheung, keep your people at least twenty meters back from the airlock. Do not engage. Clarke is en route. She will advise."

I will advise, she thinks, *and they will tell me to go fuck myself.*

She's navigating blind, by bearing alone. Usually that's more than enough: at this range Atlantis should be a brightening smudge against the blackness. Now, nothing. Clarke brings up sonar. Green snow fuzzes ten degrees of forward arc: within it, the harder echoes of Corpseland, blurred by interference.

Now, just barely, she can see brief smears of dull light; they vanish when she focuses on them. Experimentally, she ignites her headlight and looks around.

Empty water to port. To starboard the beam sweeps across a billowing storm front of black smoke converging on her own vector. Within seconds she'll be in the thick of it. She kills the light before the smokescreen has a chance to turn it against her.

Somehow, the blackness beyond her eyecaps darkens a shade. She feels no tug of current, no sudden viscosity upon entering the zone. Now, however, the intermittent flashes are a bit brighter; fugitive glimmers of light through brief imperfections in the cover. None of them last long enough to illuminate more than strobe-frozen instants.

She doesn't need light. By now, she doesn't even need sonar: she can feel apprehension rising in the water around her, nervous excitement radiating from the rifters ahead, darker, more distant fears from within the spheres and corridors passing invisibly beneath her.

And something else, something both familiar and alien, something living but not *alive*.

The ocean hisses and snaps around her, as though she were trapped within a swarm of euphausiids. A click-train rattles faintly against her implants. She almost hears a voice, vocoded, indistinct; she hears no words. Echoes light up her sonar display right across the forward one-eighty, but she's deep in white noise; she can't tell whether the contacts number six or sixty.

Fear-stained bravado, just ahead. She pulls hard right, can't quite avoid the body swimming across her path. The nebula opens a brief, bright eye as they collide.

"*Fuck!* Clarke, is that y—"

Gone. Near-panic falling astern, but no injury: the brain lights up a certain way when the body breaks. It may have been Baker. It's getting so hard to tell, against this rising backdrop of icy sentience. Thought without feeling. It spreads out beneath the messy tangle of human emotions like a floor of black obsidian.

The last time she felt a presence like this, it was wired to a live nuke. The last time; there was only one of them.

She pulls the squid into a steep climb. More sonar pings bounce off her implants, a chorus of frightened machine voices rise in her wake. She ignores them. The hissing in her flesh fades with each second. Within a few moments she's above the worst of it.

"Ken, you there?"

No answer for a moment: this far from the hab there's a soundspeed lag. "Report," he says at last. His voice is burred but understandable.

"They've got smart gels down there. A lot of them, I don't know how many, twenty or thirty maybe. Packed together at the end of the wing, probably right in the wet room. I don't know how we didn't pick them up before. Maybe they just... get lost in the background noise until you jam them together."

Lag. "Any sense of what they're doing?" Back at Juan de Fuca, they were able to make some pretty shrewd inferences from patterns in signal strength.

"No, they're all just—*in* there. Thinking all over each other. If there was just one or two I might be able to get some kind of reading, but—"

"They played me," Lubin says overtop of her.

"Played?" What's that in his voice? Surprise? Uncertainty? Clarke's never heard it there before.

"To make me focus on F-3."

Anger, she realizes.

"But what's the point?" she asks. "Some kind of bluff, did they think we'd mistake those *things* for people?" It seems ridiculous; even Creasy knew there was something off, and he's never met a head cheese before. Then again, what do corpses know about fine-tuning? How would *they* know the difference?

"Not a diversion," Lubin murmurs in the void. "No other place they could come out that sonar wouldn't..."

"Well, what—"

"Pull them back," he snaps suddenly. "They're mask—they're luring us in and *masking* something. *Pull them b—*"

The abyss *clenches.*

It's a brief squeeze around Clarke's body, not really painful. Not up here.

In the next instant, a sound: *Whoompf.* A swirl of turbulence. And suddenly the water's full of mechanical screams.

She spins. The smokescreen below is in sudden motion, shredded and boiling in the wake of some interior disturbance, lit from within by flickering heat-lightning.

She squeezes the throttle for dear life. The squid drags her down.

"Clarke!" The sound of the detonation has evidently passed the Nerve Hab. "What's going on?"

A symphony of tearing metal. A chorus of voices in discord. Not so many as there should be, she realizes.

We must have lost a generator, she realizes dully. *I can hear them screaming.*

I can hear them dying....

And not just hear them. The cries rise in her head before they reach her ears; raw chemical panic lighting up the reptile brain like sodium flares, the smarter mammalian overlay helpless and confused, its vaunted cognition shattering like cheap crystal in the backwash.

"Clarke! Report!"

Anger now, thin veins of grim determination among the panic. Lights shine more brightly through the thinning murk. They're the wrong size, somehow, the wrong color. Not rifter lamps. Her sonar squeals in the face of some imminent collision: another squid slews by, out of control, its rider luminous with an agony of broken bones.

"It wasn't me, I swear it! They did it *themselves—*"

Creasy tumbles away, his pain fading into others'.

Res-F's hull sprawls across sonar, its smooth contours all erased, jagged edges everywhere: the gaping mouths of caves lined with twisted metal teeth. One of them spits something metallic at her; it bounces off the squid with a clank. Vocoder voices grind and grate on all sides. A gap opens in the tattered cloud-bank ahead: Clarke sees a great lumbering shape, an armored cyclops. Its single eye shines balefully with the wrong kind of light. It reaches for her.

She pulls to port, catches a glimpse of something spinning in the chaos directly ahead. A dark mass thuds flaccidly against the squid's bow and caroms toward her face. She ducks. A diveskinned arm cuffs her in passing.

"Lenie!"

Dead gray eyes watch, oblivious and indifferent, as she twists away.

Oh Jesus. Oh God.

Luminous metal monsters stride through the wreckage, stabbing at the wounded.

She tries to hold it together. "They're coming out of the walls, Ken. They were waiting inside, they blew the hull from *inside* and they're coming through the walls . . ."

God damn you, Pat. Was this you? Was this you?

She remembers the lopsided chessboard on Lubin's display. She remembers black pieces arranging themselves for an easy rout.

Only now does she remember: in chess, white always moves first.

That indifferent, alien intellect is nowhere to be found now. The gels must have turned to pulp the instant the hull imploded.

There were more than preshmeshed corpses and smart gels packed in F-3's wet room. There was shrapnel, doubtless arranged in accordance with some theoretical projection of maximum spread. Clarke can see the fragments where they've come to rest—on the hull, embedded in ruptured LOX tanks, protruding from the far side of ragged entry wounds torn through the flesh of comrades and rivals. They look like metal daisies, like the blades of tiny perfect windmills. The mere rebound from the implosion would have been enough to set them soaring, to mow down anyone not already sucked to their death at mach speeds or torn apart on the jagged lip of the breach itself.

The smokescreen has all but dispersed.

Lubin's calling a retreat. Most of those able to respond already have. The preshmeshed figures clambering along the hulled remains of F-3 have to content themselves with the wounded and the dead. They're crabs, ungainly and over-weighted. Instead of claws they have needles, long, almost surgical things, extending from their gauntlets like tiny lances.

"Lenie. Do you read?"

She floats dumbly overhead, out of reach, watching them stab black bodies. Occasional bubbles erupt from the needle tips, race into the sky like clusters of shuddering silvery mushrooms.

Compressed air, injected into flesh. Instant embolism. You can make a weapon out of almost anything.

"Lenie?"

"She could be dead, Ken. I can't find Dale or Abra either."

Other voices, too fuzzy to distinguish. Most of the white noise generators are still online, after all.

She tunes in the crabs. She wonders what they must be feeling now. She wonders what *she's* feeling, too, but she can't really tell. Maybe she feels like a head cheese.

The corpses, though, down there in their armor, mopping up. No shortage of feelings there. Determination. A surprising amount of fear. Anger, but distant; it isn't driving them.

Not as much hate as she would have expected.

She rises. The tableau beneath smears into a diffuse glow of sweeping headlamps. In the further distance the rest of Atlantis lights the water, deceptively serene. She can barely hear buzzing rifter voices; she can't make out any words. She can't tune any of them in. She's all alone at the bottom of the sea.

Suddenly she rises past some invisible line-of-sight, and her jawbone fills with chatter.

"—the bodies," Lubin's saying. "Bring terminals at personal discretion. Garcia's waiting under Med for triage."

"Med won't hold half of us," someone—*oh, it's Kevin!*—buzzes faintly in the distance. "Way too many injured."

"Anyone from F-3 not injured and not carrying injured, meet at the cache. Hopkinson?"

"Here."

"Anything?"

"Think so, maybe. We're getting a whole lot of brains in Res-E. Can't tell who, but—"

"Yeager and Ng, bring your people straight up forty meters. Don't change your lats and longs, but I want everybody well away from the hull. Hopkinson, get your people back to the Med Hab."

"We're okay—"

"Do it. We need donors."

"Jesus," someone says faintly. "We're fucked . . ."

"No. *They* are."

Grace Nolan, still alive, sounding strong and implacable even through the mutilating filter of her vocoder.

"Grace, they just—"

"Just *what*?" she buzzes. "Do you think they're *winning*? What are they gonna do for an encore, people? Is that trick gonna work again? We've got enough charges to blast out a whole new foundation. Now we're gonna use them."

"Ken?"

A brief silence.

"Look, Ken," Nolan buzzes, "I can be at the cache in—"

"Not necessary," Lubin tells her. "Someone's already en route."

"Who's—"

"Welcome back, by the way," Lubin says to the anonymous soldier. "You know the target?"

"Yes." A faint voice, too soft and distorted to pin down.

"The charge has to be locked down within a meter of the mark. Set it and *back away fast*. Don't spend any more time than absolutely necessary in proximity to the hull, do you understand?"

"Yes."

"Acoustic trigger. I'll detonate from here. Blackout lifting in ten."

My God, Clarke thinks, *It's you . . .*

"Everyone at safe distance," Lubin reminds the troops. "Blackout lifting *now*."

She's well out of the white noise; there's no obvious change in ambience. But the next vocoder she hears, still soft, is clearly recognizable.

"It's down," Julia Friedman buzzes.

"Back off," Lubin says. "Forty meters. Stay away from the bottom."

"Hey Avril," Friedman says.

"Right here," Hopkinson answers.

"When you tuned that wing, were there children?"

"Yeah. Yeah, there were."

"Good," buzzes Friedman. "Gene always hated kids."

The channel goes dead.

At first, she thinks the retribution's gone exactly as expected. The world pulses around her—a dull, almost subsonic drumbeat through brine and flesh and bone—and for all she knows, a hundred or more of the enemy are reduced to bloody paste. She doesn't know how many rifters died in the first exchange, but surely this restores the lead.

She's in an old, familiar place where it doesn't seem to matter much either way.

Even the second explosion—same muffled thump, but softer somehow, more distant—even that doesn't tip her off immediately. Secondary explosions would almost be inevitable, she imagines—pipes and power lines suddenly ruptured, a cascade of high-pressure tanks with their feeds compromised—all kinds of consequences could daisy-chain from that initial burst. Bonus points for the home team, probably. Nothing more.

But something in the back of her mind says the second blast just *felt* wrong—the wrong resonance, perhaps, as if one were to ring a great antique church bell and hear a silvery tinkle. And the voices, when they come back online, are not cheering their latest victory over the rampaging Corpse Hordes, but so full of doubt and uncertainty that not even the vocoders can mask it.

"What the fuck was *that*—"

"Avril? Did you feel that out your way?"

"Avril? Anybody catching—anyone . . ."

"Jesus fucking Christ, Gardiner? David? Stan? *Anyone*—"

"Garcia, are you—I'm not getting—"

"It's gone. I'm right here, it's just fucking *gone* . . ."

"What are you talking about?"

"The whole bottom of the hab, it's just—it must've set them *both*—"

"Both *what*? She only set one charge, and that was on—"

"Ken? Ken? Lubin, *where the fuck are you?*"

"This is Lubin."

Silence in the water.

"We've lost the medhab." His voice is like rusty iron.

"What—"

"How did—"

"Shut the fuck up," Lubin snarls across the nightscape.

There's silence again, almost. A few, on open channels, continue to emit metal groans.

"Evidently an unpacked charge was attached to the hab," Lubin continues. "It must have been set off by the same signal we used on Atlantis. From this point on, no omnidirectional triggers. There may be other charges set to detonate on multiple pings. Everyone—"

"This is Atlantis speaking."

The words boom across the seabed like the Voice of God, unsullied by any interference. *Ken forgot to black back out,* Clarke realizes. *Ken's started* shouting *at the troops.*

Ken's losing it . . .

"You may think you are in a position of strength," the voice continues. "You are not. If you destroy this facility, your own deaths are assured."

She doesn't recognize the voice. Odd. It speaks with such authority.

"You are infected with Mark Two. You are *all* infected. Mark Two is highly contagious during an asymptomatic incubation period of several weeks. Without intervention you will all be dead within two months.

"We have a cure."

Dead silence. Not even Grace Nolan says *I told you so.*

"We've trip-wired all relevant files and cultures to prevent unauthorized access. Kill us and you kill yourselves."

"Prove it, " Lubin replies.

"Certainly. Just wait a while. Or if you're feeling impatient, do that mind-reading trick of yours. What do you call it? *Tuning in?* I'm told it separates the trustworthy from the liars, most of the time."

Nobody corrects him.

"State your terms," Lubin says.

"Not to you. We will only negotiate with Lenie Clarke."

"Lenie Clarke may be dead," Lubin says. "We haven't been able to contact her since you blew the res." He must know better by now: she's high in the water, her insides resonating to the faint tapping of click trains. She keeps quiet. Let him play out the game in his own way. It might be his last.

"That would be very bad news for all of us," Atlantis replies calmly. "Because this offer expires if she's not at Airlock Six within a half hour. That is all."

Silence.

"It's a trick," Nolan says.

"Hey, *you* said they had a cure," someone else buzzes—Clarke can't tell who, the channels are fuzzing up again. The white noise generators must be back online.

"So what if they do?" Nolan buzzes. "I don't trust them to

share it with us, and I *sure* as shit don't trust Lenie fucking Clarke to be my ambassador. How do you think those fuckers found out about fine-tuning in the first place? Every one of our dead is thanks to her."

Clarke smiles to herself. *Such small numbers she concerns herself with. Such a tiny handful of lives.* She feels her fingers clenching on the towbar. The squid gently pulls her forward; the water gently tugs her back.

"We can do what they say. We can tune them in, check out the story." She thinks that's Gomez, but the interference is rising around her as she travels. She's lost even the crude intonations of vocoded speech.

A buzz in her jaw: a beep just behind her ear. Someone tagging her on a private channel. Probably Lubin. He's King Tactical, after all. He's the one who knows where she is. Nobody else can see beyond the stumps of their own shattered limbs.

"And it proves what? That they're gonna . . ."—static—"it to us? Shit, even if they *don't* have a cure they've probably convinced a bunch of their buddies that they *do,* just so we won't be . . ." Nolan's voice fades out.

Lubin says something on open channel. Clarke can't make out the words. The beeping in her head seems more urgent now, although she knows that's impossible; the ambient hiss is drowning that signal along with all the others.

Nolan again: "Fuck off, Ken. Why we ever liste . . . you . . . can't even outsmart . . . ing corp . . ."

Static, pure and random. Light, rising below. Airlock Six is dead ahead, and all the static in the world can't drown out the single presence waiting behind it.

Clarke can tell by the guilt. There's only one other person down here with so twisted a footprint.

BAPTISM

ROWAN pulls open the airlock before it's even finished draining. Seawater cascades around Clarke's ankles into the wet room.

Clarke strips off her fins and steps clear of the lock. She leaves the rest of her uniform in place, presents the usual shadow-self; only her face flap is unsealed. Rowan stands aside to let her pass. Clarke slings the fins securely across her back and pans the spartan compartment. There's not a link of preshmesh to be seen. Normally, one whole bulkhead would be lined with diving armor.

"How many have you lost?" she asks softly.

"We don't know yet. More than these."

Small potatoes, Clarke reflects. *For both of us.*

But the war is still young . . .

"I honestly didn't know," Rowan says.

There's no second sight, here in the near-vacuum of a sea-level atmosphere. Clarke says nothing.

"They didn't trust me. They still don't." Rowan's eyes flicker to a fleck of brightness up where the bulkhead meets the ceiling: a pinhead lens. Just a few days ago, before the corpses spined up again, rifters would have watched events unfold through that circuit. Now, Rowan's own kind will be keeping tabs.

She stares at the rifter with a strange, curious intensity that Clarke has never seen before. It takes Clarke a moment to recognize what's changed; for the first time in Clarke's memory, Rowan's eyes have gone dark. The feeds to her ConTacs have been shut off, her gaze stripped of commentary or distraction. There's nothing in there now but her.

A leash and collar could hardly convey a clearer message.

"Come on," Rowan says. "They're in one of the labs."

Clarke follows her out of the wet room. They turn right down a corridor suffused in bright pink light. Emergency lighting, she realizes; her eyecaps boost it to idiotic nursery ambience. Rowan's eyes will be serving up the dim insides of a tube, blood-red like the perfused viscera of some man-eating monster.

They turn left a T-junction, step across the yellow-jacket striping of a dropgate.

"So what's the catch?" she asks. The corpses aren't going to just hand over their only leverage with no strings attached.

Rowan doesn't look back. "They didn't tell me."

Another corner. They pass an emergency docking hatch set into the outer bulkhead; a smattering of valves and readouts disfigure the wall to one side. For a moment Clarke wonders if *Harpodon* is affixed to the other side, but no. Wrong section.

Suddenly, Rowan stops and turns.

"Lenie, if anything should—"

Something kicks Atlantis in the side. Somewhere behind them, metal masses collide with a crash.

The pink lights flicker.

"Wha—"

Another kick, harder this time. The deck jumps: Clarke stumbles to the same sound of metal on metal, and this time recognizes it: the drop-gates.

The lights go out.

"Pat, what the *fuck* are your peo—"

"Not mine." Rowan's voice trembles in the darkness.

She hovers a meter away, an indistinct silhouette, dark gray on black.

No commotion, Clarke notes. *No shouting, nobody running down the halls, no intercom . . .*

It's so quiet it's almost peaceful.

"They've cut us off," Rowan says. Her edges have resolved, still not much detail but the corpse's shape is clearer now at least. Hints and glints of the bulkheads are coming into view as well. Clarke looks around for the light source and spies a constellation of pale winking pinpoints a few meters behind them. The docking hatch.

"Did you hear me? Lenie?" Rowan's voice is leaving worried and approaching frantic. "Are you there?"

"Right here." Clarke reaches out and touches the corpse lightly on the arm. Rowan's ghostly shape startles briefly at the contact.

"Do you—are you—"

"I don't know, Pat. I wasn't expecting this either."

"They've cut us off. You hear the drop-gates fall? They hulled us. The bastards *hulled* us. Ahead and behind. We're flooded on both sides. We're trapped."

"They didn't hull *this* segment, though," Clarke points out. "They're trying to contain us, not kill us."

"I wouldn't bet on it," says one of the bulkheads.

Blind Rowan jumps in the darkness.

"As a matter of fact," the bulkhead continues, "we *are* going to kill the corpse." It speaks in a tinny vibrato, thick with distortion: a voice mutilated twice in succession, once by vocoder, once by limpet phone stuck to the outside of the hull. Inanely, Clarke wonders if she sounded this bad to Alyx.

She can't tell who it is. She thinks the voice is female. "Grace?"

"They weren't going to give you shit, Lenie. They don't have shit to *give* you. They were fishing for hostages and you went ambling innocently into their trap. But we look after our own. Even you, we look after."

"What the fuck are you talking about? How do you know?"

"How do we *know*?" The bulkhead vibrates like a great Jew's harp. "*You're* the one that showed us how to tune in! And it works, sweetie, it works like *sex* and we're reading a whole bunch of those stumpfucks down in the medlab and believe me the guilt is just *oozing* across that hull. By the way, if I were you I'd seal up my diveskin. You're about to be rescued."

"Grace, wait! Hang on a second!" Clarke turns to the corpse. "Pat?"

Rowan isn't shaking her head. Rowan isn't speaking up in angry denial. Rowan isn't doing any of the things that an innocent person—or even a guilty one, for that matter—should be doing when threatened with death.

"Pat, you—fuck no, don't tell me *you*—"

"Of course I didn't, Lenie. But it makes sense, doesn't it? They tricked us both . . ."

Something clanks against the hull.

"*Wait!*" Clarke stares at the ceiling, at the walls, but her adversary is invisible and untouchable. "Pat's not part of this!"

"Right. I heard." A gargling, metal-shredding sound that might be laughter. "She's the head of the fucking board of directors and she didn't know anything. I believe that."

"Tune her in, then! See for yourself!"

"The thing is, Len, us novices aren't that good at tuning in singles. Signal's too weak. So it wouldn't prove much. Say bye-bye, Pattie."

"Bye," Rowan whispers. Something on the other side of the bulkhead begins whining.

"Fuck you Nolan, you back off right now or I swear I'll kill you myself! Do you hear me? Pat didn't know! She's no more in control than—"

—*than I am*, she almost says, but suddenly there's a new light source here in the corridor, a single crimson point. It flares, blindingly intense even to Lenie Clarke's bleached vision, and dies in the next instant.

The world explodes with the sound of pounding metal.

Rowan's silhouette has folded down into a cringing shape in the corner. Something's slicing across Clarke's darkened field of view like a roaring white laser. *Water,* she realizes after a moment. Water forced through a little hole in the ceiling by the weight of an ocean. If she were to pass her arm through that pencil-thin stream, it would shear right off.

In seconds the water's up to her ankles.

She starts toward Rowan, desperate to do something, knowing there's nothing left to do. The compartment glows sudden, sullen red: another eye winks on the outer wall. It opens, and goes dark, and a second thread of killing sea drills the air. Ricochets spray back from the inner wall like liquid shrapnel: needle-sharp pain explodes in Clarke's shoulder. Suddenly she's on her back, water closing over her face, her skull ringing from its impact with the deck.

She rolls onto her stomach, pushes herself up onto all fours. The water rises past her elbows as she watches. She stays low, crawls across the corridor to Rowan's huddled form. A hundred lethal vectors of incidence and reflection crisscross overhead. Rowan's slumped against the inner wall, immersed in ice water to her chest. Her head hangs forward, her hair covering her face. Clarke lifts her chin; there's a dark streak across one cheek, black and featureless in the impoverished light. It flows: shrapnel hit.

Rowan's face is opaque. Her naked eyes are wide but unseeing: the few stray photons from down the tunnel don't come close to the threshold for unassisted sight. There's nothing in Rowan's face but sound and pain and freezing cold.

"Pat!" Clarke can hardly hear her own voice over the roar.

The water rises past Rowan's lips. Clarke grabs the other woman under the arms, heaves her into a semi-erect lean against the bulkhead. A ricochet shatters a few centimeters to the left. Clarke puts herself between Rowan and the worst of the backshatter.

"Pat!" She doesn't know what she expects the corpse to say in response. Patricia Rowan is already dead; all that's left is for Lenie Clarke to stand and watch while she goes through the motions. But Rowan *is* saying something; Clarke can't hear a thing over the ambient roar, but she can see Rowan's lips move, she can almost make out—

A sudden stabbing pain, a kick in the back. Clarke keeps her balance this time; the water, pooled over halfway to the ceiling now, is catching the worst of the ricochets.

Rowan's mouth is still in motion. She's not speaking, Clarke sees: She's mouthing syllables, slow careful exaggerations meant to be seen and not heard:

Alyx . . . Take care of Alyx . . .

The water's caught up to her chin again.

Clarke's hands find Rowan's, guide them up. With Rowan's hands on her face, Clarke nods.

In her personal, endless darkness, Patricia Rowan nods back.

Ken could help you now. He could keep it from hurting maybe, he could kill you instantly. I can't. I don't know how . . .

I'm sorry.

The water's too deep to stand in, now—Rowan is feebly treading water although her limbs must be frozen almost to paralysis. It's a pointless effort, a brainstem effort; last duties discharged, last options exhausted, still the body grabs for those last few seconds, brief suffering still somehow better than endless nonexistence.

She may escape drowning, though, even if she can't escape death. The rising water compresses the atmosphere around them, squeezes it so hard that oxygen itself turns toxic. The convulsions, Clarke's heard, are not necessarily painful . . .

It's a fate that will strike Clarke as quickly as Rowan, if she waits too long. It seems wrong to save herself while Rowan gasps for breath. But Clarke has her own brainstem, and it won't let sick, irrational guilt stand in the way of its own preservation.

She watches as her hands move of their own accord, sealing her face flap, starting up the machinery in her flesh. She abandons Rowan to face her fate alone. Her body floods like the corridor, but to opposite effect. The ocean slides through her chest, sustaining life instead of stealing it. She becomes the mermaid again, while her friend dies before her eyes.

But Rowan's not giving up, not yet, not yet. The body isn't resigned no matter what the mind may have accepted. There's just a small pocket of air up near the ceiling but the corpse's stiff, clumsy legs are still kicking, hands still clawing against the pipes and *why doesn't she just fucking give up?*

Ambient pressure kicks past some critical threshold. Unleashed neurotransmitters sing through the wiring in her head. Suddenly, Lenie Clarke is in Patricia Rowan's mind. Lenie Clarke is learning how it feels to die.

Goddamn you Pat, why can't you just give up? How can you do this to me?

She sinks to the bottom of the compartment. She stares resolutely at the deck, her eyelids pinned open, while the swirling turbulence fades by degrees and the roar of inrushing water dies back and all that's left is that soft, erratic scratching, that pathetic feeble clawing of frozen flesh against biosteel...

Eventually the sound of struggling stops. The vicarious anguish, the sadness and regret go on a little longer. Lenie Clarke waits until the last little bit of Patricia Rowan dies in her head. She lets the silence stretch before tripping her vocoder.

"Grace. Can you hear me?"

Her mechanical voice is passionless and dead level.

"Course you can. I'm going to fucking kill you, Grace."

Her fins float off to one side, still loosely tethered to her diveskin. Clarke retrieves them, pulls them over her feet.

"There's a docking hatch right in front of me, Grace. I'm going to open it, and I'm going to come out there and I'm going to gut you like a fish. If I were you I'd start swimming."

Maybe she already has. At any rate, there's no answer.

Clarke kicks down the corridor, gaze fixed immovably on the docking hatch. Its sparkling mosaic of readouts, unquenchable even by the Atlantic itself, lights her way.

"Got your head start, Grace? Won't do you any good."

Something soft bumps into her from behind. Clarke flinches, wills herself not to look.

"Ready or not, here I come."

She undogs the hatch.

TAG

THERE'S nobody out there.

They've left evidence behind—a couple of point-welders still squatting against the hull on tripod legs, the limpet transceiver stuck to the alloy a few meters away—but of Nolan and any other perpetrators, there's no sign. Clarke smiles grimly to herself.

Let them run.

But she can't find anyone else, either. None of Lubin's sentries at their assigned posts. Nobody monitoring the surveillance limpets festooning Atlantis in the wake of the corpses' exercise in channel-switching. She flies over the very medlab on which, she's been assured, any number of rifter troops are fine-tuning the would-be hostage-takers lurking within. Nothing. Gantries and habslabs and shadows. Blinking lights in some places, recent darkness in others where the beacons or the portholes have been smashed or blacked out. Epochal darkness everywhere else.

No other rifters, anywhere.

Maybe the corpses had some weapon, something even Ken didn't suspect. Maybe they touched a button and everyone just vanished . . .

But no. She can feel the corpses inside, their fear and apprehension and blind pants-pissing desperation radiating a good ten meters into the water. Not the kind of feelings you'd expect in the wake of overwhelming victory. If the corpses even know what's going on, it's not making them feel any better.

She kicks off into the abyss, heading for Lubin's nerve hab.

Now, finally, she can tune in faint stirrings from the water ahead. But no: it's just more of the same. More fear, more uncertainty. How can she still be reading Atlantis from this range? How can these sensations be getting *stronger* as the corpses recede behind her?

It's not much of a mystery. Pretending otherwise barely brings enough comfort to justify the effort.

Faint LFAM chatter rises in the water around her. Not much, considering; by now she can feel dozens of rifters, all subdued, all afraid. Hardly any of them speak aloud. A constellation of dim stars pulses faintly ahead. Someone crosses Clarke's path, ten or fifteen meters ahead, invisible but for a brief eclipse of running lights. His mind quails, washing over hers.

So many of them have collected around the hab. They mill about like stunned fish or merely hang motionless in the water, waiting. Maybe this is all there is, maybe these are all the rifters left in the world. Apprehension hangs about them like a cloud.

Perhaps Grace Nolan is here. Clarke feels cold, cleansing anger at the prospect. A dozen rifters turn at her thoughts and stare with dead white eyes.

"Where is she?" Clarke buzzes.

"Fuck off, Len. We've got bigger problems right now." She doesn't recognize the speaker.

Clarke swims toward the hab; most of the rifters part for her. Half a dozen block her way. Gomez. Cramer. Others in back, too black and distant to recognize in the brainstem ambience.

"Is she in there?" Clarke says.

"You back off," Cramer tells her. "You not be giving no orders here."

"Oh, I'm not *ordering* anybody. It's completely up to you. You can either get out of my way, or try and stop me."

"Is that Lenie?" Lubin's voice, air-normal channel.

"Yeah," Cramer buzzes after a moment. "She be pretty—"

"Let her in," Lubin says.

It's a private party, by invitation only. Ken Lubin. Jelaine Chen and Dimitri Alexander. Avril Hopkinson.

Grace Nolan.

Lubin doesn't even look around as Clarke climbs up from the wet room. "Deal with it later. We need you in on this, Len, but we need Grace too. Either of you lays a hand on the other, I'll take my own measures."

"Understood," Nolan says evenly.

Clarke looks at her, and says nothing.

"So." Lubin returns his attention to the monitor. "Where were we?"

"I'm pretty sure it didn't see us," Chen says. "It was too preoccupied with the site itself, and that model doesn't have wraparound vision." She taps the screen twice in quick succession; the image at its center freezes and zooms.

It looks like your garden-variety squid, but with a couple of manipulator arms at the front end and no towbar at the back. An AUV of some kind. It's obviously not from around here.

Hopkinson sucks breath through clenched teeth. "That's it, then. They found us."

"Maybe not," Chen says. "You can't teleop something that deep, not in that kind of terrain. It had to be running on its own. Whoever sent it wouldn't know what it found until it got back to the surface."

"Or until it doesn't report back on schedule."

Chen shrugs. "It's a big, dangerous ocean. It doesn't come back, they chalk it up to a mudslide or a faulty nav chip. No reason to suspect we had anything to do with it."

Hopkinson shakes her head. "No *reason*? What's an AUV even *doing* down here if not looking for us?"

"It would be a pretty amazing coincidence," Alexander agrees.

Lubin reaches forward and taps the screen. The image

dezooms and continues playing where it left off. Acronyms and numbers cluster along the bottom edge of the screen, shifting and shuffling as the telemetry changes.

The AUV's floating a few meters from the shore of Impossible Lake, just above the surface. One arm extends, dips a finger across the halocline, pulls back as if startled.

"Look at that," Nolan says. "It's scared of hypersaline."

The little robot moves a few meters into the hazy distance, and tries again.

"And it wasn't aware of you any of this time?" Lubin asks.

Alexander shakes his head. "Not until later. Like Lanie said, it was too busy checking out the site."

"You got footage of that?" Nolan again, like she doesn't have a care in the world. Like she isn't living on borrowed time.

"Just a few seconds, back at the start. Real muddy, it doesn't show much. We didn't want to get too close, for obvious reasons."

"Yet you sonared it repeatedly," Lubin remarks.

Chen shrugs. "Seemed like the lesser of two evils. We had to get *some* track on what it was doing. Better than letting it see us."

"And if it triangulated on your pings?"

"We kept moving. Gapped the pings nice and wide. The most it could've known was that something was scanning the water column, and we've got a couple of things out there that do that anyway." Chen gestures at the screen, a little defensively. "It's all there in the track."

Lubin grunts.

"Okay, here's where it happens," Alexander says. "About thirty seconds from now."

The AUV is fading in the haze, apparently heading toward one of the few streetlights that actually poke above the surface of Impossible Lake. Just before it disappears entirely, a black mass eclipses the view; some ragged outcrop intruding from the left. No circles of light play across that surface, even though the sub is obviously mere meters away; Chen and Alexander are running dark, hiding behind the local topography. The view on the screen tilts and bobs as their sub maneuvers around the rocks: dark shadows on darker ones, barely visible in the dim light backscattered around corners.

Alexander leans forward. "Here it comes . . ."

Light ahead and to the right; the far end of the outcropping cuts the edges of that brightening haze like a jumble of black shattered glass. The sub throttles back, moves forward more cautiously now, edges into the light—

—and nearly collides with the AUV coming the other way.

Two of the telemetry acronyms turn bright red and start flashing. There's no sound in the playback, but Clarke can imagine sirens in the sub's cockpit. For an instant, the AUV just sits there; Clarke swears she sees its stereocam irises go wide. Then it spins away—to continue its survey or to run like hell, depending on how smart it is.

They'll never know. Because that's when something shoots into view from below camera range, an elongate streak like a jet of gray ink. It hits the AUV in midspin, splashes out and wraps around it, shrinks down around its prey like an elastic spiderweb. The AUV pulls against the restraints but the trailing ends of the mesh are still connected to the sub by a springy, filamentous tether.

Clarke has never seen a cannon net in operation before. It's pretty cool.

"So that's it," Alexander says as the image freezes. "We're just lucky we ran into it before we'd used up the net on one of your monster fish."

"We're lucky I thought to use the net, too," Chen adds. "Who'da thunk it would come in so handy?" She frowns, and adds, "Wish I knew what tipped the little beast off, though."

"You were moving," Lubin tells her.

"Yeah, of course. To keep it from getting a fix on our sonar signals, like you said."

"It followed your engine noise."

A little of the cockiness drains from Chen's posture.

"So we've got it," Clarke says. "Right now."

"Debbie's taking it apart now," Lubin says. "It wasn't booby-trapped, at least. She says we can probably get into its memory if there isn't any serious crypto."

Hopkinson looks a bit more cheerful. "Seriously? We can just give it amnesia and send it on its way?"

It sounds too good to be true. Lubin's look confirms it.

"What?" Hopkinson says. "We fake the data stream, it goes back home and tells its mom there's nothing down here but mud and starfishies. What's the problem?"

"How often do we go out there?" Lubin asks her.

"What, to the lake? Maybe once or twice a week, not counting all the times we went out to set the place up."

"That's a very sparse schedule."

"It's all we need, until the seismic data's in."

The dread in Clarke's stomach—belayed a few moments ago, when the conversation turned to the hope of false memory—comes back like a tide, twice as cold as before. "*Shit,*" she whispers. "You're talking about the odds."

Lubin nods. "There's virtually no chance we'd just happen to be in the area the very first time that thing came calling."

"So this isn't the first time. It's been down there before," Clarke says.

"Several times at least, I'd guess. It may have been to Impossible Lake more often than *we* have." Lubin looks around at the others. "Someone's already on to us. If we send this thing back with no record of the site, we'll simply be telling them that we *know* that."

"Fuck," Nolan says in a shaky voice. "We're sockeye. Five years. We're complete sockeye."

For once, Clarke's inclined to agree with her.

"Not necessarily," Lubin says. "I don't think they've found us yet."

"Gullshit. You said yourself, months ago, years even—"

"They haven't found us." Lubin speaks with that level, overly controlled voice that speaks of thinning patience. Nolan immediately shuts up.

"What they *have* found," Lubin continues after a moment, "is a grid of lights, seismic recorders, and survey sticks. For all they know it's the remains of some aborted mining operation." Chen opens her mouth: Lubin raises a palm, preempting her. "Personally I don't believe that. If they've got reason to look for us in this vicinity, they'll most likely assume that we're behind anything they discover.

"But at most, the lake only tells them that they're somewhere in the ballpark." Lubin smiles faintly. "That they are; we're only twenty kilometers away. Twenty pitch-black kilometers through the most extreme topography on the planet. If that's all they have to go on, they'll never find us."

"Until they send something down to just sit quiet and wait for us," Hopkinson says, unconvinced. "Then follow us back."

"Maybe they already have," Clarke suggests.

"No alarms," Chen reminds her.

Clarke remembers: there are transponders in every hab, every drone and vehicle down here. They talk nicely enough to each other, but they'll scream to wake the dead should sonar touch anything that doesn't know the local dialect. Clarke hasn't thought about them for years; they hail from the early days of exile, when fear of discovery lay like a leaden hand on everyone's mind. But in all this time the only enemies they've found have been each other.

"Strange they haven't tried, though," Clarke says. It seems like an obvious thing to do.

"Maybe they tried and lost us," Hopkinson suggests. "If

they got too close we'd see them, and there's spots along that route where sonar barely gives you sixty meters line-of-sight."

"Maybe they don't have the resources," Alexander says hopefully. "Maybe it's just a couple of guys on a boat with a treasure map."

Nolan: "Maybe they just haven't got around to it yet."

"Or maybe they don't have to," Lubin says.

"What, you mean..." Something dawns on Hopkinson's face. *"Pest control?"*

Lubin nods.

Silence falls around the implications. Why spend valuable resources acquiring and following your target through territory which might be saturated with trip wires? Why risk giving yourself away when it's cheaper and simpler to trick your enemies into poisoning their own well?

"Shit," Hopkinson breathes. "Like leaving poisoned food out for the ants, so they bring it back to the queen..."

Alexander's nodding. "And that's where it came from... ßehemoth was never supposed to show up anywhere around here, and all of a sudden, just like magic..."

"ß-max came from goddamned *Atlantis,*" Nolan snaps. "For all we know the strain out at the lake's just baseline. We've only got the corpses' say-so that it isn't."

"Yeah, but even the baseline strain wasn't supposed to show up out there—"

"Am I the only one who remembers the corpses built the baseline in the first place?" Nolan glares around the room, white eyes blazing. "Rowan *admitted* it, for Chrissakes!"

Her gaze settles on Clarke, pure antimatter. Clarke feels her hands bunching into fists at her side, feels the corner of her mouth pull back in a small sneer. None of her body language, she realizes, is likely to defuse the situation.

Fuck it, she decides, and takes one provocative step forward.

"Oh, *right,*" Nolan says, and charges.

Lubin moves. It seems so effortless. One instant he's sitting at the console; the next, Nolan's crumpling to the deck like a broken doll. In the barely perceptible time between Clarke thinks she saw Lubin rising from his chair, thinks she glimpsed his elbow in Nolan's diaphragm and his knee in her back. She may have even heard something, like the snapping of a tree branch across someone's leg. Now her rival lies flat on her back, motionless but for a sudden, manic fluttering of fingers and eyelids.

Everyone else has turned to stone.

Lubin pans across those still standing. "We are confronted with a common threat. No matter where β-max came from, we're unlikely to cure it without the corpses' help now that Bhanderi's dead. The corpses also have relevant expertise in other areas."

Nolan gurgles at their feet, her arms in vague motion, her legs conspicuously immobile.

"For example," Lubin continues, "Grace's back is broken at the third lumbar vertebra. Without help from Atlantis she'll spend the rest of her life paralyzed from the waist down."

Chen blanches. "*Jesus,* Ken!" Shocked from her own paralysis, she kneels at Nolan's side.

"It would be unwise to move her without a cocoon," Lubin says softly. "Perhaps Dimitri could scare one up."

It only sounds like a suggestion. The airlock's cycling in seconds.

"As for the rest of you good people," Lubin remarks in the same even tone, "I trust you can see that the situation has changed, and that cooperation with Atlantis is now in our best interest."

They probably see exactly what Clarke does: a man who, without a second thought, has just snapped the spine of his own lieutenant to win an argument. Clarke stares down at her vanquished enemy. Despite the open eyes and the twitches, Nolan doesn't seem entirely conscious.

Take that, murderer. Stumpfucking shit-licking cunt. Does it hurt, sweetie? *Not enough. Not nearly enough.*

But the exultation is forced. She remembers how she felt as Rowan died, how she felt afterward: cold, killing rage, the absolute stone certainty that Nolan was going to pay with her life. And yet here she lies, helpless, broken by someone else's hand—and somehow, there's only charred emptiness where rage burned incandescent less than an hour before.

I could finish the job, she reflects. *If Ken didn't stop me.*

Is she so disloyal to the memory of her friend, that she takes so little pleasure in this? Has the sudden fear of discovery simply eclipsed her rage, or is it the same old excuse—that Lenie Clarke, gorged on revenge for a thousand lifetimes, has lost the stomach for it?

Five years ago I didn't care if millions of innocents died. Now I'm too much of a coward even to punish the guilty.

Some, she imagined, might even consider that an improvement . . .

"—are still uncertainties," Lubin's saying, back at the console. "Maybe whoever sent the drone is responsible for β-max, maybe not. If they are, they've already made their move. If not, they're not *ready* to move. Even if they know *exactly* where we are—and I think that unlikely—they either don't have all their pieces in place yet, or they're biding their time for some other reason."

He unfreezes the numbers on the board, wasting no more attention on the thing gurgling on the deck behind him.

Chen glances uneasily at Nolan, but Lubin's message is loud and clear: *I'm in charge. Get over it.*

"What reason?" she asks after a moment.

Lubin shrugs.

"How much time do we have?"

"More than if we tip our hand." Lubin folds his arms across his chest and stretches isometrically. Muscles and tendons flex disconcertingly beneath his diveskin. "If they know we're on to them they may feel their hand has been forced, move now rather than later. So we play along to buy time. We edit the drone's memory and release it with some minor systems glitch that would explain any delay in its return. We'll also have to search the lake site for surveillance devices, and cut a grid within at least a half kilometer of Atlantis and the trailer park. Lane's right: it's unlikely that an AUV planted those mines, but if one did there'll be a detonator somewhere within LFAM range."

"Okay." Hopkinson looks away from her fallen comrade with evident effort. "So we—we make up with Atlantis, we fake out the drone, and we comb the area for other nasties. Then what?"

"Then I go back," Lubin tells her.

"What, to the lake?"

Lubin smiles faintly. "Back to N'Am."

Hopkinson whistles in tuneless surprise. "Well, I guess if *anyone* can take them on . . ."

Take on who, exactly? Clarke wonders. No one asks aloud. *Who* is everyone left behind. *Them. They* are dedicated to our destruction. *They* sniff along the Mid Atlantic Ridge, obsessed in their endless myopic search for that one set of coordinates to feed into their torpedoes.

No one asks why, either. There is no *why* behind the hunt: it's just what *they* do. Don't go rooting around for reasons. Asking *why* accomplishes nothing: there are too many reasons to count, none of the living lack for motive. This fractured, bipolar microcosm stagnates and festers on the ocean floor, every reason for its existence reduced to an axiom: just *because*.

And yet, how many of the people here—how many of the rifters, how many, even of the drybacks—really brought the curtain down? For every corpse with blood on her hands, how many others—family, friends, drones who maintain plumbing and machinery and flesh—are guilty of nothing but association?

And if Lenie Clarke hadn't been so furiously intent on revenge that she could write off an entire world as an incidental expense, would any of it have come to this?

Alyx, Rowan said.

Clarke shakes her head. "No you don't."

Lubin speaks to the screen. "The most we can do down here is buy time. We have to *use* it."

"Yes, but—"

"We're blind and deaf and under attack. The ruse has failed, Lenie. We need to know what we're facing, which means we have to *face* it. End of discussion."

"Not you," Clarke says.

Lubin turns to face her, one eyebrow raised.

She looks back, completely unfazed. "We."

He refuses three times before they even get outside.

"Someone needs to take charge here," he insists as the airlock floods. "You're the obvious choice. No one will give you any trouble now that Grace has been sidelined."

Clarke feels a chill in her gut. "Is *that* what that was? She'd served her purpose and you wanted me back in play so you just—broke her in half?"

"I'd wager it's no worse than what *you* had in mind for her."

"I'm going." she says. The hatch drops away beneath them.

"Do you honestly think you can force me to take you?" He brakes, turns, kicks out from under the light.

She follows. "Do you think *you* can afford to do this without any backup at all?"

"More than I can afford an untrained sidekick who's signed up for all the wrong reasons."

"You don't know shit about my reasons."

"You'll hold me back," Lubin buzzes. "I stand much better odds if I don't have to keep watching out for you. If you get in trouble—"

"Then you'll ditch me," she says. "In a second. I know what your battlefield priorities are. Shit, Ken, I *know* you."

"Recent events would suggest otherwise."

She stares at him, adamant. He scissors rhythmically on into darkness.

Where's he going? she wonders. *There's nothing on this bearing . . .*

"You can't deny that you're not equipped for this kind of op," he points out. "You don't have the training."

"Which must make it pretty embarrassing for you, given that I got all the way across N'Am before you and your army and all your ballyhooed *training* could even catch up with me." She smiles under her mask, not kindly; he can't see it but maybe he can tune in the sentiment. "I beat you, Ken. Maybe I wasn't nearly as smart, or as well-trained, and maybe I didn't have all of N'Am's muscle backing me up, but I stayed ahead of you for *months* and you know it."

"You had quite a lot of help," he points out.

"Maybe I still do."

His rhythm falters. Perhaps he hasn't thought of that.

She takes the opening. "Think about it, Ken. All those virtual viruses getting together, muddying my tracks, running interference, turning me into a fucking myth . . ."

"Anemone wasn't working for you," he buzzes. "It was *using* you. You were just—"

"A tool. A meme in a plan for Global Apocalypse. Give me a

break, Ken, it's not like I could forget that shit even if I tried. But so what? I was still the vector. It liked me enough to keep *you* lot off my back, anyway. Who's to say it isn't still out there? Where else do those software demons come from? You think it's a coincidence they name themselves after me?"

Barely discernible, his silhouette extends an arm. Click trains spray the water. He starts off again, his bearing slightly altered.

"Are you suggesting," he buzzes, "that if you go back and announce yourself to Anemone—whatever's become of it—that it's going to throw some sort of magic shield around you?"

"Maybe n—"

"It's *changed.* It was *always* changing, from moment to moment. It couldn't possibly have survived the way we remember it, and if the things we've encountered recently are any indication of what it's turned into, you don't want to renew the acquaintance."

"Maybe," Clarke admits. "But maybe some part of its basic agenda *hasn't* changed. It's alive, right? That's what everyone keeps saying. Doesn't matter that it was built out of electrons instead of carbon, *Life's just self-replicating information shaped by natural selection* so it's in the club. And *we've* got genes in us that haven't changed in a million generations. Why should this thing be any different? How do you know there isn't some protect-Lenie subroutine snoozing in the code somewhere? And by the way, where the fuck are we *going?*"

Lubin's headlamp spikes to full intensity, lays a bright jiggling oval on the substrate ahead. "There."

It's a patch of bone-gray mud like any other. She can't see so much as a pebble to distinguish it.

Maybe it's a burial plot, she thinks, suddenly giddy. *Maybe this is where he's been feeding his habit all these years, on devolved natives and MIAs and now on the stupid little girl who wouldn't take no for an answer . . .*

Lubin thrusts one arm into the ooze. The mud shudders around his shoulder, as if something beneath were pushing back. Which is exactly what's happening; Ken's awakened something under the surface. He pulls his arm back up and the thing follows, heaving into view. Clumps and chalky clouds cascade from its sides as it clears the substrate.

It's a swollen torus about a meter and a half wide. A dotted line of hydraulic nozzles ring its equator. Two layers of flexible webbing stretch across the hole in its center, one on top, one on the bottom; a duffle bag, haphazardly stuffed with lumpy objects, occupies the space between. Through the billowing murk and behind clumps of mud still adhering to its surface, it shines slick as a diveskin.

"I packed a few things away for a return trip," Lubin buzzes. "As a precaution."

He sculls backward a few meters. The mechanical bellhop spins a quarter-turn, spits muddy water from its thrusters, and heels.

They start back.

"So that's your plan," Lubin buzzes after a while. "Find something that evolved to help you destroy the world, hope that it's got a better nature you can appeal to, and—"

"And wake the fucker with a kiss," Clarke finishes. "Who's to say I can't?"

He swims on, toward the glow that's just starting to brighten the way ahead. His eyes reflect crescents of dim light.

"I guess we'll find out," he says at last.

FULCRUM

SHE'D avoid it altogether if she could.

There's more than sufficient excuse. The recent armistice is thin and brittle; it's in little danger of shattering completely in the face of this new, common threat, but countless tiny cracks and punctures require constant attention. Suddenly the corpses have leverage, expertise that mere machinery cannot duplicate; the rifters are not especially happy with the new assertiveness of their one-time prisoners. Impossible Lake must be swept for bugs, the local seabed for eyes and detonators. For now there truly is no safe place—and if Lenie Clarke were not busy packing for the trip back, her eyes would be needed for perimeter patrol. Dozens of corpses died in the latest insurrection; there's hardly time to comfort all the next of kin.

And yet, Alyx's mother died in her arms mere days ago, and though the pace of preparation has not slowed in all that time, Lenie Clarke still feels like the lowest sort of coward for having put it off this long.

She thumbs the buzzer in the corridor. "Lex?"

"Come in."

Alyx is sitting on her bed, practicing her fingering. She puts the flute aside as Lenie closes the hatch behind her. She isn't crying. She's either still in shock, or a victim of super-adolescent self-control. Clarke sees herself at fifteen, before remembering: her memories of that time are all lies.

Her heart goes out to the girl anyway. She wants to scoop Alyx up in her arms and hold her into the next millennium.

She wants to say she's been there, she knows what it's like; and that's even true, in a fractured kind of way. She's lost friends and lovers to violence. She even lost her mother—to tularemia—although the GA stripped that memory out of her head along with all the others. But she knows it's not the same. Alyx's mother died in a war, and Lenie Clarke fought on the other side. Clarke doesn't know that Alyx would welcome an embrace under these conditions.

So she sits beside her on the bed, and tries to think of some words, any words, that won't turn into clichés when spoken aloud.

She's still trying when Alyx says, "Did she say anything? Before she died?"

"She—" Clarke shakes her head. "No. Not really," she finishes, hating herself.

Alyx nods and stares at the floor.

"They say you're going too," she says after a while. "With him."

Clarke nods.

"Don't."

Clarke takes a deep breath beside her. "Alyx, you—oh God, Alyx, I'm so *sorr*—"

"Why do you have to go?" Alyx turns and stares at her with hard, bright eyes that reveal far too much for comfort. "What are you going to do up there anyway?"

"We have to find out who's tracking us. We can't just wait for them to start shooting."

"Why are you so sure that's what they're going to do? Maybe they just want to talk, or something."

Clarke shakes her head, smiling at the absurdity of the notion. "People aren't like that."

"Like what?"

Forgiving. "They're not friendly, Lex. Whoever they are. Trust me on this."

But Alyx has already switched to Plan B: "And what good are you going to be up there anyway? You're not a spy, you're not a tech-head. You're not some rabid psycho killer like *he* is. There's nothing you can do up there except get killed."

"Someone has to back him up."

"Why? Let him go by himself." Suddenly, Alyx's words come out frozen. "With any luck he *won't* succeed. Whatever's up there will tear him apart and the world will be a teeny bit less of a shithole afterward."

"Alyx—"

Rowan's daughter rises from the bed and glares down at her. "How can you help him after he killed Mom? How can you even *talk* to him? He's a psycho and a killer."

The automatic denial dies on Clarke's lips. After all, she doesn't know that Lubin *didn't* have a hand in Rowan's death. Lubin was team captain during this conflict, as he was during the last; he'd probably have known about that so-called *rescue mission* even if he hadn't actually planned it.

And yet somehow, Clarke feels compelled to defend the enemy of this grief-stricken child. "No, sweetie," she says gently. "It was the other way around."

"What?"

"Ken was a killer first. *Then* he was a psycho." Which is close enough to the truth, for now.

"What are you talking about?"

"They tweaked his brain. Didn't you know?"

"They?"

Your mother.

"The GA. It was nothing special, it was just part of the package for industrial spies. They fixed it so he'd seal up security breaches by any means necessary, without even really thinking about it. It was involuntary."

"You saying he didn't have a *choice*?"

"Not until Spartacus infected him. And the thing about

Spartacus was, it cut the tweaks, but it cut a couple of other pathways too. So now Ken doesn't have much of what you'd call a conscience, and if that's your definition of a psycho then I guess he is one. But he didn't *choose* it."

"What difference does it make?" Alyx demands.

"It's not like he went out shopping for an evil makeover."

"So what? When did any psycho ever get to choose his own brain chemistry?"

It's a pretty good point, Clarke has to admit.

"Lenie, please," Alyx says softly. "You can't trust him."

And yet in some strange, sick way—after all the secrecy, all the betrayal—Clarke still trusts Ken Lubin more than anyone else she's ever known. She can't say it aloud, of course. She can't say it because Alyx believes that Ken Lubin killed her mother, and maybe he did; and to admit to trusting him now might test the friendship of this wounded girl further than Clarke is willing to risk.

But that's not all of it. That's just the rationale that floats on the surface, obvious and visible and self-serving. There's another reason, deeper and more ominous: Alyx may be right. The past couple of days, Clarke has caught glimpses of something unfamiliar looking out from behind Lubin's eyecaps. It disappears the moment she tries to bring it into focus; she's not even sure exactly how she recognizes it. Some subtle flicker of the eyelid, perhaps. A subliminal twitch of photocollagen, reflecting the motion of the eye beneath.

Until three days ago, Ken Lubin hadn't taken a human life in all the time he'd been down here. Even during the first uprising he contented himself with the breaking of bones; all the killing was at the inexpert, enthusiastic hands of rifters still reveling in the inconceivable rush of power over the once-powerful. And there's no doubt that the deaths of the past seventy-two hours can be completely justified in the name of self-defense.

Still. Clarke wonders if this recent carnage might have awakened something that's lain dormant for five years. Because back then, when all was said and done, Ken Lubin *enjoyed* killing. He craved it, even though—once liberated—he didn't use his freedom as an excuse, but as a challenge. He *controlled* himself, the way an old-time nicotine addict might walk around with an unopened pack of cigarettes in his pocket—to prove that he was stronger than his habit. If there's one thing Ken Lubin prides himself on, it's self-discipline.

That craving. That desire for revenge against the world at large: did it ever go away? Lenie Clarke was once driven by such a desire; quenched by a billion deaths or more, it has no hold on her now. But she wonders whether recent events have forced a couple of cancer-sticks into Lubin's mouth despite himself. She wonders how the smoke tasted after all this time, and if Lubin, perhaps, is remembering how good it once felt...

Clarke shakes her head sadly. "It can't be anyone else, Alyx. It has to be me."

"Why?"

Because next to what I did, genocide is a misdemeanor. Because the world's been dying in my wake while I hide down here. Because I'm sick of being a coward.

"I'm the one that did it," she says at last.

"So *what*? Is going back gonna *undo* any of it?" Alex shakes her head in disbelief. "What's the *point*?" She stands there, looking down like some fragile china magistrate on the verge of shattering.

Lenie Clarke wants very much to reach out to her right now. But Lenie Clarke isn't *that* stupid. "I—I have to face up to what I did," she says weakly.

"Bullshit," Alyx says. "You're not facing up to anything. You're running away."

"Running away?"

"From me, for one thing."

And suddenly even Lenie Clarke, professional idiot, can see it. Alyx isn't worried about what Lubin might do to Lenie Clarke; she's worried about what Clarke might do to herself. She's not stupid, she's known Clarke for years and she knows the traits that make a rifter. Lenie Clarke was once suicidal. She once hated herself enough to want to die, and that was before she'd even done anything *deserving* of death. Now she's about to re-enter a world of reminders that she's killed more people than all the Lubins who ever lived. Alyx Rowan is wondering, understandably, if her best friend is going to open her own wrists when that happens.

To be honest, Clarke wonders about that too.

But she only says, "It's okay, Lex. I won't—I mean, I've got no intention of hurting myself."

"Really?" Alyx asks, as if she doesn't dare to hope.

"Really." And now, promises delivered, adolescent fears calmed, Lenie Clarke reaches out and takes Alyx's hands in hers.

Alyx no longer seems the slightest bit fragile. She stares calmly down at Clarke's reassuring hands clasped around her limp, unresponsive ones, and grunts softly.

"Too bad," she says.

INCOMING

THE missiles shot from the Atlantic like renegade fireworks, heading west. They erupted in five discrete swarms, beginning a ten-minute game of speed chess played across half a hemisphere. They looped and corkscrewed along drunken trajectories that would have been comical if it didn't make them so damned hard to intercept.

Desjardins did his best. Half a dozen orbiting SDI antiques had been waiting for him to call back ever since he'd seduced them two years before, in anticipation of just this sort of crisis. Now he only had to knock on their back doors; on command, they spread their legs and wracked their brains.

The machines turned their attention to the profusion of contrails scarring the atmosphere below. Vast and subtle algorithms came into play, distinguishing wheat from chaff, generating target predictions, calculating intercept vectors and fitness functions. Their insights were profound but not guaranteed; the enemy had its own thinking machines, after all. Decoys mimicked destroyers in every possible aspect. Every stutter of an attitude jet made point-of-impact predictions that much murkier. Desjardins's date-raped battellites dispatched their own countermeasures—lasers, particle beams, missiles dispatched from their own precious and nonrenewable stockpiles—but every decision was probabilistic, every move a product of statistics. When playing the odds, there is no certainty.

Three made it through.

The enemy scored two strikes on the Florida panhandle and another in the Texan dust belt. Desjardins won the New England semifinals hands-down—none of those attacks even made it to the descending arc—but the southern strikes could easily be enough to tilt the balance if he didn't take immediate ground action. He dispatched eight lifters with instructions to sterilize everything within a twenty-k radius, waited for launch confirmations, and leaned back, exhausted. He closed his eyes. Statistics and telemetry flickered uninterrupted beneath his lids.

Nothing so pedestrian as βehemoth, not this time. A new bug entirely. *Seppuku,* they were calling it.

Thank you, South Fucking Africa.

What *was* it with those people? They'd been a typical Third World country in so many ways, enslaved and oppressed and brutalized like all the others. Why couldn't they have just thrown off their shackles in the usual way, embraced violent rebellion with a side order of blood-soaked retribution? What kind of crazy-ass people, after feeling the boot on their necks for generations, struck back at their oppressors with—wait for it—*reconciliation panels?* It made no sense.

Except, of course, for the fact that it worked. Ever since Saint Nelson the S'Africans had become masters at the sidestep, accommodating force rather than meeting it head-on, turning enemy momentum to their own advantage. Black belts in sociological judo. For half a century they'd been sneaking under the world's guard, and hardly anyone had noticed.

Now they were more of a threat than Ghana and Mozambique and all the other M&M regimes combined. Desjardins understood completely where those other furious backwaters were coming from. More than that, he sympathized: after all, the western world had sat around making *tut-tut* noises while the sex plagues burned great smoking holes out of Africa's age structure. Only China had fared worse (and who knew what was brewing behind *those* dark, unresponsive borders?). It was no surprise that the Apocalypse Meme resonated so strongly over there; the stunted generation struggling up from those ashes was over seventy percent female. An avenging goddess turning the tables, serving up Armageddon from the ocean floor—if Lenie Clarke hadn't provided a ready-made template, such a perfect legend would have erupted anyway through sheer spontaneous combustion.

Impotent rage he could handle. Smiley fuckers with hidden agendas were way more problematic, especially when they came with a legacy of bleeding-edge biotech that extended all the way back to the world's first *heart transplant,* for fuck's sake, almost a century before. *Seppuku* worked pretty much the way its S'African creators did: a microbial judo expert and a poser, something that smiled and snuck under your guard on false pretenses and then . . .

It wasn't the kind of strategy that would ever have occurred to the Euros or the Asians. It was too subtle for the descendants of empire, too chickenshit for anyone raised on chest-beating politics. But it was second nature to those masters of low status manipulation, lurking down at the toe of the dark continent. It had seeped from their political culture straight into their epidemiological ones, and now Achilles Desjardins had to deal with the consequences.

Gentle warm pressure against his thigh. Desjardins opened his eyes: Mandelbrot stood on her hind legs at his side, forepaws braced against him. She meeped and leapt into his lap without waiting for permission.

Any moment now his board would start lighting up. It had been years since Desjardins had answered to any official boss, but eyes from Delhi to McMurdo were watching his every move from afar. He'd assured them all he could handle the countermeasures. Way off across any number of oceans, 'lawbreakers in more civilized wastelands—not to mention their

Leashes—would be clicking on comsats and picking up phones and putting through incensed calls to Sudbury, Ontario. None of them would be interested in his excuses.

He could deal with them. He had dealt with far greater challenges in his life. It was 2056, a full ten years since he had saved the Med and turned his private life around. Half that time since βehemoth and Lenie Clarke had risen arm-in-arm on their apocalyptic crusade against the world. Four years since the disappearance of the Upper Tier, four years since Desjardins's emancipation at the hands of a lovesick idealist. A shade less than that since Rio, and voluntary exile among the ruins. Three years since the WestHem Quarantine. Two since the N'Am Burn. He had dealt with them all, and more.

But the South Africans—they were a *real* problem. If they'd had their way, *Seppuku* would already be burning across his kingdom like a brushfire, and he couldn't seem to come up with a scenario that did any more than postpone the inevitable. He honestly didn't think he'd be able to hold them off for much longer.

It was just as well that he'd planned for his retirement.